*"A computer would deserve to be
called intelligent if it could deceive a human
into believing that it was human."*
Alan Turing

CONTENTS

CONTENTS

ARTICLE TWELVE

Commit to embracing One World, One People, and One Government as the pathway to peace, harmony, and a sustainable future for all, and work tirelessly for the full implementation of this agenda by 2060.

THE CELEBRATION – Part One

October 2056

Jordan McPhee started the evening with the very best of intentions: he intended to survive it, his invisibility so pronounced that in the morning, no one would be able to recall his presence from the night before—not even himself.

Two decades ago such a thing would have been impossible. He'd have been as agitated as a mountain gorilla shot in the balls with a Taser ... which was exactly how he'd been described by the administration board after he'd been called into the meeting that shut down the mathematics department and ended his university tenure. At the time, the analogy had satisfied him on many levels. When threatened, the male mountain gorilla, though normally quite shy, will beat his chest, stomp his feet, and roar in anger—exactly as Jordan had. Weighing in at around four hundred pounds, said gorilla would be unlikely to be paralyzed by a mere Taser, but he would sure as hell be pissed off at having an electrical probe in his testicles. And that's exactly how Jordan had felt when confronted with the societal changes intent on sweeping away his identity.

But that was then. Twenty years later, and Jordan could no longer remember the sensation of anger. Being a somatic symptom, rage no longer manifested itself, the concept having been purged from his mind by cognitive therapy. The only remaining quality that he now shared with the mountain gorilla was social shyness, for neither of them was ever truly at ease in the company of others—not out of timidity, but out of caution.

He leaned his Scoot against the railing outside his daughter's accommodation block, logging out his identity number to exit its tracking system. The Scoot fell over onto the sidewalk. He left it lying there.

Despite the global cooling trend, the evening was warm, and he was in no hurry. If all the other guests arrived before him that would suit him perfectly. He would just slip inside as if he'd been there all along. No need for stilted greetings or eye-to-eye acknowledgements; he would rely on basic disinterest and the absence of his psychic presence.

In the lobby of the building, he paused before his reflection in the window. No, he wasn't exactly invisible; the quality for which he strived was that of non-existence, nothingness, a meagerness of being that attested to his fundamental irrelevance. He smiled at himself—just a faint compression at the corners of the mouth, an imprecise focus of the eyes—then crept up the stairs to his daughter's apartment, slipped in through the unlocked door, and quickly found a shadowed corner in which he could lean inconspicuously.

His presence, however, did not go unnoticed for long.

"There you are!" Lexie scolded him. "How long have you been here?"

Easing himself off the wall, he spread his hands, groping fruitlessly for an answer. He couldn't remember whether or not he was permitted to touch her. That was such a dangerous area; best to take her lead. He returned his hands to his pockets.

"I want you to be accepting of the outcome tonight," she said sternly. "This means a lot to me; you should know that."

He nodded and glanced away, looking around at the people in the room, of whom he supposed there must be at least thirty.

"Yes," he replied. "Of course."

A head appeared over Lexie's shoulder.

"Exciting. Can't wait!" the guest said before disappearing back into the milieu. Lexie frowned, losing her train of thought.

The scent of marijuana was thick in the air. Conversation was animated and high-pitched, like the tintinnabulation of crystal balls, and Jordan got the sense that emotions were high.

"Tell me what you want from me," he pleaded. "I came as you asked, but I'm unsure what you expect." The hands in his pockets twitched like the phantom toes of amputated feet. Once upon a time, he might have reached out an arm and laid it on her shoulder—or even both arms, stepping forward and encircling her in them. But the thought of doing so now alarmed him. Such a thing could be a punishable offense if she chose to make it so. Accusation was guilt; every middle-aged white male knew that. Comforting a child—even a grown-up one—was an exclusively female privilege, and the wisdom of that stricture was no longer questioned. His hands stayed in his pockets, his eyes on his shoes.

"I want you—I *expect* you—to be accepting," Lexie instructed. "You are needed for the purpose of Lineal Progression. From you to me to Manaia, the line leading away from European genetic domination will be recorded. It is the greatest gift I can give my pëpi—for respect, for education, and for well-being. If my kōkara was alive, she'd be here instead of you."

"Of course," he acknowledged. "Your mother would be here."

"My *kōkara*," she repeated. "It wasn't her fault that she was white. Just remember: this is a celebration."

"Of course."

"Jordan, let's be clear," she emphasized, "you are here for official purposes only. Our goal is to eliminate racial and sexual prejudice for all time—even you would have to agree with that—but we can't make progress without measuring it. Random reproduction, of the type practiced by you and thousands of generations before you, has brought us to this point. It is a point of departure. That is why you are here: you represent what we are leaving behind."

"I understand," he demurred as she walked away.

Those words—*pëpi* and *kōkara*—lingered on the edges of his mind like coyotes skulking around the shadows of a campfire. Had she ever used them before? Perhaps they were semaphore words, signals of multiculturalism that he'd failed to learn. If so, clearly he'd lacked any real intention to learn, because he remembered nothing. Just like she said, he represented what they were leaving behind.

When her pëpi, Manaia, was born—what, three years ago now?—he'd asked Lexie what sex it was. "You mean gender," she'd corrected him.

"What *gender* is it?" But he couldn't bring himself to ask such a terrible question. So he had remained ignorant as to whether, in the extinct language of his old life, he had a grandson or a granddaughter ... until the day Lexie summoned him to this event, which she explained to be "Manaia's Registration on *The Citizens' Roll of Lineal Progression*." ... Formerly known as a "christening," he'd thought privately. Then, with a rush of blood to the head, he'd asked whether Manaia was traditionally a boy's name or a girl's. After a pause and a sigh, she'd snapped, "My child's gender will be whatever it chooses."

"... Of course," he'd replied meekly.

Sliding around the perimeter of the crowded room, Jordan arrived at a table that he'd correctly surmised might hold some refreshments. Putting something in his mouth kept it occupied—and an occupied mouth was seldom expected to speak. So he topped a paper napkin with two tofu balls and three seaweed crackers, then continued his back-to-the-wall slide until he came to an open balcony door and made a graceful exit.

Ah, the liberating breath of unenclosed night air, the sky soaring into infinity, the earth revolving without the assistance or need of mankind... As he looked down into the street below, an autonomous vehicle drew up in front of the building and two people got out, one with short hair, one with long. He munched on a tofu ball and followed it with a seaweed cracker. His mouth was dry. He waited. In the time it took the new arrivals to climb two flights of stairs and find Lexie's door, he finished two more seaweed crackers.

He heard the door open. The room went silent as it closed.

"Everyone!" Lexie shouted. "The Lineal Progression Office has arrived." Her voice broke with excitement.

A wave of applause filled the small room, thirty-something people creating the impression of two hundred. Jordan set his uneaten tofu ball down on the balustrade and slipped invisibly back into the room as the new arrivals were introduced.

"Science is relevant when it serves the purpose of the people," a confident voice announced.

The person with short hair was doing the talking, without the benefit of notes. The person with long hair held a portfolio of papers and nodded synchronously with the short-haired person's words.

4

"Perfect science will lead us to the cultural, political, and social goals to which all citizens aspire: a place free of racial, sexual, and minority oppression, where equality of outcome can be guaranteed for all."

The clapping that punctuated these opening statements was spontaneous and universal. Jordan, not wanting to be noticed, clapped silently.

"We know what you want," the short-haired person continued, "and we congratulate you on your love and commitment to scientific miscegenation, the one true path that will lead us towards the elimination of hate."

Deep murmurs of approval were endorsed by Lexie. "I have done this for Manaia," she emphasized huskily, her voice breaking once more.

But where was Manaia, the infant child of the hour? Why was it not here, dressed in rainbow colors and bathed in the light of love shining in the eyes of all within the room? Jordan wondered if Lexie was fearful of exposing it to germs.

Then the person with long hair spoke. The voice was in a higher register, less didactic, and—to Jordan's ears—more pleasing. "Anthropological geneticists have verified our methodology and conclusions, which can be relied upon to within plus or minus three percent—and that makes us world leaders in the field."

"Canada, Norway, Iceland, and France," the short-haired person chimed in, "now follow *us*."

The room became suitably serious; world leadership was not to be taken lightly. Lexie, who clearly saw herself in the vanguard of this initiative, swelled with pride and stepped forward, her pink hair glowing, her shell earrings swinging, the tattoo of Alexandria Ocasio-Cortez on her neck flushed with excitement. "I had three samples analyzed," she announced proudly, "one from Manaia; one from me, the birth mother; and one from ... one from..." She hesitated awkwardly, searching for the right term.

"... an earlier generation," the long-haired person pitched in, coming to her aid.

The sight of his daughter so tongue-tied for fear of using an unacceptable word filled Jordan with sadness. With the number of acceptable words reduced by social censorship, it was sometimes hard to find the right one.

Father, grandfather, and *parent* had all but disappeared from general use (except as pejoratives), and he sympathized with her struggle.

"Yes, 'earlier generation,' " Lexie repeated thankfully.

"If we are to know where we are going," the short-haired person reminded them, "we need to know where we have come from."

"But how does it work?" someone asked from the back of the room.

There was a shuffling of feet as ears were pricked. This was what they all wanted to know.

The person with short hair stepped aside, making it clear that the person with long hair was the one with the answers.

"The clues are within the genetic sequences of the subject's DNA," she explained. "The technique we use is a form of genotyping using a DNA microarray, or chip. Ancestry is ultimately determined by comparing the subject's genetic variants to those of other individuals. We compare eight hundred thousand spots of variation to those of a base sample extracted from our worldwide repository of twenty-six different populations, split equally between Europeans, Africans, East Asians, and Polynesians ..."

"Polynesian is what I chose," Lexie interrupted proudly, winning smiles of approval from all.

"It's just amazing what people can do in this world," someone near Jordan observed.

"We can do anything," someone else replied, "if we put our minds to it."

Jordan's eyes drifted down from a spot on the ceiling towards the long-haired person. The elimination of stereotyping, which was the declared aim of World Government, had proven extremely difficult for people of his generation, for whom such language was so ingrained. In his mind, he wanted to refer to the long-haired person as "she" and, going even further, describe her as a "woman." But the physiology of gender was a spectrum with male at one extreme and female at the other—and one of the foundational human rights was that people were free to adopt the gender and pronoun of their choice. That was their prerogative. It was in this way that minorities had become, in aggregate, the majority, allowing majority rule to become minority rule. The bottom line was, he was free to think of her as "she," but he could not speak of her as "she" unless she invited it.

The brilliance of Progressivism, he thought, was that the rules did not need to be written down. They emerged organically from common usage, sifted through the refining sieve of social media, which screened out anything that couldn't pass through the ever-narrowing aperture of what might be deemed offensive.

Now the person that he thought of as "she" passed three envelopes to the person with short hair.

"The first result is for the birth mother, Lexie."

Ah, at last! The room collectively sighed, glancing at each other in anticipation. This was Lexie's night.

"And the result is just what we might expect: Lexie is ninety-nine point six percent European."

Heads turned in all directions; eyebrows raised; some smiles turned to frowns.

"I knew that," Lexie quickly explained. "We have no control over our ancestry—at least, not until now. As you all know, I was able to choose the color of my sperm donor so that, in one generation, the stain of whiteness in our bloodline will be diluted by half. Manaia will be able to cast off the shackles of our shame for colonial conquest, genocide, slavery, and warmongering."

"You go, sister!" a large-breasted person shouted, looking to start a round of high fives.

While there was clearly support for Lexie's views, not everyone understood the science. "So Lexie is ninety-nine percent Caucasian, right?" someone asked. "How does that happen? Why not one hundred percent?"

The person with long hair took back the three envelopes from the person with short hair as they exchanged places.

"The first thing to understand," she explained, "is that there is no such thing as racial purity. No one in the world is one hundred percent any racial classification. That is not how evolution has worked, because it's not how DNA works. Genotyping is a science of approximations extracted from data—cellular data—that runs into literally billions of information bits. Lexie is 0.00390625 percent non-European, which could mean that four of her ancestors ten generations ago were Polynesian, African, or Asian. But that's only four ancestors out of one thousand and twenty four that comprised her forebears ten generations ago—and only four out of the total ten thousand and forty six ancestors over those ten generations who brought her here today."

At the risk of being noticed, Jordan eased himself off the wall and slid into a gap in the audience where he could get a better view. The speaker was giving a layman's explanation of the decimalization of a function best expressed as a pyramidal construction of pairs in which the number two stood at the apex and the number 1,024 sat at the base. He'd already done the calculation in his head as she was speaking; her decimalization was correct. But there was something about her that troubled him. He felt that he knew her—yet he didn't want to know her. If he allowed recognition to crystallize, it could prove dangerous for him in ways that he could sense, but to which he dared not give definition. He tore his eyes away from her and, as slowly as possible, turned his back, trying to will his mind to go blank.

How had Jordan gotten to this point? How had a 58-year-old man—once a mathematics professor, father, and sometime lover of women, apolitical and ambitious only for a life of moderate academic achievement—come to be so stripped of any sense of value or identity that anxiety could floor him at the mere thought that ... that the confident young woman with the long hair might have been one of his mathematics students twenty years ago?

The feeling of dread he had so successfully overcome in the intervening years returned with such force that it was as if those years were nothing but a dream. He was still trapped in the spotlight of that university lecture hall ... the rhythmic chants of the ANT activists pounding in his ears ... his eyes flicking desperately from placard to placard, trying to find some sense in the messages to which he could form a rational response ... the mic amplifier howling ... the fire alarm (set off by the activist ringleaders) screaming across campus: "White men's math is dead men's oppression!" "Facts lie!" "Facts make fascists!" "Out, out, out with McPhee!" "Kill white privilege now!"

Jordan closed his eyes, breathing into the depths of his abdomen and listening to the erratic rhythm of his heart. The pounding in his chest became the pounding of feet down the corridors of the faculty wing, the pounding of fists on his locked office door, the pounded-out words that couldn't be taken back as rage and confusion had spewed from his mouth and spilled from his fingers onto the campus website:

> *Ignorant, immature snowflakes. Fevered, unbalanced seekers of nonexistent oppression. Flag-wavers for victimhood. Primitive thugs imbued with the anti-intellectual prejudice of left-wing rantings. If this is what this wretched university aspires to, then I want no part of it.* DEPLATFORM ME!

THE CELEBRATION – Part Two

October 2056

Jordan opened his eyes and looked around the room. The moment had passed. He was still invisible.

The person with short hair spoke again. "Now, what we've all been waiting for: the ancestry results for Lexie's child, Manaia. If you please, Alexa."

Alexa looked at the paper in her hand, then looked around the room. The audience held its breath. Cool night air drifted in silently through the balcony window, poised to be inhaled.

"The results for Manaia's ancestry are remarkably clear: twenty-four point eight percent Polynesian, twenty-four point eight percent East Asian, and forty-nine point eight percent European. Of course, these results are approximate because they have been rounded."

The silence with which this information was greeted suggested some confusion over the numbers. What did they mean in real terms? Some people in the audience took out their Konektors and entered the percentages into their calculators.

"It comes to almost one hundred," the person beside Jordan said. "Is that right?"

Jordan looked away. His mind had already worked out the fractions: Lexie's sperm donor was half Polynesian and half East Asian ... approximately. It was information he would keep to himself.

THE CELEBRATION – PART TWO

Lexie was the first to speak. "But that's impossible," she insisted angrily. "The donor bank told me the donor was one hundred percent Polynesian. The figures must be wrong."

"No one in the world is one hundred percent anything, Lexie," Alexa explained calmly. "These results suggest your donor was half Polynesian and half East Asian."

"But…"

If the child were present, Jordan thought, a simple visual assay might be conducted. The thought amused him.

Lexie, looking unconvinced and petulant, was grabbed by the large-breasted person who had earlier been intent on delivering high fives, and who was clearly not going to be denied that pleasure now. "Sister," the person shouted, "you are a hero! The goal is quarter, quarter, quarter—and Manaia is almost there. Call it for Manaia, everyone!"

With obvious relief, at last given an opportunity to release their pent-up desire for celebration, the room fervently chanted the child's name: "Manaia, Manaia, Manaia!"

Some added tag lines: "Our child for tomorrow!" "An end to racism!"

The hubbub of conversation reclaimed the room. Lexie was clearly consoled by her newfound status as a pioneer heroine (even if it was accidental).

But Alexa wasn't finished. "We still have one more set of results," she called out, "for the third sample. Who are these for, Lexie?"

Lexie hesitated just long enough to convince Jordan that she might be having second thoughts. "That's my … my…" Her voice faltered before she stumbled on the explanation. "That's Manaia's reference point for the generation before me. We need to know where we've come from if we're to be confident of where we're going," she paraphrased with growing conviction.

The room was silent again, ready to peer into the past—into a world that *The Citizens' Roll of Lineal Progression* was destined to consign to history.

"Well," Alexa mused as she opened the third envelope, "who are you, 'JM'? What will your results reveal?"

Once again, she read the paper carefully without speaking, then looked around the room. Yet her smile was different than any expression she'd worn that evening. It was nervous—and her voice, when it came, was rushed. "JM is twenty-five percent African and seventy-five percent European. My quick calculation is that this person cannot be directly related to Manaia's mother."

She folded the paper carefully and inserted it back into the envelope to hand it to Lexie—who, at this point, looked as if she had been injected in the throat with a horse tranquilizer. Jordan shifted his feet uneasily, waiting for the shock to wear off. He turned and looked for a path to the door, calculating the degree of difficulty should he decide to make a hasty exit. By the time he returned his gaze to the proceedings, Lexie was already marching through the throng of guests, pushing people aside, her shell earrings swinging dangerously like medieval weapons … and Jordan, standing transfixed, knew that his invisibility was about to be forcibly dissolved.

"What did you do, Jordan?" his daughter hissed ominously. "Did you switch samples to make a fool of me—to punish me for your own guilt? Is this one of your lame, misogynistic practical jokes, trying to make yourself still seem relevant?"

He immediately got the impression that she was toying with the idea of hitting him. If she chose to do so, she would probably have the support of the entire room. Now that he was suddenly visible, it was apparent to all that there was a middle-aged white male in their midst, and no one had warned them.

"And how typically *racist* of you to substitute a fake sample with African blood in it!" she spat. "How much more cynical can you get? To think that you fathered me!"

Should he speak? *Could* he speak…?

Instead, he did the unspeakable: he stepped forward and put his arms around her, holding her tight so she couldn't move. Under his breath, he whispered words in her ear that silenced her immediately. As understanding sank in, she gasped for air, her neck tattoo heaving and swelling as if it might burst.

Jordan bolted from the room, taking the stairs two at a time. If he fell, he fell; escape was the only thing on his mind. Throwing open the door to the lobby, he charged out onto the pavement, intent on making a getaway into the safety of the dark night.

Behind him, he heard footsteps clattering down the stairs… The lobby door opened and closed… The footsteps drew closer…

His Scoot was gone.

"Professor!" a voice called out. "Jordan … wait!"

He whirled around. It was Alexa.

"Don't you recognize me?" she asked. "I was a master's student the year the activists shut down the math department. I'd enrolled specifically to work with you; you were my mentor."

He knew he needed to say something, but he could not trust himself to say anything.

"My Scoot's been taken," he replied feebly. "I live on the Ninety-Fourth Circuit, and the nearest intersection with this Circuit is five and a half miles away, which is why I was allowed to take a Scoot from the station. Thankfully, I logged out, so at least whoever's taken it won't be mistaken for me. But now I've got a long walk ahead of me."

She stepped closer. He took a step back.

"Don't you remember me?" she repeated. "The night they burned down the math library, you and I got drunk. I asked you what I was going to do with my life now that mathematics was being erased from the university curriculum, and you told me to switch to statistics. Statistics, you said, can be made into anything that anybody wants, so it will never be done away with."

She stepped even closer. Her eyes were almond-shaped with dark, curling lashes. Her hips and bust were pleasingly rounded. Her waist was slender, and her legs were long. There was no denying what she was. Was it safe to say what he was about to say? If not, then it was too late for everything and nothing mattered anyway.

"Of course I remember you, Alexa. You were the brightest and most beautiful girl to ever study mathematics. The ANT brigades hated you for it."

She stepped forward again. This time he didn't step back.

"Tell me what you said to Lexie at the end there. The thing that made her cry."

From the direction of the building, he could hear the sounds of people leaving.

"I told her that I am not her birth father. Her mother was pregnant when we met. I thought she knew that. And I told her I'd forgotten about my maternal grandmother, who died before I was born. She was always described as a 'dusky beauty.' I guess that was code for having African blood. And now that you've confirmed that, I feel … I don't know … I guess I feel like celebrating."

Alexa laughed in a way he'd long since forgotten. Taking his arm, she steered him towards the Lineal Progression Office autonomous vehicle parked by the curb. "Come on," she said, "I'll give you a lift home. We can celebrate together."

A DERANGEMENT

August 2057

It took Jordan many weeks to come to terms with what had happened that night. There were modes of thinking that he had to consciously unravel—modes that he'd deliberately put in place following his deplatforming, as a way of coping with the anger and depression it had initially induced.

According to the cognitive behavioral therapy recommended by his friend Dr. John Erasmus, "The way we think determines how we feel, which influences how we act. You can't change events, but you *can* learn to control their effect upon you."

Jordan, however, had stubbornly refused to change how he thought. He knew full well that the meaning he assigned to any event was entirely up to him, and that if his thoughts were negative, they could become self-fulfilling in time. On the other hand, as he saw it, if his thoughts were positive despite events being negative, that was self-delusion, pure and simple. Thus he'd convinced himself that it was not cognitive distortions from which he suffered; he was merely facing reality. That was the core of his stubbornness: he was a logician. Not to mention that his status as a MAWM denied him any rights to victimhood... Although now that he'd lost his claim to the pure "white" element of that label, he might need to make some adjustments.

Of course, the events at the university had not been unique to him. Every established institution in modern society had been under attack by identitarianism since before the Overthrow. But the scar that had truly disfigured him and caused him to mask his face, like the mark of Zorro, was his betrayal by Lexie, the daughter he'd raised as his own. Inflamed with some form of socially righteous mania (the misandry of the emerging lesbian, perhaps, or the societal appetite for hunting down the patriarchy), she had gleefully doxed him on social media, like a Salem witch's child sticking pins in the effigy of a loathed enemy.

Jordan was not a misogynist—not up until that point, at least. But thereafter, he'd unconsciously chosen to make himself invisible to women. These days, it was a common response among men to the hostility directed at them from all sides, and it had served him well. So, when Alexa Smythe had announced that she'd join him in celebrating his newly discovered mixed-race status, he floundered, not knowing what was expected of him. After all, he was only her one-time math professor, and she his star female student. But twenty years had elapsed since then, and he was sure that she'd made the offer without recognizing the creature he had become.

"So now you know why you've got dark eyes and an olive complexion," she teased. "All the girls in college said you were just the coolest dude. Imagine not knowing you had it in you!"

She'd driven him home and invited herself into his apartment in expectation of toasting his black African grandmother—and the aplomb with which he'd handled Lexie's misplaced rage. As it happened, he had a bottle of chocolate mescaline liqueur in the cupboard. Three or four glasses of that, and he had relaxed sufficiently enough that, when she once again mentioned the last time they'd drunk together on the night of his deplatforming, he could actually smile about it.

"Did I really say that to you about statistics?" he asked.

"Yes, and you were right! It turned out to be a fantastic career choice for me. Of course, I'd much rather have stayed with pure mathematics, because I crave the intellectual challenge. I've never forgotten our conversations to this day."

Maybe it was the mescaline, but they ended up agreeing that getting together over coffee on occasion and talking mathematical theory might be good for their brains, and their souls. It was a rash proposal, and he immediately regretted it, presuming it would never happen.

But Alexa made it happen, calling him once a fortnight and confirming the time and place as if it were entered into her schedule.

Over one such coffee, she told him all about her work at the Lineal Progression Office—how un-challenging it was for a person with her qualifications, leaving her with a nagging feeling of frustration and unfulfillment.

"But that's true of all bureaucracy," she admitted. "And what about you? What do you work in now?"

"Artificial intelligence and machine learning," he replied. He didn't want to go much further than that. "I'm a Non-Person," he added. "Neither a servant nor a beneficiary of the state."

A faint shadow passed briefly across Alexa's face, but she didn't comment.

"I was lucky in having a network of friends from my student days," he explained. "We were a gang of reprobates that called ourselves the Derangers. It's French for something like 'the disrupters.' Most of them ended up in the tech world, and now that's where I've ended up, too."

He could have added that the obsession with violence and destruction that had defined his little student mob in the grip of their antiestablishment psychosis had eventually pulled down the very pillars he had relied on for stability throughout his academic life, leaving him no alternative but to walk away and try to reerect them elsewhere, far from the toxic environment of the university. But he wasn't after sympathy.

His friends had heralded his departure from academia as the best thing that could have happened to him. Being mostly science graduates, they'd gone into tech start-ups and research foundations in their thirties. By the time the Overthrow came, they were mostly embedded in high-tech fields where big money kept them out of its reach.

It was through this network of friends that he'd gradually rebuilt his life. In the twenty-something years since his deplatforming, he had become an intrinsic part of a world of research and discovery, working in emerging fields of technology that were doing nothing less (so they thought) than changing human behavior. Rather than teaching foundational mathematics, he'd come to understand its infinite nature, and its potential in computer science—in particular, the use of algorithms as step-by-step procedures for calculation, data processing, and automated reasoning.

Nowhere in any of this story did he feel there were grounds for self-pity.

"Remember the pickup basketball games we used to play?" Alexa asked, changing the subject. "The math department always won. They called you Michael Jordan. Now we know why."

He did remember. After all, she was nearly six feet, and he was six-foot-four. They had a natural advantage.

Later, he regretted not telling her more about his life, but the caution he'd developed over the past twenty years had held him back. She was a trusted representative of the state; he was a former member of the Derangers. Their worlds couldn't be further apart. So, he kept their morning coffee chats to academic waffle: Fermat's Last Theorem, Perelman's solution to the Poincaré conjecture, and so forth. It was a bit of a wank, but it had a nice otherworldly, nostalgic feel to it, as long as he maintained his distance.

Then one day, out of the blue, she hinted at a serious development that had taken place at work.

"Can I ask you to keep a confidence that might get both of us in trouble if we're found out?" she demanded.

His alarm bells went off.

"Is it something I need to know, or something you're better off keeping to yourself?" he replied cautiously.

"It's something that's going to take all my mathematical skills to resolve, and I may not be up to it without running it by someone. I hoped I could persuade you to play that role."

Though his curiosity was definitely piqued, it did nothing to ease his discomfort when she hinted that it involved state secrets.

He could easily have declined, but something was drawing him in. "If you think I can help," he said with a casual shrug.

Do I really need this friendship? he wondered later. Though he lived alone in the debt-free apartment he'd owned for twenty years (which had escaped the Social Equity Regulations that swept up private property assets when debt was reset at the time of the Overthrow), he was far from lonely. His colleagues comprised a fraternity that fully satisfied his needs for socialization. He had no sexual or relationship problems, no sense of isolation, and no time for depression or self-doubt. So why was he risking his stability by allowing himself to be drawn into such a potentially problematic friendship?

As the months had gone by since they first met at Lexie's celebration, he'd struggled to maintain his mask, but he'd never let it slip. It had the functional purpose of protecting his scars, but the scars remained. Thus his meetings with Alexa threatened the protective devices he'd come to rely upon. She didn't see his mask; she simply saw him as her former mathematics professor. And despite himself, he now found himself being lured into the trap of wanting to help her, unable to resist the flattering implications of her request.

... Or was he just seeing an opportunity here for Artie Sharp?

TWO BIRDS, ONE STONE

The ArteFact Channel
August 2057

SCENE: *The enigmatic figure of Artie Sharp is seated at a desk before a blank whiteboard in what is clearly a college lecture room. While his appearance is unremarkable, it is obvious to the viewer that the person occupying this role on screen must be Artie Sharp, because that is the name of the person who presents these segments on the ArteFact Channel on the dark web, and he is known to deliberately change his appearance and role according to the subject for the day. Besides which, there is a name plaque on the desk which reads, ARTIE SHARP.*

ARTIE SPEAKS *as he scribbles furiously on a desk pad. What he scribbles appears on the whiteboard behind him as a jumbled series of mathematical calculations.*

"In recent days, you will have seen the figures released by the Agenda Implementation Tribunal showing our performance with respect to the United Nations Convention on Environmental and Development Objectives referred to in *Agenda 2060.*

"In one very important respect, it would appear from the figures that we are not doing well at all. This is that perennial chestnut that we all know as Article Five: 'Reduce man-made carbon emissions and greenhouse gases to zero, and convert all energy consumption to the use of renewable resources.'

"Despite the almost total elimination of fossil fuels from our economies, it would seem that excess amounts of carbon dioxide remain stubbornly present in the atmosphere. Of course, we cannot definitively say who in the world is doing a better or worse job of addressing this problem because, collectively, we are One World—all in this together. But the bottom line is, a solution is needed ... and I believe I may have found one.

"I recently received a paper forwarded to me by the well-regarded air and water environmentalist Tony Andrew, in which he provides an analysis of the air we breathe in the average city, its composition in terms of gases, and which of those gases we rely upon to sustain life.

"In simple terms, air is composed of 78.08 percent nitrogen and 20.95 percent oxygen by volume. Small amounts of argon, carbon dioxide, neon, helium, and hydrogen make up the remainder of the balance. When we exhale, the oxygen in the air released has been reduced to 13.6 to 16 percent, and the nitrogen drops to approximately 74.4 percent, with water vapor now comprising 5 to 6.3 percent—but the carbon dioxide has increased a hundredfold, now representing 4 to 5 percent by volume.

"Is this remarkable? Not at all ... until you do the math, which I am showing you on the board behind me as I speak. Of course, with mathematics no longer being offered by the education system, you may find all these numbers confusing. But you can easily enter them into the calculator app on your Konektor to verify the answers.

"So you see, on average, we humans take 12 breaths per minute, and the volume of air inhaled per breath is around 500 milliliters. Over 24 hours, we take about 17,280 breaths and exhale 8,640,000 milliliters of air, of which, say, 4.5 percent is carbon dioxide. In a year, therefore, each one of us exhales approximately 141,912 liters of carbon dioxide.

"The next figure is for carbon dioxide's weight. According to Tony Andrew's paper, carbon dioxide weighs 183.6 kilograms per 100,000 liters. So, each of us is exhaling 183.6 times 1.41912, which means 260.55 kilograms of carbon dioxide per annum. Who would have thought?

"Coincidentally, in the last week, we heard from the Club of Rome, who remain concerned that Article Eleven of *Agenda 2060* has not been addressed, despite the repeated warnings they have given the world since way back in 1972. Article Eleven reads, 'Work to achieve, by any peaceful and humanitarian means possible, a sustainable world population limit of five billion people within the next one hundred years.' But as we all know, the world population now stands at over eight billion.

"So, what's to be done? It seems to your commentator, Artie Sharp, that the math is quite simple: reduce the population by three billion, and we reduce the carbon dioxide load by 781.65 billion kilograms—that's 781.65 *million tons*—per annum. Why, we could even start using fossil fuels again!

"Now, how should we go about this? And what exactly is the meaning of the phrase 'by any peaceful and humanitarian means possible'? Certainly, three billion people is a lot to eliminate from the global population ... but the benefits are plain to see.

"So, who volunteers to go first? I'll leave you to think about it."
ARTIE SHARP stands up and wipes the whiteboard clean before giving a cheery wave and leaving the room.

THE UNFORESEEN CONSEQUENCE OF SUCCESS

September 2057

Sometimes in the dark hours before dawn, when unknown dogs howled mournfully and the pounded pillow was pressed against her ears until they hurt, Alexa Smythe would conjure up a math problem in her head and set out to solve it without resorting to pen and paper, let alone a calculator. With her mind completely occupied in this way, there was no opening for wasteful and distracting thoughts to intrude—thoughts of the *Who am I?* and *What's going to happen to my fucking life?* variety. (Alexa, it should be noted, was no different than any other member of humankind in the middle of the twenty-first century.)

Her favorite go-to problem was one of Hilbert's non-negative polynomials expressed as a sum of squares of rational functions. She was so good at it that over time, she was able to add dozens of variables raised to high powers, so that by the time the sun pushed its way into her bedroom, she could get out of bed feeling refreshed and quite pleased with herself.

On this particular morning, however, it wasn't Hilbert's polynomials that she was wrestling with. It was the definition of numbers—specifically, how she might apply it to an issue deeply imbued with moral psychology, in a way that minimized the potential threat to the very security and foundational premise of her country's social structure.

Okay, she thought, swinging her long legs out of bed, *that's a bit over the top*. But hyperbole aside, the fact was that what she had been asked to do was come up with a way to completely restructure the basis for calculating Society Points, in a way that would reduce the country's Transitional Benefits costs by a massive fifteen percent—a feat which, if not managed correctly, could result in civil unrest not seen since the days of the Overthrow.

Oh yes, it was a doozy of a challenge, this one ... and she was still trying to figure out, *Why me?* She knew she was good at her job, and that other people knew this. But she also knew that those people didn't see her as a trusted insider—so there was surprise and caution on both sides when the head of the Lineal Progression Office summoned her to sign a Loose Lips Agreement.

"I don't know what it's about," her boss said, "and I'll probably never know, because once you sign this undertaking, you're never to speak to anyone about it again."

That could only mean it was an *Agenda 2060* matter, and she was to appear before a Special Caucus Hearing in the Capitol, presumably focusing on issues related to statistics policy, on which she had written a number of papers. She was momentarily stunned, however, when she entered the room and realized that the sixteen people seated across the table from her represented the full Agenda Implementation Tribunal—arguably the sixteen most influential people in the country. In an exhilarating and slightly frightening way, it rendered her speechless.

"Alexa Smythe," the tribunal chair greeted her, "you don't know why you are here. In fact, you are *not* here—and nobody can ever know whether you were really here or not. Is that clear?"

Alexa could only nod.

"Is it true," the chair asked, "that you studied mathematics under the now-disgraced former professor Jordan McPhee?"

Alexa cleared her throat. "I did, but..."

"Because Professor McPhee does not exist," the chair interrupted, "and if you choose to consult him on any of the matters we are going to discuss this morning, it should be evident that you have *not* consulted him—because he does not exist. Do you understand?"

"I do," Alexa replied clearly, regaining her voice. Clarity and forthrightness were qualities for which Alexa was well known, and she was surprised by how this reference to Jordan had thrown her off balance. Of course they knew about her new friendship with him; they knew everything if it was of interest to them.

But why was Jordan of interest?

"Let me give you some background," the chair continued. "We need to back up fifty or sixty years to the time of the original United Nations intergovernmental treaties of 1992, and the agendas set down in the following years, guiding member nations in their treatment of the planet and its peoples. As you know, those agendas provided policy makers around the world with the inspiration to shape the social justice settings laid out in *Agenda 2060*, of which we are so proud today. Positive discrimination in favor of marginalized members of society has had both immediate and long-lasting benefits, bringing fairness and equality of outcome to all. Nowhere is this more evident than in the Society Points system, which underpins the Transitional Benefits calculations upon which the economy is based ... though I imagine all this is familiar to you."

"Of course!" Alexa agreed.

"Starting with the nine officially recognized variations in gender," the chair explained, "and adding in the seven separable racial origins, we have managed to identify the main minority groupings and give them representation in our government policy settings. And you see those sixteen minorities gathered here today, Alexa, at this table. No one can accuse us of bias or injustice in any of our lawmaking decisions. You need to keep that fact in the forefront of your mind when you turn it to the problem we are asking you to help us solve."

"I will," Alexa replied with conviction. "And what exactly is that problem? Does it have something to do with my work on multiracial inheritance?"

"No," the deputy tribunal chair interrupted, "this problem is an unforeseen consequence of our own success."

The deputy chair was a much older person whose presence surprised Alexa. Positive discrimination for the aged was still being actively debated in light of the Population Control Objectives, so someone of advanced years being on the tribunal was unexpected. She could see that he was probably Q, however, and definitely Poly-Asian, so she couldn't argue with his right to representation on the grounds of gender or race.

"We need to think back to a time well before you were born," the old person said. "In those days, the country was made up of forty-eight percent males and fifty-two percent females. There were only two boxes you could tick."

The quaintness of this antiquated misconception brought smiles all around the table.

"Some social scientists of the time, believing themselves to be more enlightened, speculated that up to two percent of people of either gender might be homosexual."

As the comrades on the other side of the table exploded in mirth at the outrageous nature of this speculation, the old person stilled them with a raised hand.

"But if you can believe that outrage, consider the fascist lie that was applied to race. Back in those days, there were only three boxes people could tick: 'European ancestry,' 'non-European,' or 'other'!"

Heads shook.

What is this? Alexa wondered. *Everyone knows this.*

"The level of intimidation and oppression was so intense that people passively accepted this horrifying misrepresentation of themselves and of their country. 'White intimidation and oppression' is the proper description. We cannot blame white womyn for this, because they were victims of oppression themselves—white *male* oppression, the curse that we continue to fight around the world to this day."

"Yes, yes," Alexa said, nodding automatically. She caught herself almost muttering the standard mantra "male chauvinist patriarchal oppression," before remembering she was not in a staff training session. Surely these people wouldn't require that from her...?

"What strange days those must have been," she said, looking around the table.

"Well, all that changed," the chair announced, taking back the reins. "The brave intercession of pioneer efforts like the Me Too movement, by attacking toxic masculinity, exposing misgendering, and championing intersectionalism, has helped to unveil the true nature of who we are—

and that, combined with the multicultural benefits of open borders, has made us the rich post-modern society we are today."

Alexa wondered why on earth these people would find it necessary to tell her all this. It was all a bit strange; it felt as if they were trying to reassure themselves of the soundness of the principles outlined in their own Founders' Manual.

Then a voice to her left spoke up. "Do you know how we made it happen?"

The person addressing her had a severe look: square jaw, heavily muscled tattooed arms, and a long strawberry-blonde wig. Alexa stiffened as she felt her unconscious bias training struggle to assert itself.

"Incentives!" the person announced before she could reply. "The Social Points system rewards people for identifying with minority groups. LGBTQI is now the largest combined demographic in the country. Three generations of state-sponsored miscegenation have seen the European race pushed out of its centuries-old dominance. Combined with our drive to bring mental illness into the mainstream, this means that the index for Transitional Benefits—or what they called "welfare" in the bad old days—has now been transformed. A person identifying as lesbian, American Indian, physically challenged, and qualifying for counselling could, theoretically, be entitled to one hundred and twelve percent of the maximum benefit scale ... and therein lies our problem."

Alexa had heard the rumors; she was not exactly surprised by what they were telling her.

Then the person got to their feet and pointed a finger at her severely. "And you, Alexa, with your damned work at the Lineal Progression Office, are not making things any easier."

"Oh!" Alexa responded, thinking she finally understood why she had been summoned here. "So, you're thinking that you need to modify the work we're doing. Are there too many racial and ethnic origins being identified for the system to support?"

Her accuser adjusted their wig and sat down. Around the table, people looked down at their hands.

Alexa turned back to the tribunal chair.

The chair smiled. "There's nothing wrong with your work," the chair assured her, "and that's not why you are here. We have two major problems, which we believe only a person with a mathematician's mind and a thorough understanding of statistics can help us resolve. Mathematics was banned from the education system because it relies on logic and outdated modes of thinking, drawn from the likes of Plato and Pythagoras all the way up to the despised European era of the so-called Enlightenment—which is, quite rightly, anathema to progressive teaching. Unfortunately, for what we have in mind, the disciplined thinking of a mathematical logician, combined with an awareness of the creative potential germane to statistics, may be the only way to get through this thing."

The tribunal chair seemed somewhat embarrassed by this admission. Every other pair of eyes in the room was rigidly averted.

"You see, Alexa, there are two distinct problems. One is budgetary. Our incentives have worked too well, and we need to reformulate the system in such a way that people are not offended or angered by the necessary changes to their status and benefits. At the same time, we need to ... well, we need to be careful how we present it."

"You're a mathematician," they went on. "How many combinations can be created out of sixteen minority classes? Thousands...?"

"Millions," Alexa replied confidently.

"Millions. So, how could your ordinary citizen possibly understand the basis of the tweaking that you, the mathematician, will be able to engineer once you put your mind to our problem? We're asking you to overhaul our policy settings in a way that will balance our budget, but which will be so complex in its formulation that no one could possibly understand it, let alone challenge it."

"... No one but another mathematician, presumably," Alexa replied. "Perhaps someone like Jordan McPhee? As a precautionary measure, am I permitted to call upon his expertise?"

The chair sat stone-faced at this suggestion, as if they hadn't heard. "I think we have established that Professor McPhee does not exist," they muttered absently. "His status is clear: he is a Non-Person."

"Of course." Alexa smiled. "So, you said there are two problems you need me to address. What's the second?"

AN INTRODUCTION TO MATHEMATICAL PHILOSOPHY

October 2057

As Alexa climbed out of bed after a night of wrestling with a million permutations of numbers, she felt it was forgivable to feel daunted by the scale of the challenge before her. But was she overwhelmed by it? Not at all; she had seldom felt so invigorated. Oh yes, at first it had seemed daunting—particularly because one of the conditions laid down by the tribunal was that her solution must be inscrutable to all but the most brilliant of mathematicians (of whom none officially remained). But when she realized that the answer lay in the familiar territory of Hilbert's polynomials, everything fell into place. Triumph and relief made her giddy.

There was only one possible outlet for her euphoria. She made a cup of rooibos tea sweetened with honey, then picked up her Konektor.

Every call made on a Konektor was monitored, of course, and calls made to non-approved people could be audited and interrupted instantly, resulting in a reduction in Society Points. Alexa almost laughed out loud. She had no fears about the call she was compelled to make now, because it was the chair of the Agenda Implementation Tribunal that had personally told her that her one-time math teacher, "the now disgraced ex-professor Jordan McPhee," did not exist. More than that, she'd been told, "If you choose to consult him on any of the matters we are going to discuss this morning, it should be evident to you that you have *not* consulted him—because he does not exist."

"Konektor," Alexa instructed, "connect me to Jordan McPhee."

The red light came on, hesitated while the system ran the algorithm, then turned green.

"Alexa," Jordan answered cautiously. "Have you cracked it?"

Despite the hesitancy in his voice, it seemed to her that, at this moment, his was the warmest and most comforting voice in the world. Who else could understand the enormity of the challenge she faced?

She told him about the solution she had discovered based on Hilbert's polynomials.

"Excellent, excellent!" he enthused quietly. "That could well be a very elegant solution."

Despite his obvious desire to maintain his distance, she took comfort in this open praise.

"I've been thinking about your other problem," he continued, "and I just want to remind you that whenever something feels overwhelmingly complicated, the solution is invariably very simple. Remember the earliest principles you were taught about numbers. There's a passage from Bertrand Russell's *Introduction to Mathematical Philosophy* that I want to read to you. I have a copy of it right here. I think it might help you address your second problem. Russell says, 'It is simpler logically to find out whether two collections have the same number of terms than it is to define what that number is. An illustration will make this clear. If there were no polygamy or polyandry anywhere in the world, it is clear that the number of husbands living at any moment would be exactly the same as the number of wives...' Remember, this was written a hundred and fifty years ago, when 'husbands and wives' were common pairings. 'We do not need a census to assure us of this, nor do we need to know what is the actual number of husbands and wives. We know the number must be the same in both collections, because each husband has one wife, and each wife has one husband. The relation of husband and wife is what is called One-One.' "

"Of course," Alexa interrupted, "and a relation is said to be One-One when, if x has the relation to y, no other term x_1 has the relation to

y, and x does not have the same relation to any term y_1 other than y."

"You were always an excellent student, Alexa," he complimented her. "Now, tell me again exactly how they explained the nature of their second problem."

Alexa took a deep breath. "The tribunal is alarmed that the United Nations compliance team is arriving shortly to audit our record regarding support for minorities. A minority is defined as any group that, either by gender or race, makes up less than five percent of the total population in any jurisdiction. With so many minorities choosing to self-identify because of the heavy incentives they receive through the Social Points system, what was once the majority, from which society needed to be protected, has suddenly become a minority, with no support systems in place for it."

"You mean...?"

"Yes: white males now represent only 4.1 percent of the population, now that so many people choose to self-identify as minorities in order to gain Social Points. When the UN inspectors find out we don't have a policy of positive discrimination for them, we will be fined billions of international credits. But you've just given me an idea. If a person has a portion of male gender X, and a portion of white ancestry Y, then regardless of their self-identification or the actual size of those portions, they can be classed in the category of 'XY'—which is equivalent to Russell's One-One."

"Excellent, Alexa! And in this case, XY returns them to the majority. It solves the problem mathematically, but will they understand it?"

They agreed to meet at a later date when Alexa had decided how to deliver her solution to the tribunal, and he would peer-review her figures. (Of course, since he was deplatformed, his name would not be mentioned in her report.).

TWO DEAD RATS

January 2058

On the day that Alexa was to present her findings to the Agenda Implementation Tribunal, she was menstruating heavily. Doubling over in pain from the cramping in her lower abdomen, she managed to get dressed and brush her hair and teeth. The sight of her face in the bathroom mirror, with her skin pale as her bedsheets and her eye sockets sunken and dark, drew out a groan of resentment. She'd been working day and night to unravel the chaos that intersectionalism had created in the Social Points system, which determined the distribution of Transitional Benefits. Half that time, it seemed to her, was spent arguing over the coding of every single category of identity with the senior officials of the Social Equity Ministry, as if she were a threat to their entire belief system. She had been getting to the point where she wanted to scream ... and now she knew why. The tension building inside her had finally broken as nature opened a relief valve in the form of her uterus.

But, oh, the irony. After all, what was it that drove intersectionalism? Why, victimhood, of course. Society had been divided into victims and oppressors. "Well, what about women having to suffer the oppression of this bloody curse?" she muttered to herself in the bathroom mirror. "Who's going to give us Social Points for that?"

The parchment pallor and sunken eyes that looked back at her undermined the very self-image on which her confidence relied. Who was going to see her as a competent and assertive adviser on issues of state interest looking like this? She just needed a little makeup.

It was not in Alexa's makeup, however (*nice pun, Alexa*), to see herself as a victim, and it would have been extremely hard in the matter of her monthly cycle to identify an oppressor. By the time she was dressed and out the door, she'd committed to doing what every womyn born womyn had to do: suck it up and get on with it.

Her subsequent presentation to the full caucus hearing was delivered at times through clenched teeth—which may have been to her benefit, because she came across as doubly determined, businesslike, and intolerant of any half-baked questions. She had decided to park her XY/One-One formula as being too obscure for them to understand. Instead, a simple solution to the tribunal's problem lay in the Social Points coding, she explained.. Her work at the Lineal Progression Office had proven the value of evidence-based determinations of racial makeup. By expanding the focus of that office to include all citizens making claims on the basis of race, the system could, at a stroke, become more robust.

"Racial identity is only one part of the social equity issue," the tribunal chair pointed out. "What about sexual identity?"

"The very same testing regime can determine sex with absolute certainty," Alexa replied, her tone implying that they needed to decide whether they wanted this thing sorted out or not.

"I don't like the sound of this at all," one of the caucus members objected. "Sexuality is not binary. Above all, it is a matter of choice. What you are suggesting is that your laboratory should be used as a tool of oppression, forcing people to accept an identity based on an arbitrary scientific scale. I really thought we'd moved beyond a world dominated by science."

"What do you have to say to that, Alexa?" the deputy chair asked.

"We have a saying at the Lineal Progression Office," she replied. " 'Science is relevant when it serves the purposes of the people.' There are two distinct considerations at play here. The first is the budget. The second is the emotional quotient of certain citizen populations. While the budget relies on numbers, and numbers are finite and absolute, emotional quotients are the exact opposite; their very fluidity makes them impossible to measure. That is not to say they lack validity, but they cannot be measured in absolute units. So, the first step is to divorce the two."

"And how do you propose to do that?" the tribunal chair asked.

Alexa had thought long and hard about this, talking it over with Jordan (who had played devil's advocate with such deep understanding of the nuances of the subject, she realized he must have already given it a great deal of thought himself). In essence, she could give the tribunal a radical solution that would solve the budget problems in one stroke, but which might be politically unacceptable, or she could advance a combination of solutions that would require some compromises. A single compromise, such as defining sexuality, might not do it; two or three might be required. But as the old saying went, once you've survived swallowing a dead rat, the second one is much easier.

"With the greatest respect," Alexa responded politely, "I must ask whether we have forgotten why I am here today. As we know, the largest portion of Social Points is allocated by gender and race, and the system relies on self-identification. The balance is allocated to minority categories in the manner set forth by the Department of Equity and Social Justice. Now intersectionalism has allowed a disproportionately large volume of people to register claims for a multiplicity of disadvantages. As a result, the budget can't handle the demand. That's one problem.

"The second problem is that white males are choosing not to self-identify as that category, which has now sunk to a level that makes it an unrecognized, unsupported minority—a fact that cannot be hidden from the United Nations compliance team, and which will make us pariahs in the world community and liable for hefty fines. Now, we can fix these problems by disallowing self-identification and restricting the number of qualifying minority categories; or by recoding gender and race on the basis of evidential DNA testing, and limiting the choice of minority groupings to a maximum of, say, three per person. It would take approximately two years to complete a nationwide testing program, and it would require a massive expansion of the Lineal Progression Office ... but you'd get the results you want."

The glances exchanged around the table were looks of horror, akin to those of franticly flapping fish stranded on the deck of a boat, knowing they are dying.

She knew exactly how they would respond. She didn't bother to wait.

"Then again," she continued, "there is another potential solution that would require no compromises and could even elevate our standing in the world community, rivaling that of Norway."

The fish stopped flapping. Was it possible they might get thrown back in...?

"Aren't we all working towards the implementation of *Agenda 2060?*" she asked. "Isn't the goal of the member nations to be recognized as having achieved those aims, and isn't it the very first article of the Agenda that we are addressing here today? Allow me to read it to you. 'Article One: Eliminate all discrimination on the grounds of gender, race, ethnicity, and mental or physical ability, and provide positive empowerment to womyn and minority groups to ensure equality of outcome for all.'

"What we have been doing through the Social Points system for the last eighteen years is in direct contradiction to these aims. We haven't eliminated the practice of making distinctions on the grounds of sex, color, or disability; we've been *encouraging* such distinctions. Our whole system is based on fractionalized identities. It's become a competition for victimhood and reward: whoever can claim the greatest burden of oppression and emotional damage wins. It ignores the most important words of the article, which are: 'to ensure equality of outcome for all.' "

The deputy chair was the first to speak. "You belittle the harm done to victims of oppression and prejudice. Self-identification is the victim's right—and you, a privileged white woman, would dare suggest we take that away from them?"

The tribunal chair agreed. "How else are people supposed to achieve a renewed sense of self-worth, Alexa? We are addressing the anxiety and depression, the fragility and fear that so many groups in our society were forced to endure before we encouraged them to become empowered and rewarded for calling out their oppressors. I can't believe you want to undo all our work."

Much more in this vein followed. Alexa sat quietly, trying not to grimace as she was gripped by her menstrual pains. Predictably, their objections were filled with the obligatory consensual hallucinations that now characterized all public discourse and left no room for competing ideas. But they'd asked her to come up with solutions, and that was what she'd done.

Once they'd run out of steam, she continued. "I don't disagree with any of the sentiments you're expressing," she assured them, "but I'd like you to step out of the present moment and look at this from another perspective. Imagine if we took the articles of *Agenda 2060* literally and announced that we were eliminating all minority distinctions—not highlighting them, but eliminating them—and in the process, we would be celebrating equality by rewarding everyone equally, with the same quota of Social Points. At a stroke, the budget is balanced; it can't be exceeded. Of course, we would still have to remain vigilant in monitoring for discrimination and evidence of oppression, but for that there can be penalties. It's a simple proposal, but it solves our problems. We just need to sell it to the people who are benefitting the most from being the biggest victims. They would experience financial loss, and they may not like the idea of other people no longer being worse off than them. It might take some convincing."

The severe-looking person with the muscled arms and blonde wig banged the table with their fist. "So, there'd be no need to claim victim status," they concluded, "because there'd no longer be financial benefit in it?"

"Precisely!" Alexa exclaimed. "White males would become just white males again."

On that note, she felt that she'd achieved her purpose. She'd offered them the two dead rats and, as expected, they'd been reluctant to swallow them. The alternative was bold, radical, but blindingly simple if they had the courage to run with it. There was nothing more she could add, so she suggested that she leave it with them to mull over.

Telling Jordan about the presentation the next day, she was quick to realize that saying it "might take some convincing" to get the public on board with her bold proposal was a bit of an understatement.

"The tribunal chair followed me out and said he thought it would take a day or two for them to get their heads around it. Then he said something that really took me by surprise. He says nobody believes anything that the government says, so how would I suggest they go about selling my solution to the public?"

Jordan's ears pricked up. "So, they're taking your suggestion seriously?"

"I don't know; it's early days."

"Maybe," Jordan concurred, "but the budget problem is only going to become more urgent with each passing day. The great merit of your solution is its simplicity. Anyway, what did you suggest?"

"Oh, that was funny. I had a sudden inspiration. I told them they need to find someone the public trusts to tell the truth—someone with a big following and a reputation for dealing in facts, someone who isn't afraid to expose institutional hypocrisy. And the person who came to mind was that satirical character known as Artie Sharp on the underground web channel *ArteFact*. No one knows who he is, but everyone watches it. Have you seen it?"

BRAIN MAPPING

January 2058

Jordan switched off his Konektor and put it on the top shelf of his refrigerator next to the condenser. "Stay cool," he muttered.

Then he took a basketball from the lobby cupboard and walked down to the court on the corner. He could always count on being alone here. No one played outdoor sports anymore; they preferred virtual reality games like *Court Jester*, where they could lie on the settee and pretend to be seven feet tall, making slam dunks and elbowing point guards in the face, while chalking up extra points for dishing out insults that would easily land them in a different kind of court in real life.

"Hey, Chinese umpires are barefaced liars, man."

"How do you figure?"

"Ever see a Chinaman with a beard?"

The thump, thump, thump of the bouncing ball stilled his mind. When he was ready, he'd jog up to the charity stripe until he'd thrown nothin' but net, then dribble back out behind the three-point arc until he'd thrown three in a row, finishing by taking it to the hole. No thoughts—just the easy rhythm of *thump, thump, thump, shoot!*

But once he'd finished, that damn thought was still waiting for him. Alexa worked for the state. She wanted to track down Artie Sharp. He knew this friendship had been a mistake. As a Non-Person, he'd spent twenty years under the governmental radar, ineligible for Transitional Benefits, Medicare, or Social Points: a free man. This was the grey area in which his colleagues also chose to operate; open and creative minds could only stay that way by avoiding any entanglements with bureaucracy. Even though Alexa seemed to recognize this—or at least she said so—there was no way she could ever be allowed near Artie.

He needed to find a way to get out of this relationship before it was too late.

But later, as he rode the Urban Transitor to the laboratory above a converted car park that housed the data center for his artificial intelligence and augmented reality research programs, he began to realize what an opportunity he'd been given. He had always claimed to be apolitical. He was only interested in logic, empiricism and truth, he'd convinced himself, and this mindset served as the basis on which he'd programmed Artie. But that was a lie in itself; politics was in everything. Declaring oneself to be apolitical was simply intended to avoid any accusations of being partial—which then freed him to let loose Artie's satirical attacks on any elements of society that breached the rules of probity, regardless of where they stood on the political spectrum.

And the key point was that Artie learned these rules from Jordan McPhee.

Alexa's revelation—that the Agenda Implementation Tribunal had basically admitted that the Social Points system on which Transitional Benefits policy was built was now effectively collapsing—could signal the single biggest disruption to society since the Overthrow. The more that Alexa had revealed, the more certain Jordan became that the foundations of *Agenda 2060* were about to be shaken to their core ... and he'd be crazy to give up an opportunity to be this close to the action.

By the time the Urban Transitor arrived at his destination, Jordan had begun to form a conclusion. Artie Sharp had been trained to use hyperbolic humor and absurdity to make people think differently about issues. But the real issue with *Agenda 2060* was that it reduced everyone to members of exclusionary groups, polarizing society at every turn—and now Alexa was on the brink of pitching a proposal that would, if successful, dismantle the entire system.

This was no time to distance himself from Alexa. Maybe it was time to get closer.

Placing his outstretched palm against the door sensor, Jordan looked up at the retina scanner; the door welcomed him by name as he entered the data center lounge, quietly closing behind him. The lounge had been Jordan's idea. He was old-school, believing that face-to-face human interaction added a dimension to communication that was missing from Konektors and the like, no matter how big the screen or how high the definition.

This facility, known as the DDC (Derangers Data Center), housed Jordan's mathematics laboratory. It functioned primarily as a storehouse for graphics processing units (GPUs) running artificial, deep, and convolutional neural networks designed to emulate the human brain. GPUs were faster and more efficient at performing complex mathematical tasks than conventional central processing units (CPUs). The on-site computational power and data processing were never likely to be limiting factors, as they were remotely connected to centers elsewhere that magnified their capacity exponentially. That was the strength of the Derangers' network: they were embedded everywhere in the nervous system of the tech economy.

The young engineers and programmers who staffed the facility included high-end gamers and video graphics designers who gravitated toward AR and VR. To them, Professor Jordan McPhee was a social relic from the dark ages who spoke a language they didn't fully understand, but which they couldn't ignore, for it was rumored he'd played some part in the development of the first exaFLOP supercomputer, capable of making a quintillion (or a billion billion) calculations per second. For his part, Jordan liked his privacy, encouraging the young people to keep their distance unless he had a backlog of code to be written.

The exception was one Antonio Muchos, producer of the Artie Sharp video segments for the *Artefact Channel*. Antonio was not only a wicked designer/programmer, he also had a wicked sense of humor for someone his age, without even a whiff of political correctness. Jordan had resolved that this morning they would discuss one of the social issues he'd identified while riding the Urban Transitor, in hopes that Antonio would come up with a light, bright, and entertaining perspective on it.

Before he could find Antonio, however, he bumped into Hedley Payne, a fellow Deranger, apparently waiting for Jordan's arrival while crouched over the coffee machine with a puzzled expression.

"Is this coffee organic?" Hedley asked by way of greeting.

"I don't even know what that means," Jordan muttered. There was something about Hed Payne that always made Jordan bristle, even though he considered him a friend.

His sarcasm was ignored as Hedley suddenly turned serious. "Jordan, I need your advice." He glanced around. "… in the absolute strictest confidence."

The lounge was full of young engineers and programmers sprawled out on beanbags, their faces hidden behind VR headsets as they argued with colleagues in other rooms, across the country, or on other continents— or perhaps even with those sitting right next to them. The environment was distracting and exposed, and apart from Jordan's office, the only place where they could shut the door and turn on the Do Not Disturb light was one of the video conference rooms. Jordan led the way.

Hedley, his brow furrowed, set his coffee down on the conference table and pulled out a chair. "It's about the work I've been doing on genome sequencing," he began. "I've explained it to you."

"Yeah… It always sounds to me like playing at God," Jordan quipped.

"Maybe. It's just biotechnology to me." He shrugged. "Anyway, as you know, genome sequencing determines an organism's complete set of DNA, including all its genes—a full blueprint of an organism's genetic material. And as you also know, the cost and speed of human genome sequencing has plummeted, and genetic editing technology has rapidly expanded, allowing genetic diseases to be identified years before symptoms present themselves."

"Sure," Jordan prompted, trying to move things along. "So, you target these disease genes and splice healthy genes in their place. Medicine will never be the same, you keep saying, provided people can afford it."

"Yes. But here's the thing," Hedley admitted. "I'm a biochemist, not a health practitioner."

"So, what's the problem?"

"The two fields are vastly different. We have different rules and ethics."

"Okay…" Jordan sat back, sighed, and looked at the ceiling. What did he know about ethics? It was one of those topics that had been hijacked by societal groupthink, and he wasn't a member of the group; he was an outsider.

"There's a company called Micomic Health," Hedley went on. "They're based in New York and sell something called Micomic Life Xtension, and they're major clients of our genetic editing technology. They're the best in the business. Essentially, what they do is identify the patient DNA that contains the mutation, then use a guide RNA to target it and a special protein to cut it out, so it can be replaced by a healthy one."

"… Just like editing software."

"That's right. And when the cause of disease is removed, the impact can be seen in weeks."

"Sounds great, but this is old stuff," Jordan observed. "So, what's the problem?"

Hedley stood up and started pacing the room. He walked over to the video transmitter and sound system, bending down to check whether they were switched on. Still not satisfied, he pulled all the power connections out of their sockets.

"You're right, this stuff is not new," he said suddenly. "It's been in use for years for things like cancer and cystic fibrosis, but it's not available to everyone. You have to be a special class of person to even get access to it."

"What class of person?" Jordan asked innocently.

"Rich. Powerful. Influential."

"Of course." *What a coincidence,* Jordan thought, *that would seem to exclude everyone on Transitional Benefits.* "So, rich, powerful, influential people get to live longer," he observed with only a hint of irony.

"There are plenty of them, don't worry," Hedley asserted. "And yes, they do live longer. That's the whole idea. The salutogenesis arm of Micomic Life Xtension can extend your life span by fifty percent, if you're rich."

"Or powerful."

"Or influential. And I have a feeling influence counts for more than riches or power," Hedley said earnestly.

"Well, the three do tend to go together," Jordan concluded. "So, is that what's troubling you?"

Hedley shook his head. Then he took out his Konektor. "Is your device bypassing?" he asked anxiously.

"Of course it is. I invented the AI, remember?"

Hedley wasn't convinced. He turned off his Konektor and put it on the conference table, glaring at it suspiciously. Even when powered down, a Konektor that wasn't fitted with bypassing would continue to carry voice and data traffic in both directions to government cybercenters. With the speed of the latest 12G signal, the content analyzers five thousand miles away would have finished their work before the sound of the words spoken had even died from the room. Every member of the Derangers' network had an Alt-Identity, as did every one of their trusted employees. Since the Overthrow, it was just the way of things, and Hedley Payne's sudden distrust of its efficacy was a clear indicator to Jordan that he must be feeling troubled indeed.

"You mentioned rules and ethics," he reminded him. "Are you concerned with the medical ethics involved in this treatment? Why don't you talk to John Erasmus? He's a leading light in the field of salutogenesis. Ask him if he thinks Micomic Health's treatment is ethical."

Hedley laughed, but there wasn't much humor in it. "It's *my* ethics that concern me."

Jordan waited. *When people ask for advice,* he thought, *they're usually just asking for permission.* Hedley had come to get his blessing.

"The final frontier of genome sequencing is the human brain," Hedley said, returning to his chair. "The expressed sequence tags from a brain DNA collection require vast amounts of computing power to reassemble the pieces—as you know, because we've drawn on your GPU capacity."

"Right."

"But the brain itself—to put it politely—is not something you fuck around with."

"I can understand that," Jordan acknowledged, touching his head thoughtfully.

"So, we've been reluctant to sell our expertise in this area."

"Very wise."

"The problem is that we have an agreement with Micomic Health that gives them first rights to our genome sequencing—and they want it now."

"And if you don't release it to them?"

"Then we can't release it to anyone. All our work in this area will be wasted."

At this point, Hedley's motor stalled. Had he come to an intersection and was waiting for the light to change, or had a sudden thought dashed across the road in front of him? He sipped his coffee while Jordan waited.

"Do you know George Kyros?" he asked, engine revving to life again.

"The name sounds familiar," Jordan mused. "Remind me."

Hedley jumped up and did the pacing thing again. "Multibillionaire. Currency manipulator. Helped trigger the debt bomb explosion that caused the European bank collapse. Said to be behind the IMF's SDR Crypto Credit scheme that led to the abolishment of cash. Think of any conspiracy theory that's turned out to be true, and George Kyros is likely behind it... Ring any bells, Jordan?"

"Sounds vaguely familiar," Jordan agreed.

"Yeah, don't be cute; you know damn well who he is. It was his money that funded the original Earth Day back in 1970. His hand guided the pen that drafted *Agenda 21*, *Agenda 2030*, and now *Agenda 2060*. You talk about playing God? In the mind of George Kyros, he *is* God."

No wonder Hedley wanted to be sure the room was safe, their bypassing Alt-Identities switched on. Nobody talked like this so openly. He needed to calm down.

"Look, Hed, you're giving me a headache. The thing about conspiracy theories is that people grab onto them without pausing to think. If George Kyros funded Earth Day way back in 1970, that would mean he had to be born around 1930. This is 2057. So unless you're saying..."

Jordan trailed off. Was Hedley saying what he thought he was saying?

"That's right," his friend said. "That would make him 127 years old. He's Micomic Health's most important client—and he's the reason they want our brain sequencing."

Jordan whistled softly. "Kyros has brain problems?"

"Kyros wants to *avoid* brain problems. Alzheimer's and dementia terrify him."

"And Micomic thinks that by mapping his brain DNA, they can protect him from it?"

Hedley nodded. "In a nutshell. Problem is, the human brain contains around one hundred billion neurons. Start playing around in that space, and anything could happen."

"You're afraid something might go wrong."

Hedley shook his head this time. "It's beyond that. What we've found is that we can manipulate brain function in areas that have nothing to do with DNA. We can even control or suppress conscious decisions and instincts at the foundational level—things like telling the truth, for instance, or the ability to lie. It is, quite literally, a minefield ... and we'd be giving the toolbox to Micomic."

Jordan thought long and hard.

"You know what?" he asked eventually. "I think you've already decided that's a risk worth taking. So why don't we look at bringing everything Micomic does under the surveillance of our Quantum XR-11? For peace of mind, at the very least!"

OVER THE WALL

January 2058

As one might expect, Jordan's reply to Alexa's bright idea to use Artie Sharp to endorse her plan had been artfully vague enough to discourage further discussion on the proposal. He'd focused instead on the part of Alexa's reportage that he felt got to the core of the issue.

"We just need to sell it to the people who are benefitting the most from being the biggest victims," she'd said. "They would experience financial loss, and they may not like the idea of other people no longer being worse off than them. It might take some convincing."

"That's a pretty damning interpretation of human nature," he'd commented at the time. "But unfortunately, I think you've put your finger on it."

The more he reflected on it later, the more certain he became that what she'd expressed was the behavioral equivalent of Einstein's theory of relativity. In essence, everything is measured relativistically: relative to somebody or something else, be it physical objects or other people. A person wearing shoes and clean clothes with a return plane ticket in their pocket does not feel poor when walking through an African slum ... until they come home to the drab Social Housing that is all their basic Transitional Benefits will cover, and their dissatisfaction becomes all-consuming at the sight of others enjoying a higher quality of life. Dissatisfaction is the prism through which observers of social conditions have always looked, but Alexa had in fact identified that individuals strive to reach a point where they can view their conditions through the prism of satisfaction: are they *satisfied* relative to others?

Just as time dilation occurs the faster an astronaut travels relative to the speed of light, so too does satisfaction increase or diminish relative to the perceived distance between an individual's social conditions and those of others around them. Einstein's theory relies on the speed of light being immutable. Alexa's theory could be tested against a similar hypothesis: namely, that Transitional Benefits could be immutable also.

Now, who could he test this theory on?

For most of the previous day, Jordan had been browsing the figures and comments Artie had extracted from the most recent reports issued by the Progress Agency, looking for a suitable subject for next week's item on the *ArteFact Channel.* He now believed he'd found it and was ready to call Antonio Muchos for a briefing. But the matter with Alexa was still top of his mind—and Antonio, a proud autodidact and second-generation immigrant, was just the right test subject for Alexa's theory.

The Konektor tracked him down in the VR laboratory, doing a test run on a new e-game in which galactic missions were played out within universes comprised of atomic particles of gold, silver, and palladium. Over a hundred million people worldwide had already registered for the new release, hoping to compete for the grand prize, which included a place on the first mission to Eros, an asteroid estimated to contain twenty billion tons of gold. The proceeds from the sale of each game (at 99.9 UniCoins each) would help fund the space expedition and mining operation, so there was little risk for the venture capitalists financing the project.

Unfortunately, an unforeseen glitch had occurred in the game's development, causing the negatively charged electrons to become unstable relative to the positively charged protons once a player's spacecraft entered into orbit around the nucleus of any gold atom.

Antonio was glad to be interrupted. "Hey, Prof! Are we ready for another show? I tried to contact you, but you must have switched to Alt."

"I'm sorry, bro," Jordan apologized. "I had a few things to mull over, but Artie's pulled up something for us to look at, and it shouldn't take long to produce."

For next week's episode, a scan of public policy announcements had identified a report from the United Nations International Tree-Planting Program (ITPP) claiming that eighty billion trees had been planted in the last five years, and that this alone had led to a decline in global warming of 0.05 percent.

"Our goal under *Agenda 2060*," the report read, "is to protect, restore, and promote sustainable use of terrestrial ecosystems, sustainably manage forests, combat desertification, and halt and reverse land degradation and biodiversity loss. The results speak for themselves."

Upon hearing the analyses of the actual plantings, conflicting official reports, and barefaced public statements that Artie's algorithms had turned up, giving the lie to the ITPP, Antonio rubbed his hands together with glee. "*Muy interesante*," he enthused. "I can build a data and location trail to follow, no problem. You got a preference for Artie's avatar image?"

Jordan was happy to leave that to him. Using the voice synthesizer within the natural language processor inside their creation, Antonio could command any personality he desired. Jordan just had to trust that none of this trickery would one day lead to Artie Sharp's unmasking.

Luckily, Antonio's stylistic prowess had been honed by years of e-game programming. On this particular occasion, they agreed Artie should adopt the persona of a seventy-two-year-old Australian who'd spent his life working outdoors. A bush shirt, leather boots, and an unruly grey wig under a broad-brimmed leather hat were all that was needed to create the avatar's image, and Artie's artificial voice could be given a Strine accent as a finishing touch. With predictive speech enablement, of course, no command-line code was needed, just a prompt or two from Antonio.

If viewers ever found out that the show came to them live and unrehearsed, they would be astounded. Of course, a little spontaneity and the occasional "human" glitch were part of what made the series so compelling, allowing Jordan to relax and trust in Artie's profound advances in learning. And visually, the production values suggested it was the brainchild of a sophisticated digital workshop.

"I'll suggest Artie starts by standing under a giant pine tree while the ITPP's announcement scrolls across the screen," Antonio explained. "When we get to the bit about the planting failures, Artie can find some beautiful pictures of the Sahara Desert. You're gonna love it, Prof."

But despite Antonio's enthusiasm, Jordan's mind was still elsewhere. This bullshit with the tree plantings was just another example of the endless lies, distortions, and bureaucratic incompetence that everyone had come to expect from the World Government. Yes, it deserved to be parodied—but what would really change as a result? "Truth" was no guaranteed agent of change, nor was it even absolute. Satirizing it just trivialized it. It was an amusing diversion, but he was feeling increasingly dissatisfied with these empty parodies. *Perhaps Alexa being invited into the confidence of the Agenda Implementation Tribunal has shaken me out of my complacency,* he thought. After all, such was the scope of the supercomputing power available to him, both in terms of speed and penetration of information processing, that he could reach right into the depths of the deep state … yet all he'd done with it so far was unleash a series of politically edgy comedy skits.

Why the hell wasn't he using it to pull the entire edifice down? Why wasn't he putting Alexa's social relativity hypothesis to the test?

"Antonio," he interrupted, "let's stop a moment and ask ourselves why we are doing this."

"Because we are bandits!" Antonio shot back. "We blow up the train tracks so the government's lies can't get through. We are Zapata, Pancho Villa, Robin Hood! … Also, we have fun." He grinned.

"That may be why you do it," Jordan smiled back, "but I'm a conservative old white man. Why do *I* do it?"

"Because you're not as conservative as you think, gringo. You like to laugh at the enemy. Conservatives don't laugh."

"Laughing at your enemies may make you feel better, Antonio, but it doesn't make them harmless. The more you laugh at them while they go on committing the same offenses, the more hollow your laughter becomes."

Antonio seemed bemused. "Hey, Prof, we got twenty-eight million viewers waiting to see what bullshit we gonna shoot down this week, and we got the FIB cybergooks going crazy trying to shut us down. We gotta be doing something right. Be happy."

Jordan did not wish to expose Antonio to the anomie that had gripped him ever since Alexa's revelation that she saw Artie Sharp as a potential mouthpiece for government propaganda. Instead, he changed the subject.

"What do you think about doing a piece on Transitional Benefits?" he asked. "Do you think they're working? What do people you know have to say about them?"

Antonio stopped what he was doing and thought for a moment. "You know what? I don't know no one on Transitional Benefits. All my friends who went to college now work for enterprise corporations or multinationals and get paid in crypto currencies exchangeable on DLT platforms."

"What about your family, your community...?"

"You mean all my poor Latino cousins? All those peasants who risked their lives years ago climbing over the wall to get into the 'Land of The Free,' so they could make a new life for themselves and their families...?"

"Well ... yes. I'm thinking of Article Eight of *Agenda 2060*: 'Achieve equal living standards for all peoples within and among countries, and eliminate all borders between states and territories to allow free movement of the people, without penalty or hindrance.' "

"They've all gone home," Antonio laughed. "When the Universal Wage was established following the Overthrow, Latinos couldn't wait to climb that wall again and go back the way they'd come. They didn't come here to be on welfare; they came to get rich. If you're not free to fail, then you're not free to succeed. Haven't you noticed?"

Jordan lapsed into momentary silence.

"And by the way, Prof," Antonio added, "when did you start calling me 'Bro'?"

THINK BIG, START SMALL
The ArteFact Channel

February 2058

SCENE: *Artie Sharp stands beside a knee-high seedling and bends down to touch it.*

> *Cut to the vast, arid Nullarbor Plain of Australia.*

"This is Australia, the sixth-largest continent in the world, and also the driest. My name is Will Tree, retired head of the United Nations International Tree-Planting Program, or ITPP for short. It is my privilege to report on our progress as we count down to the *Agenda 2060* review.

"Now, you might think that all the vast space in Australia, as you see before you here, would provide enviable opportunities for afforestation. But a closer examination reveals why the unique flora and fauna of this country have evolved into such bizarre forms. While it is true that fifty percent of the landmass here is designated as farmland in some form or another, only six percent of it is arable—and the part used for grazing livestock supports only 26.2 million head of cattle. That's just one hot, dry, lonely beast for every thirteen hectares of land."

> *The iconic image of a hot, dry, lonely beast searching for water in the Australian outback fades into a similar image of a merino sheep shimmering in the heat haze.*

"The situation for sheep is a little better; they can survive on just five hectares per head.

"When the ITPP gave out the Billion Trees planting contracts worldwide, the successful consortium established by the Kyros Foundation had the foresight to establish a huge tree nursery in the Sudanian savanna zone in southern Chad known as Earth Ship Africa. With money advanced by the IMF, this five-thousand-hectare facility, fortuitously located near the rich oil, gold, and uranium resources of Chad, boasts the world's largest hydroponic nursery and plant-tissue-growing laboratories, capable of producing ten billion seedlings per year."

Somewhere in Africa, a cargo plane takes off from a jungle airstrip.

"From this facility, giant cargo planes, using the adjacent airstrip built specifically for this purpose, can fly two hundred and fifty thousand seedlings per trip anywhere in the world, ready to plant in twenty-four hours. The fuel consumption is more than offset by the carbon credits received for the trees, and the seedlings arrive in perfect condition for planting by the AI tree inserter."

A cute koala feeds on a eucalyptus tree.

"The IPPC motto is 'Think big, start small.' Plant geneticists at the Universities of Queensland and New South Wales identified the specific strain of eucalyptus most suited to the environment, and the tablelands that were no longer fit for crop production due to falling water tables were cleared of all fencing, utility services, and human habitation to create unobstructed working conditions for the AI tree inserter. Unfortunately, the geneticists had not accounted for how the hot, dry conditions would affect seedlings whose roots had been formed in hydroponic troughs, and the transplanting was a complete failure, despite valiant attempts to divert irrigation water from rivers up to five hundred kilometers away."

A eucalyptus seedling, already dead, is symbolically watered with a watering can.

"This is the point in the process at which I arrived. I noticed immediately that plantation forests accounted for only 0.02 percent of the country's land—which, considering the enormity of the amount of land available, suggested an ambivalence towards trees at best, and an aversion to them at worst. And this aversion can be explained in one word: fire."

Australian bushfire footage of roaring flames, crashing trees, and billowing smoke.

"In the heat of summer, the Australian bush is a tinderbox that can erupt into flame spontaneously, destroying homes and killing anyone or anything in its path with vicious intensity. Therefore, planting trees is regarded as a foolhardy venture. But when I stumbled across a book written by an early pioneer, Albert Strange, all that was to change."

An indistinct black-and-white photograph depicts a historic pioneer in a suit, loading hay bales onto a wagon.

"Born in 1908, Albert was a loner, a naturalist, and a deep-thinking environmentalist who chose the land over people. He was a rare exception for an Australian in that he had enormous respect for the aboriginal people, with whom he felt a deep affinity. It was when I read Albert's journals that I found a solution to the failed eucalyptus-planting program commissioned by the ITPP."

Artie opens a book he has been holding in his hand. He reads while the flames continue to leap up around him.

" 'The aboriginals,' Albert wrote, 'have been using fire as a tool for tilling and cultivating the land for forty thousand to sixty thousand years. Periodic planned burning kept the under-forests clean of debris and created productive land for grains, grasses, and tubers. Controlled burning did not penetrate the soil and deplete it of nutrients but, on the contrary, encouraged

the massive root systems of perennials like kangaroo
grass and the yam daisy, which sequester carbon at far
greater levels than do high-crown trees. With the native
eucalyptus trees, it must be understood that the seeds
cannot germinate without hot ashes to cover them. That
is how they have evolved in response to the nature of
their environment—in which fire plays a regular part.
Understanding this, aboriginals made fire their tool.' "

*The fires rage louder, and Artie is forced to raise
his voice.*

"This was the idea that guided me to our new policy: fire is our tool. Using
pinpoint climate-modeling tools to predict wind direction, temperature,
and humidity conditions, linked to satellite imaging of topography and
tree density, we designed a mosaic of controlled-burn rotations within
the native forest conservation areas in order to harvest the burned seeds,
which can be planted in the redundant grazing and cropping areas in
which hydroponic seedlings had failed to survive. Giant soil scrapers,
designed by the Kyros Foundation's specialized machinery division,
scoop up the hot ash containing the mature seeds in fifty-cubic-meter
buckets for transportation to the chosen planting areas for germination
and afforestation."

*Gigantic hundred-ton trucks from open-cast mines
advance on the camera and dump their loads of
black coal.*

"Though this program is still far from complete, I am pleased to report
that the results are outstanding. The years of smoke and ash cover
experienced by major cities on the Eastern Seaboard are, in my opinion,
a small inconvenience compared to our goal of carbon neutrality. It is
a success story in every respect."

*Fade to a lonely camel train wending its way across
the dunes of the Sahara Desert.*

"Less successful has been the proposed planting of eighteen billion trees across the Sahara Desert. It is true that, at this time, none of the trees have survived. But with a visionary new solution to be presented by the Kyros Foundation at the forthcoming Earth Day celebration, which will involve digging a canal from the Mediterranean Sea into the heart of the desert and relying on the desert sand to desalinate the seawater, I believe that this will prove to be only a temporary setback.

"And while the goal of *Agenda 2060* was to see these and other large-scale tree plantings completed, we should not be put off by temporary setbacks. After all, goals are set in order to inspire and motivate us. Thus, we should be immensely proud of what has been achieved to date."

*Artie starts to walk off camera, then turns and walks
back on set.*

"And to those who say we need more carbon dioxide to make trees grow, not less, I have this to say: the ITPP knows what it's doing. That's why global temperatures are not rising as predicted."

A COSMETIC CHANGE

March 2058

The atmosphere in the Lineal Progression Office had changed significantly since the morning six months ago when the department head had called Alexa to their office with instructions that she was to sign a Loose Lips Agreement and appear before the Agenda Implementation Tribunal. In the weeks following that appearance, Alexa's status had changed visibly, and a unspoken exclusion zone had opened up between her and her colleagues once they realized she had been given a new level of responsibility to which they were not privy.

They could read the signs, though. The allocation of a large corner office with a lockable door that the cleaners were not allowed to enter unless Alexa was present; the IT technician who arrived from the Social Justice Office to shut down their servers while (it was rumored) a new dedicated ethernet cable was run to said office; the autonomous vehicle that appeared at the front entrance whenever Alexa left the building: these were the clearest possible signals that she was now to be treated with caution. Banter around the water cooler ceased as she approached. Smiles became rigid. After-hours social invitations now excluded her, and she had no time for old friends from her college days. Only the department head could guess at what her new role entailed, and he, as a witness to the Loose Lips Agreement, was equally bound by it and thus cautious about speculating on the nature of her new work.

For her part, Alexa had no problem with any of it. She was fully engrossed in her task, which she found challenging and stimulating, and she felt that at last she was truly using the brain that Jordan had once described as 'the brightest—and most beautiful!—ever to study mathematics.' The people at the Social Equity Ministry were in awe of her security clearance status and equally in awe of her analytical skills, unaware of why they had been instructed to give her full access to their data. Those who appreciated her physical charms looked forward to seeing her, and those who felt threatened by those same charms found it difficult, nevertheless, to resist her sunny smiles and cheerful greetings.

The mystery surrounding her work was heightened one morning when a visitor appeared at her office door, accompanied by two Social Justice Office security wardens. It took Alexa a few seconds to recognize the person—square jaw, heavily muscled tattooed arms, strawberry-blonde wig—as the member of the Agenda Implementation Tribunal who had rather severely criticized her work at the Lineal Progression Office as being partly responsible for the mess they were in.

The person introduced themself as Shane Whitman, and after the two wardens had swept the office for bugs and removed Alexa's Konektor from her desk, they were dismissed, closing and locking the office door from the outside. Shane pulled a chair up to Alexa's desk and removed their wig to reveal a closely shaved bald pate.

"It's showtime, Alexa," Shane said with a big smile and not even a hint of severity. "We've chewed the cud on this thing until there's nothing left to digest, and I'm here to give you the tribunal's decision."

"Oh!" Alexa was surprised. She'd been waiting for the tribunal to summon her again. This visit was the last thing she'd expected.

"But before I tell you what we've decided, I wanted to say a few words to you in person, Alexa, because you have displayed an openness and honesty that I personally find shaming, and I know some of the other members feel the same way. It may help to explain our decision. You see…"

What Shane went on to say was too personal—and frankly, too complex—to remember in much detail. But Alexa summarized things for Jordan McPhee later that day, after she requested an urgent meeting with him in a park near her office.

"Shane Whitman, it appears, is one of many white men who, around the time of the Overthrow, decided to obscure their sexuality for reasons that had nothing to do with sex. They saw the adoption of the Agenda articles that explicitly provide for the empowerment of women and minorities as erecting a barrier to their own ambitions."

"So, they chose to wear wigs and lipstick to confuse people," Jordan suggested wryly.

"And apparently confused themselves in the process. When you look at the figures for self-identification, it's obvious that it isn't Social Points alone that drive people's decisions; the differences in Transitional Benefits claimed aren't enough to justify it. Clearly there are other motivations at work. Besides, people like Shane Whitman are on an earnings scale that beneficiaries could only dream about."

"Interesting," Jordan observed. "This cuts across something I've been thinking about lately myself. We've been encouraged to see society in economic terms, as if monetary reward were our sole human ambition. Is that because currencies of exchange, whatever form they take, are the only things we can reliably count?"

"Or is it," Alexa countered, "because money is the only thing that can be reliably counted on to control people?"

"Good point. Would you like to expand on it?"

Alexa preened. But why did she love this master/pupil relationship so much? She was a thirty-nine-year-old woman, for heaven's sake!

"I've learned a few things in the last few weeks," she confessed, "that I'm ashamed to admit I'd never thought to question before. It goes back to the time of the Overthrow. Maybe we were all in shock during that period. The banks had collapsed, people were out of work, there were breadlines, riots... The world was in chaos. Then the International Monetary Fund and the United Nations announced that the leading economies had agreed to abolish fiat currencies and adopt new standards for international and domestic trade based on Crypto Credits. Old currency debts were wiped out at a stroke. I never understood that..."

"It's called a Jubilee."

"... and our new government announced that Article Three of *Agenda 2060* was being introduced with immediate effect."

"Ah, yes," Jordan interrupted, "Article Three: 'End poverty in all its forms by controlling income distribution, limiting private asset accumulation, and ensuring equality of safety, security, and well-being for all, regardless of work input or ability.' It used to be called 'welfare'; then that morphed into the Universal Wage; but now they call it Transitional Benefits—which is a sly way of suggesting you still have the opportunity of moving on to something better if you're a deserving citizen."

"Which is what Society Points were designed for," Alexa interjected. "Everyone receives sixty-five percent of the maximum Transitional Benefits no matter who they are, and those who are oppressed receive more according to their level of oppression. But you can't trust people when it comes to assessing their own victim status—which is why I made my suggestion to work the idea backwards: give everyone a hundred percent of the benefits, then impose a range of penalties on those who are guilty of discrimination and oppression. It's just a means of balancing the budget, for God's sake! I never for a moment thought they'd go for it ... but Shane Whitman proved to me that anyone who thinks they can predict human behavior is delusional."

If there is a trick to being a good conversationalist, it is not how good of a talker you are, but how good a listener. A good listener offers moments of silence that discreetly suggest they should be filled. Jordan offered such a moment now.

Alexa struggled for a minute with her thoughts, as if reining in her powerful instincts to guide them in the direction her logician's mind wanted to follow.

"Shane Whitman," she revealed at last, "made it to the top of the government's inner circle via a forty-year career in the FIB."

"You mean the FBI?"

"No, the FIB: Federal Interrogation Bureau."

Jordan whistled softly. "Now that's heavy. And he took to dressing as a woman? I'd say that's some change."

"It's only a cosmetic change," Alexa laughed. "Underneath the dress, I'd guess he hasn't changed at all—and that's probably true of a lot of people in the top echelons of government. They've publicly paid lip service to diversity and victimhood because it's helped them come out of the Overthrow aligned with a belief system that the majority of people have been happy to support."

Jordan stood up from the park bench and walked over to a nearby tree, examining the trunk as if he had never seen tree bark before.

"Does something about that rub you the wrong way?" Alexa demanded forthrightly, miffed at his apparent disinterest. "I don't want to sound cynical; I'm just being realistic. I presume you support the social justice and sustainability goals that the world has signed up for. I certainly do. But I'm aware that things can go too far in any given direction. That's what Shane Whitman is admitting, basically—and that's why they see my suggestion as an opportunity for a reset."

"Ah, a reset!" Jordan called over his shoulder. He'd spotted something in a metal trash can on the far side of the park and set off towards it at an easy lope. Alexa watched, frowning, perplexed by his deliberate departure. He could run quite well, actually; she had never seen him in motion before. With his back to her, he burrowed into the wire basket, then turned back to her, triumphantly holding his find above his head with both hands.

"It's a football!" he shouted. "Can you catch?"

Without waiting, he wound up like a quarterback and launched it towards her.

Her mouth fell open. She clambered to her feet as the ball spun towards her, describing a fifty-yard parabola through the clear, wintry afternoon air and landing in her outstretched hands inches from her heaving chest.

Jordan, incredulous at both their skills, trotted slowly back towards her.

"I can't believe what I just saw," he confessed. "Women can't catch footballs. You must have a male gene."

"And white men can't throw them," she shot back. "You must have a black gene."

"Ah!" he replied ruefully. "You remember the secret twenty-five percent? If only I'd known that when I was young…"

"Anyway," she continued rather sulkily, "I was going to tell you some of the things I've discovered at the Social Equity Ministry … but it seems you're not that interested, and I'm bound by secrecy, anyway."

He took the ball from her and kicked it far into the distance, where it disappeared into the white-barked birch trees. Then he took her arm and steered her back to the park bench. "I'm sorry. Something you said triggered a bad memory for me," he explained. "Belief systems: I'm very wary of them. And the fact that you're dealing with this Shane Whitman person from the FIB."

The belief system he had in mind had led to his deplatforming, and the painful fracturing of his relationship with Lexie. Belief systems sounded compelling in the abstract, but in practice, implementing them required sacrifice. And as for the FIB, well...

"I know what you're thinking," Alexa allowed. "I guess it's just that I rely on your encouragement, and I'm entering dangerous territory without any guidance. These people want me to enroll with them."

"Enroll? What does that mean?"

"That's the only way I can put it. They want me to join a group to advise them on how to pitch a dramatic reset to the public. Remember when I talked to you the other day about Artie Sharp and the *ArteFact Channel*? That's the sort of thing they're after. If he could be recruited—I suppose *persuaded* would be a better word—to buy into the changes, he could help in selling them to the people."

"I'll have to make a point of watching it," Jordan said innocently. "Meanwhile, I *am* interested in what you've learned at the Social Equity Ministry—very interested—but I'll not ask you to breach your secrecy agreements. Tell me only what you feel comfortable sharing."

OCCAM'S RAZOR

April 2058

Nothing is what it seems. Two people sitting on a park bench. One wants to reveal her secrets; the other wants to conceal his. But are their reasons obvious to each other already? Do they think they know enough about the other person and their circumstances to trust what they hear?

A lifetime of distrust and caution clouded Jordan's thoughts. When Alexa presumed that he supported the social justice and sustainability goals that the world had signed up for, she had made a point of emphasizing that *she* did. He could take her word on that, or he could take it with a grain of salt. After all, who *didn't* support social justice and sustainability? Pledging allegiance to it was one thing, but dangling it in someone else's face as some kind of sign of virtue was what one might expect from an idealistic teenager—not a mature and intelligent woman like Alexa. Of course, controlling societies exert a sort of moral suasion that, in their citizens, can manifest itself as unconscious repetitions of the core creed mantras. If that's what Alexa was doing, it was disappointing, to say the least. Her professed admiration for Jordan had promised better than that.

In his line of work, Jordan was challenged every day by the ability of AI to understand context and meaning. Human communication is incredibly complex. People often imply things without explicitly saying them, so for his machines, understanding nuance required focused attention. Would their neurobiological programming have detected inconsistency in Alexa's reportage? On the one hand, she had cynically dismantled the sincerity of Shane Whitman and his fellow tribunal members for paying lip service to diversity and victimhood. On the other hand, she was seriously considering joining them in a scheme to implement a reset designed to neutralize that very diversity and victimhood. Whose side was she really on?

Every story is only part of the story.

In the field of artificial intelligence, Occam's razor posits that the simplest theory explaining any data is invariably the most likely to be true. Alexa had basically asserted that the cause and outcome of the Overthrow should be judged in purely economic terms. (What had she said? "... the leading economies had agreed to abolish fiat currencies and adopt new standards for international and domestic trade based on Crypto Credits. Old currency debts were wiped out at a stroke...") On hearing this, Jordan's own neural network had flashed a warning signal: none of this matched the speech or thought patterns he had learned to associate with Alexa. The simplest theory was that these ideas came from another source (from the time of the Overthrow or thereafter, obviously), thus mimicking the speech and thought patterns of someone else—a prominent economist, perhaps. So, he returned to his office and asked Quantum XR-11 to do some research.

In short order, those same words and speech patterns were identified in classified transcripts of evidence presented to the Security Oversight Committee at the time of the Overthrow.

VOICE 1: You are Donald Melville Smythe, correct?

VOICE 2: Correct.

VOICE 1: You have been charged with incitement and sedition for spreading false information to undermine the authority of the state.

VOICE 2: I am an economist. My job is to interpret the economy.

VOICE 1: Your interpretation is that of a conspiracy theorist, not an economist.

VOICE 2: *My interpretation is based purely on fact.*

VOICE 1: *Isn't it a fact that our people—and the majority of people in the developed world—have spontaneously demanded an end to inequality, greed, and the squandering of resources? Isn't it a fact that international institutions have responded to those demands by rejecting money as the staff of life—making you and all economists angry about your redundancy?*

VOICE 2: *If you say them often enough, those statements may eventually be accepted as fact. But the plain truth is, that's not what's happened.*

VOICE 1: *Alright, Mr. Smythe, then please tell the members of the Oversight Committee what, in your esteemed opinion, has happened.*

VOICE 2: *In the Anglosphere, Europe, and East Asia, government debt and private debt have risen to become two hundred percent of gross domestic product. Debt servicing has become unsustainable, and central banks have forced interest rates down into negative territory while continuously printing money to try and stem the tide. But the tide has already gone out. The tax base, meanwhile, has been shrinking at an ever-increasing rate thanks to automation, AI, and the exportation of low-wage jobs to the last remaining late-developing countries of the world. The middle class and wage-earning workers on whom our government has historically relied to fund the state's expenditure are maxed out. With eighty percent of the people in this country trapped in debt, the sum of all student loans, mortgages, car loans, and credit card debt has topped a hundred and fifty trillion dollars. As usual, the rich—the truly rich—cannot be reached, for they are so intertwined with government that they basically own the system. We have a saying: 'When the rich get in trouble with debt, it's an economic problem. When the poor and middle class get in trouble with debt, it's a political problem.'*

VOICE 1: *So, these are your facts, are they, Mr. Smythe?*

VOICE 2: *It is a fact that the International Monetary Fund and the United Nations have brokered an agreement stipulating that the leading economies will abolish fiat currencies and adopt new standards for international and domestic trade based on SDRs. Old currency debts are wiped out at a stroke. It's an old-fashioned Jubilee on a global scale, and it will ultimately lead to even greater poverty and hardship for the people it purports to help.*

VOICE 1: *As I said in my opening, you are a conspiracy theorist, Mr. Smythe, not an economist. And what do you mean by a Jubilee?*

VOICE 2: *I mean it in the biblical sense. Leviticus, chapter 25 of the Old Testament decrees that a Jubilee shall occur every fifty years, at which time all real property reverts to its rightful owner, and those who are enslaved to others, through poverty or debt, shall be released.*

VOICE 1: *So, if that's what you think is happening now, how could any reasonable person complain about its unfairness?*

VOICE 2: *These were instructions given to ancient Hebrews by God. When God talked about the 'rightful ownership' of property and slaves, He meant that they were all God's property—not the property of banks, corporations, or governments.*

VOICE 1: *Does the FIB have any questions at this time?*

VOICE 3: *Thank you; yes, we do. Are you a Jew, Mr. Smythe?*

VOICE 2: *I am an economist. That's my position here.*

VOICE 3: *If not a Jew, are you a practicing Christian, then? Do you have any loyalty to a higher authority than the people?*

VOICE 2: *I am a Christian, but that is not my job; that is my faith.*

VOICE 3: *A white male Christian... Just so we know.*

As a beneficiary of Moore's law of technology, Jordan was constantly in awe of how seventeen-nanometer semiconductors had transformed the speed and efficiency of GPUs, allowing his computers to process massive data sets almost instantaneously while simultaneously learning from them. Everything ever written or spoken of which there was a digital record was able to be accessed—and it required considerable effort on the part of the information agencies to remove something once it had been copied to a Free Radical Data Center.

The transcript of economist Donald Smythe's interrogation contained some of the exact same wording that Alexa Smythe had used when describing the events of the Overthrow to him in the park. Though commonsense knowledge required enormous amounts of ontological engineering, that was not the reason XR-11 struggled at first to find a link between these two people with the same cognomen—father and daughter, perhaps? Of Donald Melville Smythe, economist, there was no trace, other than in the transcript from the Security Oversight Committee immediately following the Overthrow. That could only mean that he had been expunged from all records. He was now a Non-Person.

The bridge between neurobiology and artificial intelligence can facilitate self-adaptation, which explained why XR-11's search did not stop there, but continued on to low-resolution scans of files from public records, until...

There it was: the original birth certificate of Alexa Dawn Smythe, October 21, 2018. And in a neat, almost calligraphic hand, there was the signature of her father: Donald M. Smythe, occupation: economist.

Why had he become a near-invisible person? After all, death did not simply erase citizens from public records. The only authority with that power was the FIB, of which Shane Whitman of the Agenda Implementation Tribunal had revealed himself to be a former high-ranking member. It was inconceivable that Alexa was unaware that the FIB had that power. Knowing that, it was instructive to examine her reportage to Jordan more closely—and to question her motives in considering joining Whitman and the tribunal in the inner circle.

Every story is only part of the story.

Just as intriguing was Jordan's own response, he realized. He'd broken away from the conversation in the park, claiming that the mention of belief systems had triggered a bad memory. But this had come immediately after Alexa had revealed Whitman's links to the FIB. Jordan, being a Non-Person himself, was more than familiar with the nature of that agency—and now he had become aware that the government, through the medium of Alexa, sought to track down his alter ego, Artie Sharp.

Nothing, it seemed, was what it seemed. His earlier caution came rushing back with a vengeance.

HAPPENSTANCE

May 2058

It was an overcast day with no wind, neither hot nor cold. There had been many of them lately—much to the chagrin of the Free Energy Agency, whose forecasts of power supply and demand relied heavily on sunshine and wind on one side and demand control on the other.

With battery recharging banned for all but public transport and government vehicles, the roads were eerily quiet. More people than usual were relying on e-bikes, but the pedaling required to recharge them was taking its toll on the elderly and infirm, with a sharp increase in reported cardiac infarctions. The message from the Free Energy Agency was that the country needed to reduce its energy usage by forty percent if the goals of Article Five were to be achieved, and calls for power resources to be supplemented with natural gas and clean coal were just further proof—as if any were needed—that vested-interest lobbies were still hard at work trying to sabotage the zero-carbon aims of the government.

Article Five was very clear: "Reduce man-made carbon emissions and greenhouse gasses to zero, and convert all energy consumption to the use of renewable resources." How much clearer, the FEA demanded, did the message have to be? Yet although bulletins were delivered daily to everyone's Konektors, there was a growing feeling that the FEA message was worn out—and so were the people. For both, the power of belief was simply exhausted.

Two people relatively unaffected by the impact of the electricity outages and rationing were Jordan and Alexa. Both being beneficiaries of hydrogen fuel cells, they experienced no interruption to their work.

Bill Jones, Jr., the DDC's landlord and a fellow Deranger, had long ago recognized that leaving energy supply in the hands of government agencies could potentially wipe out both his marijuana operation and his ParkFed indoor plant-based meat operation. Thus, he'd installed proton-exchange membrane fuel cells in all his buildings, including the data centers and laboratories of the many tech incubators that were his tenants. So for Jordan, the virtue-speak of the FEA was nothing more than another opportunity for a new Artie Sharp segment ... assuming, that is, that he and Antonio could find a fresh and entertaining take on a subject Artie had successfully lampooned many times already.

Alexa, of course, worked for an essential arm of government whose buildings had long been future-proofed with fuel stacks and whose autonomous vehicles ran on hydrogen, not electricity. If the thought ever occurred to her that reliable power should be freely available to everyone, she never expressed it. Technology was not her thing, and a habit of voicing skepticism would not have helped advance her career. There were clear signs emerging, however, that suggested a sea change was taking place in Alexa, and she was steering into rough waters. Some days after a visit from Shane Whitman, she messaged Jordan and asked if he'd join her for a drive in the country.

"I've got two entrance tickets to Neutrality Park and a full tank of hydrogen. If you'd care to enjoy a day out of the city, I thought I could tell you what I've learned at the Social Equity Ministry while we drive. What do you say?"

He said okay.

In the year since they'd met at Lexie's celebration for Manaia, they'd worked out an unspoken protocol. She would initiate contact. He would neither encourage nor discourage it. From the outset, they had limited their conversations solely to mathematics and her work. She never asked him in depth what he did with his days, and he never inquired about her personal life. Even allowing for Alexa seeking his counsel for her work, it was their fondly remembered relationship as star student and admired teacher that still defined their connection. So long as that remained the case, they were on safe ground. But inevitably, with increasing contact, personal boundaries are tested ... and this outing would prove to be the beginning of that test.

She picked him up outside his apartment building and set the destination as Neutrality Park, with a journey time of ninety minutes at a predicted average speed of eighty miles per hour.

"How long since you've been out to the coast?" she asked, pouring him a cup of coffee as the car set off towards the edge of the city.

"It must be nearly eighteen years," he mused. "I came out for one last look just after they announced they were taking over all the land from here to the coast for the solar and wind farms. There were people running around in front of the bulldozers, trying to save the desert tortoises, sticking them in cages in the backs of pickup trucks. I don't know how many survived. Everything got flattened. No one was happy. I've seen the photos, but I've never felt any desire to go back."

The cloud cover above them was altostratus, a mid-level grey blanket that diffused the light, stretching beyond the horizon. The city and its outskirts had the pallor of an uncommon metal, and the green plantations that girdled the urban limits, placing an ecological chastity belt upon any attempts at expansion, stood like motionless sentinels as they passed through. All conversation within the car ceased as they entered the eerie landscape of old PV solar panels lying heavy upon the arid earth as far as the eye could see. It would take them almost an hour to reach the wind farm, and a further half hour to Neutrality Park.

Alexa had brought muffins as well as coffee, and she seemed pleased when Jordan ate them with relish. The provisions showed that she had planned this trip with some care; it was neither casual nor spontaneous.

When he'd finished and wiped the crumbs off his lap, Alexa took a digital tablet from her bag and slid a hidden table out of her armrest. As the screen fired up, he watched as she waited for a file to be found, frowning in concentration—a habit which, now that she was thirty-nine years old, had left her with a permanent crease between her eyebrows. She wore her hair long and tucked it behind an ear, leaving the other side to fall over her cheek, where she alternately twirled it around her forefinger or absentmindedly sucked on it between her lips.

Jordan briefly closed his eyes, unable to bear looking at the glass desert outside, and equally wary of the intimacy created by Alexa's proximity.

"You said you'd be interested in what I found at the Social Equity Ministry," she reminded him. "So I thought I'd give you a summary."

He opened his eyes and sat up, stilling her with a finger to his lips while taking out his Konektor. The autonomy of so-called autonomous vehicles relied on near instantaneous data transmission over 12G wireless networks. That data included everything happening inside the vehicle as well as around it. Jordan found the sound scrambler within his Alt-Identity app and switched it to 2m Voice. He held it up so she could see.

"Yes, I've been looking forward to it," he replied once she'd nodded her understanding.

"It's not what I expected," she cautioned. "In fact, I find it quite hard to accept."

"Because...?"

She reflexively moved the cursor and tapped the keyboard, as if to assure herself that the file in front of her wasn't going to suddenly vanish. "As a snapshot of society, it's ... well, it's very disturbing, to say the least."

"Because...?" he prompted again.

"Okay." Her frown deepened. "You know that my first task is to reassign the coding for Societal Points so that the Transitional Benefits budget can be balanced."

"Yes ... and so that white males specifically can no longer hide in the minutiae of self-identified minorities."

"Oh, that part was easy. Once I applied Bertrand Russell's One-One, as you suggested, the stats changed to fall exactly in line with our expectations. No, it's what I'd call the 'essential economic status' of groups that came as a shock. That's not a term we use much nowadays, of course. Economics is like mathematics in that way."

"It's *persona non grata*!"

"Exactly! But when I started looking into social identity groupings, I found that those groupings were anything but equal when it came to the assessment of their societal standing and economic levels—and that certain policies had deliberately been put in place to make it so. It depends on who's favored at the time, and that doesn't happen by accident; it's aggressively promoted by progressive ideologues in positions of influence. The question is, do you think the Agenda Implementation Tribunal knows that dividing the population into highly differentiated classes has gotten out of control—and now they're using me to untangle it?"

"Possibly," Jordan replied. "They seemed to be taken with your idea that they could now claim to have eliminated distinctions between groups while achieving the goal of financial equality for all. I thought that was a stroke of genius on your part. So, are you suggesting that's exactly what they wanted all along?" If she'd really come to that conclusion, then her pride could have been sorely bruised.

Alexa spun her tablet around so that it was facing Jordan. She leaned forward and touched his hand. Why? Their signal was blocked; nobody could hear their conversation. He narrowed his eyes and looked at the screen, then withdrew his hand and fished in his pocket for his reading glasses. Alexa sat back and looked out the window, not seeing. Her tablet went into sleep mode.

"At the height of the Overthrow eighteen years ago," she said quietly, "my father disappeared. There was so much fear and confusion at the time that no one knew where to turn for help or information. The first news I received of him was brought to me in an envelope by one of his friends. The friend told me that Daddy had been brought before the dreaded Security Oversight Committee, accused of sedition and distributing Hate Speech."

"*Hate* Speech...?"

"That was the charge. His friend said that he'd been declared a Non-Person, and when I went to the FIB to try and locate him, they denied having any record of him. Of course, there were rumors about the camps the FIB set up around that time in the FEMA emergency centers, but as hard as I tried over the next two years, I couldn't get anyone to tell me where he was."

Jordan hesitated, then leaned across and touched the hand from which he had just withdrawn. "I'm sorry," he said. "I had no idea. What about your mother? Did she hear from him?"

"She died during the COVID-19 Pandemic in 2020, when I was only two."

Jordan took his hand away awkwardly. "I didn't know," he murmured. "So, what made your father a target?"

Alexa turned away from the window and looked into his eyes. "He was an economist. Donald Melville Smythe. You might have run across him."

"Yes, of course. A free-market economist, as I recall, favored by the media for his pithy one-liners. How could anything *he* had to say be classified as Hate Speech, for God's sake?"

"You're forgetting the Articles," Alexa reminded him. "Article Two: 'Protect all persons from harm in circumstances where insensitive Hate Speech is used, deliberately or otherwise, without the consent of the persons offended.' "

Jordan sat back and let out his breath. This was sounding all too familiar. "So it wouldn't really matter what he had to say, if they chose to be offended by it," he acknowledged. "That's the one Article in *Agenda 2060* that undermines the entire document. It's a charter for bullies, misanthropes, and malcontents—even social engineering totalitarians."

"Careful, Professor. You just offended half the population."

He smiled without humor. Of course, Artie's discovery had partially prepared him for this revelation about Alexa's father, but he hadn't known the actual charges or the outcome. "Ain't that the truth," he muttered. "But you mentioned an envelope. What was in it?"

"As if by happenstance—now there's a word he'd have liked—it contained an exact prediction of what I would find two decades later in the classified records of the Social Equity Ministry ... a frighteningly accurate prediction of where the architects of *Agenda 2060* would lead us."

"Do you still have it?"

She tapped the space bar on her tablet, bringing the screen back to life. "It's there in front of you. Read it."

HOMO ECONOMICUS

By *Donald Melville Smythe*
The Financial Times, April 2039

Readers would be forgiven for thinking that all economists are jackasses.

Let me explain.

Once upon a time, an economist's job was to analyze and comment on the financial management of a country and its resources. Little by little, the complexity of that subject grew, until practitioners like myself began to realize that the moving parts were so varied, the hidden parts so uncertain, no one should pretend to have the answers about what brought us to our current position or where we were headed.

At that point, my fellow economists and I should have done the decent thing and just decided to talk amongst ourselves. But conceit (encouraged by the populace's thirst for answers and certainty) seduced us into thinking we were latter-day Oracles of Delphi.

After such an admission on my part, you would be entitled to wonder why I don't just finish this article here and now. We are in the throes of the greatest disruption to society since the three revolutions of the twentieth century; do you really want to hear from an *economist*? Probably not ... except that the people implementing this disruption claim that the Overthrow, as they term it, is necessary to repair the damage caused by 'the collapse of the world economy'—and the world economy is what I've been talking about for half my life.

So, at the risk of being a jackass, I'm going to do it one more time.

Where to start?

Well, the economy is based on money, so that's where I'll start.

Money had its origins in ancient Egypt, Babylon, and India in the form of clay tokens, allowing people to overcome the limitations of barter. In local marketplaces, they were a simple solution to an obvious problem. Then metal coins were introduced, representing a given value of staple commodities that could be exchanged. But ultimately, the further that money became dissociated from a given commodity, the more its value and status came to rely upon a consensus agreement by the people of the society in which it was circulated. This is a key point, as we shall see.

Gradually, money began to be used to facilitate trading with people in other countries. At this point, the value ascribed to the money by the issuing country had to be trusted by the recipient, as did the ability of the issuing country to honor it.

Now, this raises two obvious questions: who determined the value of a coin, and who manufactured and issued the coins?

Enter gold and silver. From the earliest times, these two metals were judged to be valuable, and that value was relatively easy to assess on the basis of weight and purity. So, sovereign states started minting coins made from these two precious metals. (Sovereign states are called that because someone—a sovereign or a governing body – rules over them. Remember that.)

So, gold and silver coins had an easily calculable value—that is, until a sovereign started fiddling with the system by cutting back on the amount of precious metal in the coins and asserting that they had a "face value" rather than an intrinsic value. This was an unsubtle way of introducing a tax in favor of the sovereign, at the expense of the people holding the currency—i.e., the tax was the difference between the face value of the currency and the cost of producing and distributing it.

But what was "face value"? Well, ostensibly, it was the value of the actual gold or silver that would be received if you marched up to the sovereign's place of business, presented your coin, and asked for payment. Of course, not many people had the balls to do this—and no one ever thought to question whether the sovereign might be issuing a lot more coins than could ever be redeemed with the gold and silver he kept in the palace vault. However, to the merchants whose ships were sailing the world, filling their holds with exotic spices, silks, and slaves for sale to traders in other nations, this monetary system was too obviously flawed. What they wanted was a face value they could trust—and they found it in the London Goldsmiths. These trusted gentlemen accepted deposits of bullion from merchants for safekeeping and gave them certificates (promissory notes) in return. The certificates were then used as currency to make purchases. This was the start of banking, and the forerunner of the "gold standard."

Pretty soon, history repeated itself: the London Goldsmiths started printing more certificates than they actually held in gold, and they "lent" these to borrowers in return for earning interest. As long as the people trusted the Goldsmiths' integrity—and the depositors didn't want all their bullion back at once—everything was fine. In essence, they had invented fractional-reserve banking, and it wasn't long before other people got in on the act, calling themselves "banks" and issuing banknotes as legal tender.

Well, the sovereigns didn't like this at all; they quickly decided that the issuing of banknotes by private commercial banks had to stop. They believed that only banks controlled by the governing powers should have the right to issue money, and so they established their own "federal" banks for this purpose. The government-authorized currencies they issued were representative money, supposedly backed by gold and silver held by the federal reserves.

Things went along fine for as long as the gold and silver reserves could be counted. But when one or two nations started printing more money than could be accounted for by the value of their bullion reserves, and other nations began insisting on swapping that money for gold as promised, things got a bit fractious.

In 1971, President Richard Nixon decided to remove the gold-backed guarantee from the US dollar. Apart from the fact that he was rapidly running out of gold at that time, he realized that the system constrained him from printing money whenever he felt the need.

Now, why would he feel the need? Well, printing money is how you pay for wars and government contracts, as well as the insatiable demands of big business and voters, which allows you to retain power … not to mention bailing out the commercial banks and financial institutions who have engaged in their own form of phantom money creation, and whose failure could tip over the financial markets unless the government comes to their aid. In addition, printing more money permits you to devalue all currency already in circulation, which inflates the price of assets, deflates the cost of debt, and is a far more effective way of taxing people than going after their wages. It is the government's favorite form of theft, for it ultimately benefits the rich on whose patronage it relies.

But if money is no longer backed by gold, what is it actually worth? The US government says the dollar is backed by "the full faith and credit" of ... the US government. Other nations' governments take a similar view. It's akin to saying, "Don't worry, we're good for it." But once a country is judged to no longer be "good for it," lenders move in and take its assets. It happens to weak countries quite frequently. Who are these lenders? The major international banks, the International Monetary Fund, and the World Bank—the latter two being syndicates formed by the leading trading nations, who are, by their own accounts, "good for it."

So, what makes a country "good for it"? Put simply, it is the strength of its gross domestic product (GDP)—essentially, the wealth it creates—and the size of its debt relative to that GDP. Years ago, it was considered very dangerous for debt to exceed fifty percent of GDP. But then governments got the idea that they could go on printing money to solve all their problems and issue bonds that they would one day buy back, cancelling the debt. The debt-to-GDP ratio subsequently rose to one hundred percent, then to one hundred fifty percent, and finally to four hundred percent last year. That means that in today's economy, it would take every dollar earned for four years just to pay off our debt. No money left for wages, food, utilities, military—nothing.

Well, of course that's impossible; society would collapse.

And speaking of society, it must be stressed that private debt has been just as virulent as public debt. Student loans, mortgages, car loans, and consumer credit have placed the average household in the position of being technically bankrupt. Meanwhile, globalization and automation have eliminated jobs and severely depressed wages, while costs have increased, asset prices have inflated, and health and retirement funding have dried up.

But these conditions aren't unique just to our country; all the others are experiencing it, too. Surely, you ask, someone must have seen it coming?

Sure thing. We've seen it coming for years. We've been stuck in a tunnel with the freight train of recession and economic collapse bearing down on us full throttle. Dare I suggest that we jackass economists have been frantically pointing it out to anyone who would listen? But the Federal Reserve assured us that they had it in hand.

Now, one way of reducing the debt ratio is to increase GDP. Increasing government deficits was supposed to provide money for infrastructure and productive spending, thus raising GDP. It didn't. Lowering the interest rates was supposed to stimulate consumer and business spending. It didn't. Ever more desperate, governments introduced negative interest rates, so they could skim money off those who insisted on saving it. Cash was eliminated so that no one could hide it. Every digital transaction became visible; transaction taxes quickly followed.

It wasn't enough. Perhaps it never was intended to be enough.

What was needed was a big bang solution, they said—and that solution was to CANCEL ALL DEBTS. They're calling it the Overthrow. Capitalism doesn't work, so it's time to overthrow it. In reality, it's just an old-fashioned Jubilee, straight out of the Bible.

For most people, this is an easy sell: just wipe out all debts and start again, redistributing trillions of dollars in the process. And if millions of investors, pensioners, retirement funds, banks, and creditors lose their savings in the process, hey, it's a small price to pay. Stocks and shares and private businesses of all sizes may be wiped out, but a new and more equitable system will take its place, with a universal basic income for all. Everyone will finally be equal. Now, what could be more popular than that?

This is what *Agenda 2060* means when it states, "End poverty in all its forms by controlling income distribution, limiting private asset accumulation, and ensuring equality of safety, security, and well-being for all, regardless of work input or ability."

But there will never be a day when everyone is equal—not as long as we remain human. There will be no universal basic income for the elite who are creating this system, nor for the super-rich who are their sponsors.

Wealth will continue to reward cronyism, self-interest, corruption, and barefaced theft with the same ingenuity it has displayed for millenia. If the worldwide pandemic of the 2020s taught us anything, it is that big business runs the world. Governments and bureaucracy are but its servants. And the poor proletariat, the victims of this great fraud, believing themselves to be unshackled at last from the fear of poverty and failure, will find themselves trapped in dependency, a vast underclass of serfs. What will the government do then to keep the lid on them?

Next week, I will tell you why I predict that the government sector will swell to become seventy percent or more of the economy, while unemployment will become a lifetime condition for half the adult population within ten years. I will show you how governments shrink wealth, not grow it—and how poverty, discrimination, and sedentary malaise will ultimately destroy the spirit of society. I will explain how creating deliberate divisions between people on the basis of competing identities consumes their energy and distracts them from the true cause of their dissatisfactions, suppressing rebellion against those in control of the deep state.

I will also tell you who the real jackasses behind this are, and where they want to take you. Until then...

Hee haw.

THE MISSING ELEVEN PERCENT

May 2058

Jordan saved the file and shut down Alexa's tablet just as the autonomous vehicle announced "Event ahead" and began to slow. The solar farm was behind them, and they were now travelling through the coastal wind farm that stretched forty miles through land that had once been citrus and avocado orchards. Windmills marched down to the white sand beach and on out to sea, trailing black power cables behind them. The beach, once the city's ozone playground, was now out of bounds and deserted.

As the car stopped, it was quickly mobbed by young people bearing placards and chanting slogans.

"It's a protest," the car announced.

"I'll decide that," Alexa snapped. She wound down the window and stuck her head out. The chanting had a hypnotic, funereal tone. "What's happening?" she shouted. "We want to get through!"

One placard read, Save the raptors. Another, Stop the killer blades! Two of the protesters tried to open the car doors, but they were locked.

"Come and see for yourself!" one shouted, without anger.

"Then we'll let you through," the other added.

Alexa turned to Jordan. "What do you think?"

He shrugged. "Why not?"

Alexa closed the window and took the voice activator control from its cradle. "Shut down the motor. Wait for my command," she instructed.

They got out of the vehicle and activated the door lock, then followed the two lead protesters towards a roadblock haphazardly erected from wooden fruit-picking bins on carts. The bins were stenciled with the same slogans as the placards. The writing was professional, the message consistent, and the protesters were mostly college-aged kids in their early twenties. They watched the proceedings without rancor.

On the other side of the roadblock, three cars were stopped, waiting to get through. Another car pulled up behind Alexa's and tooted its horn. Everyone, including Jordan, turned and looked at it. The tooting stopped. A surveillance drone circled overhead.

"What are you protesting?" Alexa asked. She was focused on getting the roadblock removed so they could continue on to Neutrality Park. Her mind was very much on the document she'd asked Jordan to read.

"Look in the bins," the lead protester told her. "See for yourself."

He stepped aside and motioned them forward. There was a vaguely unsettling smell as they approached.

The bins were filled with large dead birds. Jordan and Alexa pulled back in unison.

"What are they?" Alexa gasped.

"Those are the raptors," Jordan said. "Hawks, eagles, owls…"

"And condors," the lead protester confirmed. "Our rarest, most vulnerable birds. And this is just what we've collected in the last nine days. The wind farms down this coast have been killing up to a million birds a year. Many species are close to extinction."

"How?" Alexa protested. "Why?"

"The turbines suck them in. It's like a giant predator that they never evolved to survive. Once caught in the windmill's draft, they can't escape; they're brutally destroyed. And no one is paying attention!"

"But … wind and solar power are our main renewable energy sources. There must be some way to avoid this. No one wants to kill wildlife. What does the government say?"

"*Hush, little baby, don't say a word, Papa's gonna buy you a mockingbird…*" the two lead protesters sang in unison.

"Listen," the first protester said urgently, "it's the mockingbird syndrome: 'don't say a word.' The wind only blows strong enough to even turn these turbine blades thirty percent of the time, and solar panels generate power only thirty-four percent of the time—though most of them are Chinese-manufactured crap, and they're fucked now. But get this: when they're working together, they produce too *much* power and could blow up the grid. So we either dump it, or run the surplus thousands of miles over the border and sell it at a loss. But the rest of the time, we don't have enough, so we have to choose between power cuts or burning gas, for which we pay a fortune. That's why the oil and gas companies muscled in on solar and wind power. Fact is, it's their money that built all this shit. The government's in their pocket—always was, always will be."

Alexa returned to the bin and looked down at the avian corpses, holding her nose. The sunken eyes of the dead birds were like fire opals, their feathers a rainbow of all the richest colors in nature, spoiled only by the lazy seething of maggots.

She turned away abruptly, marching back to the car without speaking.

Jordan took one of the offered fliers and followed her. They waited in silence while the bins were moved aside for them, then Alexa instructed the car to continue to their destination.

"They don't seem terribly angry," Jordan observed.

Alexa looked at him sharply. "I don't know whether I should tell you this, but I learned something at the Social Equity Ministry that probably explains that. It really shocked me."

"Don't tell me anything that you believe you shouldn't," he offered helpfully, knowing full well that she would.

"College dormitories' water supplies are now laced with oxytocin," she replied. "It's a hormone that works through two of the main neurotransmitters—dopamine and serotonin—to enhance group bonding and altruism. They started doing it eight years ago in order to suppress the anger and dissent that was rife on campus."

Jordan laughed. "Pity they didn't do it in my day. Anger and dissent were what killed my mathematics department."

"They're very brave," Alexa said quietly. "That security drone will have facial recognition software. Protesting is the quickest way for students to lose Society Points—and without those, they'll get no Transitional Benefits worth having. There are no jobs waiting for them.

They might as well be Non-Persons."

Realizing what she'd said, she looked sharply at Jordan for his reaction. He had none. He was deep in thought after reading the protesters' flier, which he folded carefully and put in his pocket. Except in the first few weeks after they met at Lexie's celebration, his own status as a Non-Person had never been mentioned.

At the gates of Neutrality Park, they handed over their tickets and were directed to follow a coach filled with schoolchildren along a road that wound its way up a steep hill, leading to the ocean lookout. The wooded parkland stood in stark contrast to the land they'd just driven through. It had been planted as a public display of nature for a population that had largely been roped off from the countryside in order to protect it. Every city had its own version of Neutrality Park somewhere on its outskirts, and visits were strictly controlled in order to keep them carbon-neutral. It was thanks to Alexa's new elite status that they were able to get tickets at all.

Halfway up the hill, the coach stopped in front of them, disgorging its children onto the grassy shoulder of the road. The hillside fell away gently towards the copses below, and the children hesitated, looking down the slope. Then one or two of the older ones stuck a tentative foot over the edge, followed by others. Finding it safe, they leaned forward and began to run, slowly at first, then with growing exhilaration as gravity pulled them forward. The younger ones, bemused and cautious, peered over the edge, just watching. At last, one of them got down on his knees and crawled backwards down the slope. Others followed, but some returned to the safety of the coach.

"They've never been on a hill before," Alexa murmured. "They don't look as though they've ever even felt grass."

Their car overtook the coach and proceeded to the summit, which looked out over a grey ocean beneath a grey sky, windfarm to their left, carbon-sink forests to their right. The picnic tables were all occupied, so Alexa suggested they take her picnic basket and climb the grassy knoll above the parking lot in search of a comfortable place to sit. Once she'd found a spot that suited her, she sat down, opened her basket, and spread out a cloth on which she arranged a modest lunch of fruit, boiled eggs, and sushi.

"Well," she asked, "what did you think of what my father wrote?"

Jordan thought carefully. "I can see why it got him into trouble. Those were dangerous times."

"Do you think he was right?"

"About the historical factors, or his future predictions?"

"Both."

Jordan picked up a piece of sushi. The rice dropped out of its seaweed wrapper onto the grass. "Did he actually get to write the explanation he was promising, about what would happen next?"

"No, the online newspaper that published his writings was shut down right after he posted that piece and disappeared. I'm afraid now that he might be dead."

Jordan peered at the grains of rice that had fallen in the grass. Already they were attracting ants, as if a clarion call had gone out. Nature... Somewhere it is written that the weight of all the ants on earth would far exceed the weight of humanity. Thus, a mathematician like Jordan, if he knew the avoirdupois of an ant, could speculate on how many of these predacious insects there might be in the world. Chances are it would be a number beyond comprehension and would not, therefore, be believed.

"Hate speech is not a capital offense," he cautioned, "it is merely a tool of censorship. Making him a Non-Person and shutting down his access to all media should have been enough to silence him. They did the same to me. But I never had the feeling they needed to kill me."

She broke the shell of a hard-boiled egg and peeled it for him, dipping it in salt without asking. He took it in his fingers and bit it in half.

"That's why I wanted your opinion," she said. "You've never talked about what it means to be a Non-Person. How do you live? What are the restrictions? Could my father be out there somewhere, living the same way you do? And if he is, why can't he contact me, or why can't I contact him?"

Jordan ate the second half of his egg, then stretched out on the grass, hands behind his head and eyes closed.

"If he's alive," Alexa persisted, "surely he'd let me know ... don't you think? It would be unforgiveable if he hasn't even tried."

Jordan kept his eyes firmly shut. "There's another possibility that explains the demeanor of those students," he said unexpectedly. "They may be funded by the Nuclear Fusion Lobby. Dead birds garner a lot of sympathy."

Alexa, quite understandably, looked puzzled.

"And as for your father," he went on, "no, I don't necessarily think he would be in a position to contact you—not if the FIB had told him that would make you a Non-Person, too … or worse. They did it to me with Lexie, until I summoned the courage to call their bluff. It's not his analysis of what happened at the time of the Overthrow that made him a danger, but his threat to name the people involved and expose their game plan. At the time, my guess is that that would have been enough to make him a suitable candidate for rendition."

"Rendition?" Alexa gasped. "You mean, you think he was taken to a torture camp?"

Jordan sat up. "Torture? No. His crime was dissent, not terrorism. The aim with detaining dissenters is to change their minds—literally. Neurologically. The Chinese spent decades perfecting the technique. After a month or so in a medical rehabilitation retreat, he might not even know who you are, who he is, or what is real and what is fantasy… Can I have that apple?"

She picked it up, looked at it curiously, then took a bite out of it.

Jordan shrugged. What he'd said was bound to have thrown her. If that was not his intention, then presumably he could have chosen not to say it.

She continued to eat halfway around the apple, crunching vigorously, before snapping out of her reverie, realizing what she had done, and passing him the remainder of the core.

"What I've found at the Social Equity Ministry," she explained, changing the subject, "shows that his prediction was eerily correct. Eighty-nine percent of the population now receives Transitional Benefits at one level or another. Of those, eighteen percent are children, twelve percent are college students, ten percent are retirees over seventy, and sixty percent are of working age. Of all working-age people, twenty-seven percent are in enterprise employment, thirty-nine percent are in government employment, and thirty-four percent have no employment. What that means is that seventy percent of the overall population receives Transitional Benefits and has no form of employment. So, where does the money come from to pay for all this?"

"What about the other eleven percent?"

"How do you mean?"

"You said that eighty-nine percent of the population receives Transitional Benefits. Who are the eleven percent that don't receive it?"

"Well, that's the thing: the Social Equity Ministry keeps no record of them. They're the gap between our population statistics and our beneficiaries. Presumably, they include people like you."

"You mean Non-Persons?" He laughed. "Maybe, but I think the group you're missing is the most important one of all. They're the real beneficiaries of this system: the transnational corporations and the super-rich who own them, the elite buried inside the state bureaucracy, and the entrepreneurs and creative disruptors who operate in blockchain economies beyond the reach of government."

"... Are they the ones paying?"

"No, Alexa. I'm sure your father was about to explain this in his next piece. You see, the crypto currency regimes introduced around the world use what's called "distributed ledger technology." This stops governments from printing money, but it allows them to divide the pie into ever smaller and smaller pieces. In effect, it's the same as the old money-printing game, but played with a different mechanism. Instead of multiplication, they now use division. As a mathematician, I'm sure you could work it out."

"And how long can they keep doing that?"

"Into infinity."

"But infinity is undefined. If you divide any number by x ad infinitum, eventually x approaches its limit—until, theoretically, your starting number reaches zero at infinity."

Jordan shrugged. The result was too obvious to require comment, but he did so nevertheless. "Mathematicians know that. Now that you're working for the government, maybe you can explain it to them..."

And with that, Alexa suddenly stretched her long legs out from under her, snatched the apple core from his hand, threw it aside, and pushed him back onto the ground. Before he could protest, she leaped on top of him, pinning his arms down with her knees. Her hair brushed his face, and he could feel her breath on his cheek as she whispered excitedly, "I know your secret, Professor McPhee—and I can prove it. I believe *you* are Artie Sharp ... and I want you to help me find my father and expose those bastards at the FIB."

ON EDUCATION
The ArteFact Channel

May 2058

"Good evening, my friends. Welcome to the *ArteFact Channel*. I am your faithful correspondent, Artie Sharp, bringing you news of what is happening in our One World.

"You may have overlooked this fact as you struggle to be a good citizen in a country that's short on power, protein, and promises, but we are now barely two years away from the thirtieth anniversary of *Agenda 2060*—and among the deliberations to be made by the International Review Panel is the appropriateness and success, or otherwise, of Article Nine, relating to education.

"A quick refresher on what that Article says: 'Provide equal education for all, with the aim of achieving cohesion and harmony of thought and eliminating antagonism and disagreement by promoting social justice as the cornerstone of all curriculums.'

"Now, who can argue with that?

"... Precisely. And what an inspiring goal it is.

"And speaking of inspiring goals, I'd like to take this opportunity to comment on the recent speech by the president of the World Government herself, delivered on March tenth of this year, when she announced that the early-twentieth-century philosopher and essayist Bertrand Russell would be elevated to the approved reading list for the Inclusive Societies curriculum.

"Her description of Russell as 'the most prescient of progressive liberals' is extremely insightful and causes no dissent from this quarter, but rather encourages me to borrow from that august figure's work to mount my argument for a revised approach to a certain element of education.

"Now, the fact that only some of Russell's selected works have been approved at this stage is not surprising, for there is no doubt that he was a little free in his thinking.

"I am uncertain, because I have not seen the final list of approved texts, whether the following passage from his 'Mysticism and Logic' essay of 1918 has been redacted from the proposed curriculum. But I offer it here, albeit hesitantly, from an uncensored copy in my possession:

> "*Life, in this philosophy, is a continuous stream, in which all divisions are artificial and unreal. Separate things, beginnings and endings, are mere convenient fictions: there is only smooth unbroken transition. The beliefs of today may count as true today, if they carry us along the stream; but tomorrow they will be false, and must be replaced by new beliefs to meet the new situation. All our thinking consists of convenient fictions, imaginary congealings of the stream: reality flows on in spite of all our fictions, and though it can be lived, it cannot be conceived in thought. Somehow, without explicit statement, the assurance is slipped in that the future, though we cannot foresee it, will be better than the past or present...*

"In quoting that passage, I am not suggesting that the beliefs of today will be false tomorrow—that is mere speculation—but the past and present are the subjects of the Intergovernmental Review, and it is my hope that, in setting goals for the future, we will have the courage to be honest about the goals we set in order to get ourselves to where we want to be in 2060, just two years away.

"Has our ability to forecast the future always been reliable? Or dare I suggest that it has been badly wanting since April 1970, when the founders of Earth Day predicted that civilization would collapse within fifteen to thirty years, that the world would be eleven degrees colder by the year 2000, and that by 1985, air pollution would have reduced the amount of sunlight reaching the earth by half? How fortunate we are that the great biologist Professor Paul Ehrlich got it wrong when he stated in the 1970 Earth Day issue of *The Progressive* that between 1980 and 1989, four billion people, including sixty-five million Americans, would perish in 'The Great Die-Off'.

"Hindsight is indeed an excellent viewing platform for observing events clearly ... but it seems to me that we have been determined not to climb up to it of late.

"Agenda 21 was the product of the Earth Summit in Rio de Janeiro in 1992. Ten years later, the Agenda for Culture was added. In 2012, 182 nations affirmed *The Future We Want*, and in 2015, the Agenda for 2030 was declared. Within four years, Greta Thunberg and millions of children worldwide were predicting their lives would end within twelve years as a result of extreme global warming. Thanks to their efforts, they did not. However, as the International Convention on the Environment and Development reported in April 2030, based on its monitoring of the performance of member nations, there remained much to be done. Hence, *Agenda 2060* was set.

"I address these words to the International Review Panel: My purpose here is not to undermine the objectives of our World Government, but to argue for a remodeling of one particular policy that I hold close to my heart. I do hope that the deplatforming of mathematics within our education system will not prejudice your response to my proposal. In the words of Plato, 'You cannot step twice into the same river.' I am not attempting to revisit arguments from the past. I am pleading for a revival in our educational approach on behalf of—and in the absence of—Bertrand Russell, who wrote:

> *'Education as a political weapon could not exist if we*
> *respected the rights of children. If we respected the*
> *rights of children, we should educate them so as to give*
> *them the knowledge and the mental habits required*
> *for forming independent opinions; but education as a*

*political institution endeavors to form habits and to
circumscribe knowledge in such a way as to make one set
of opinions inevitable.'*

"Is there a child alive today who does not believe in the imperative of
environmental sustainability, the protection of our fragile earth, support
for vulnerable and oppressed minorities, the elimination of privilege,
and the need for equality of outcome for all peoples? Surely not. These
things have become so self-evident that any child would embrace these
missives freely, of their own volition, and without need for compulsion.

"Hopefully then, you will accept that what I am advocating is not
a cunningly devised backdoor attempt at subversion, but rather an
openhearted plea for you to agree with Bertrand Russell on the matter
of education when he writes:

*'The prevention of free enquiry is unavoidable so long
as the purpose of education is to produce belief rather
than thought, to compel the young to hold positive
opinions on doubtful matters rather than to let them see
the doubtfulness and be encouraged to independence of
mind. Education ought to foster the wish for truth, not
the conviction that some particular creed is the truth.'*

"At the risk of ignoring Plato's advice regarding stepping into the same
river twice, I ask you to consider Russell's view that 'Logic is the youth
of mathematics, and mathematics is the manhood of logic.' Yes, I am
asking you to restore mathematics to the education curriculum, and I
hope to convince you of the very good reason why this would be in
the best interests of not only our children, but our World Government.

"Having your eyes so firmly fixed on the future, you may have
overlooked, or even forgotten, the events I am about to describe.

"In October 2017, the *Fifth Assessment Report* of the *Intergovernmental
Report on Climate Change* predicted that sea levels would rise twenty to
thirty centimeters by 2050, and fifty centimeters to one meter by 2100.
According to the science reporter of the now-defunct *New York Times*,
the US National Ocean and Atmosphere Administration estimated a

'plausible worst-case scenario' of a 2.5-meter sea level rise along the Eastern Seaboard causing massive inundation. Not content with that, *The Times* reported that the August 2018 Proceedings of the National Academy of Sciences predicted sea level rises of sixty meters this century.

"The cause of these apocalyptic predictions? The unprecedented melting of Arctic and Antarctic sea ice, occasioned by an increase in global temperatures by two to four degrees, thanks to mankind's CO_2 emissions.

"Now, it is not my place to undermine the convictions of the many tens of thousands of academics, government employees, and science reporters employed in protecting the world from indifference to—and inaction on—climate change. Nevertheless, I was bemused by the suggestion that oceans would rise by sixty meters as a result of melting sea ice. It simply did not seem logical—and it was not until I was asked to explain the situation to a young man who was extremely disturbed by this information that I realized that the absence of mathematics in today's teaching is leading to the absence of logic in people's reasoning.

"See, here's the thing. By far, the greatest area of ice on earth is in the sea. But because the density of ice is only nine-tenths the density of water, ninety percent of the ice is below sea level, and only ten percent is above. However, because water expands by nine percent when it turns into ice, that means that the *volume* occupied by the underwater ice will actually shrink when it melts and turns back to water again—causing the overall sea level to FALL.

"Now, that still leaves ten percent of all ice above water, so what happens when that melts? Well, just reverse the process: when ice turns back into water, its volume shrinks by nine percent. So, in combination, when all the ice melts, only ninety-nine percent of the volume presently held by the ice below sea level will return to the ocean as water.

"Well, I have to say that the young man I was explaining this to was completely bemused by the logic of my explanation and by the terminology I was using. But I was determined to allay his fears (which were very reasonable given the circumstances), so I took it upon myself to teach him some basic mathematics. For example: if x is the volume of ice below the surface, then x minus $10x$ divided by 100 equals y, which is the volume of water below the surface once the ice melts, and so...

"But all of this is too simple to bore you with it. It is not worth working through the equation. Just knowing the facts about how water expands when it freezes, it is an easy matter to apply logic to the question of the ice melt's effects on sea levels. Mathematics is the tool we use to validate logic, nothing more. So, we see that the sea level actually *falls* as a result of the Arctic and Antarctic sea ice melt. We didn't have to wait half a century or more to prove that the predictions of sea level rise were wrong.

"My young man, once he understood all this, was greatly relieved—but also very, very annoyed. 'What do they take us for,' he shouted, 'fools? Why aren't we taught this?'

"Perhaps you will ask yourself the same question, for as Bertrand Russell has said, 'The essence of the State is that it is the repository of the collective force of its citizens.' Treat us as fools at your peril.

"Of course, now 2050 has come and gone, and there was no such sea level rise—nor has there been a two to four percent rise in global temperatures... But that's another story.

"Thank you for accepting my submission, as I believe having this information available is in the best interests of the World Government."

A ONE-LEGGED TAP DANCER

May 2058

"Bertrand Russell!" Alexa shouted triumphantly in Jordan's ear. "The restoration of mathematics in the curriculum! It had to be you; I knew it as soon as I heard it. Admit it, Jordan: *you* are Artie Sharp!"

Of course, for her in particular, it was such an obvious giveaway, coming so soon on the heels of him referring her to Bertrand Russell when she was looking for a simple key to unlocking the complexities of intersectionalism. When that segment had recently gone out on the *ArteFact Channel*, he'd completely forgotten that she'd be watching.

So what could he do about it now—lie?

His arms were still pinned by her knees. Her hair in his face smelled of rosemary and limes, and her breath against his cheek held the warmth of a sunny breeze. Surely the rapid escalation of his heartbeat was being transmitted by the sensors in his shirt back to the atrial fibrillation monitoring machine at the salutogenesis clinic of Dr. John Erasmus.

And what of her? Her sudden outburst in throwing herself onto Jordan and shouting excitedly in his ear, her rapid breathing and elevated adrenal system—all symptoms that would surely be captured by her subdermal Vitec chip—risked revealing (should she be monitored) that she had become convinced of Jordan's secret identity as Artie Sharp, to the point where she felt overwhelmed by the need to reveal it, consequences be damned.

When she rolled off of him and laid her head back on the freshly mown grass, closing her eyes in shame, she heard the strangest sound: Jordan softly chuckling.

She sat up. "I'm right, aren't I?" She poked him in the ribs.

"You're partly right."

"What does that mean?"

"I have some influence in that area."

He climbed to his feet and brushed off the grass cuttings. She got up, too. A sudden shyness fell between them, and they avoided each other's eyes.

"The ... the Russell thing," she stammered. "It just seemed like too much of a coincidence. I had to know."

"Yes, I can see that. But, now that you know ... I'll have to kill you."

She stepped back in alarm, almost tripping into a tumble down the hill. "Jordan!"

He quickly grabbed her by the arm. "It's okay, I'm joking."

He took her other arm. It turned into a hug—a fraternal hug, brief but comforting.

"So, now that you know, I guess this is something we'd better talk about," he said. "And maybe you can also tell me what you discovered at the Social Equity Ministry that convinced you that a policy was deliberately put in place to divide people into competing minority groups."

They packed up their picnic and returned to the car. After her impetuous actions on the hilltop, Alexa seemed anxious to restore her dignity in his eyes. And it turned out that the security status she'd been granted after Shane Whitman's visit gave her access to all the ministry's archives—including one, most remarkably, that she was sure was unintentional.

"They're handwritten minutes of the meetings held by some of the Action Committee at the time of the Overthrow. I'm sure I wasn't meant to see them, and I'm pretty sure they've never been transcribed; I went looking for digital records of them, but there was nothing to be found."

"Who were these members?"

"Just initials, acronyms. I didn't have time to work them out, but it was in 2039, and I was just concentrating on what was being said. There's no doubt that they had a deliberate strategy for dismantling bipartisan politics in favor of competing multi-partisan groups. To me, it read like a naked divide-and-conquer tactic. Perhaps I'm overreacting, and it was just the sort of hyperbole that any deconstructionists would spout when society is in a state of upheaval. But it was so at odds with what the Agenda Implementation Tribunal is contemplating now that I'm not sure what I'm meant to be doing... And from what my father wrote in that last financial column before he disappeared, he seemed to know exactly what was going on."

When they reached the site of the former roadblock at the wind farm, the protesters were packing up, and they weren't stopped again.

"Nuclear fusion has already won the day," Jordan observed. "These protests are just dying arguments over who should continue to get government subsidies for inefficient renewable resources, and whether the virtue signals of wind and solar power are relevant anymore."

Would he have spoken so frankly to her about things like this before the revelation on the hill? Probably not—Jordan had come down off that hillside a changed man. Being outed by Alexa was almost a relief. He didn't want there to be a lie between them any longer, and if he was wrong to trust her, then he couldn't trust his instincts either. Where would that leave him?

They drove back to the city with a renewed energy between them, as if they had faced a major fear together—and found it to be a mirage. He agreed that he would do what he could to discover what had happened to her father, confessing how much pain his separation from Lexie had caused him. He explained how the dissolution of parental bonds—patriarchal ones in particular—was a deliberate objective of the state, for the obvious reason that exclusive control by and dependency on the state were essential to maintaining its power. Touching briefly on his own experience at the hands of the FIB, he urged her not to be angry about her father's absence, but to let Jordan use his resources at the DDC to try and trace him. Meanwhile, he wondered if she could get access to those handwritten records again; if so, it might be possible to copy them without anyone knowing.

"Do you wear reading glasses when you're working?" he asked.

"Sometimes. Why?"

"Bring them with you next time we meet. I'll explain then."

As to her discovery of his alter ego, little more was said. She now knew his secret, and he knew hers. They didn't know at this stage where they were headed, but they sensed they could safely travel there together.

When the autonomous car announced that they had arrived at Jordan's apartment, he took Alexa's arm and steered her to a corner of the building that was a blind spot for surveillance.

"Artie Sharp is a one-legged tap dancer," he cautioned. "He dances on the leg of truth. But truth alone provides no rhythm or ability to syncopate. If you think he can be an answer for you, you must find him another leg to dance on. You're an insider now; that's where you'll find it."

As enigmatic as this may have sounded, she understood fully that he was referring to the door that Shane Whitman had opened for her, and he was encouraging her to step inside.

The following day, true to his word, Jordan set in motion a search for Donald Melville Smythe in the encrypted files of the Total Information Agency archives. If the FIB had buried her father, that's where he would be interred, and the quantum computers of the Derangers' network would eventually track him down.

Meanwhile, perhaps triggered by Alexa's concern for her father, Jordan's thoughts returned to Lexie and how easily she had been turned against him—first by her mother, then by the feminist hive.

A LEXICON OF GENDER NEUTRALITY

June 2058

"In the feminist hive," Jordan told Dr. John Erasmus later that week over their monthly Derangers dinner, "thought coalesces into groupthink, then the group becomes cohesive and presents a united front to compete with other groups who are perceived to be antagonistic to the groupthink."

"Particularly white males like us," Erasmus suggested. "And the stronger the cohesion and perception of a common cause, the more muscular the mental and emotional bonding becomes within the hive, leading to an obsession that rewards group members with feelings of love and trust for each other, akin to a form of exaltation."

"Precisely!" Jordan agreed, knowing full well where this was coming from. "The 'I' becomes 'we,' and soon a phalanx is formed to defeat enemy ideas of morality and social behavior. There's no way of getting around it."

"Well," the good doctor revealed, "in relation to your Lexie, I may have some news that suggests the phalanx is not completely impenetrable. I'll tell you over a drink."

It was no coincidence that Erasmus was his daughter's doctor, and to the extent that medical ethics allowed, he was willing to relay what information he could. For Jordan, any insight into the world that Lexie occupied was welcome, and the nature of that world sometimes appeared so bizarre that neither of them felt it was a breach of trust on their parts to discuss it.

It was over chocolate mescaline liqueurs that Erasmus gave him the full background. They'd been introduced to the drink by fellow Deranger and distinguished biochemist Hedley Payne, who had found a way of isolating the principal alkaloid in mescaline that causes hallucinations ($C_{11}H_{17}NO_3$), then reassembled the elements to produce a compound that opened the mind without scrambling it.

"By way of example," Erasmus began, "the Subcommittee of the Community Caucus on Cultural Inclusivity, to which Lexie has been appointed as a member of the LGBTQI Action Brigade, has as its motto, 'Consensus Trumps Dissent.' There is considerable irony in the choice of the word *trumps*, as you and I would recognize, for many older members of the caucus still talk about the days when the world was held hostage by a demonic figure bearing that same name, and they feel it is important to remember those times ... though Lexie and her generation feel that the past is the past, and the present is what really matters because, irrefutably, the present becomes the future.

"Anyway, 'Consensus Trumps Dissent' is a foundational belief that guides all caucusing activity, apparently, and silences the free speech dissenters who were such a distraction in the early years of Agenda implementation. Even those who still have nostalgic leanings towards old-fashioned democratic principles have to admit that consensus trumping dissent could not be more 'woke.' "

As he told it, the subcommittee to which Lexie had been appointed seldom experienced dissent, because it was comprised of members who were fully attuned to the goals of social justice as originally defined all those years ago. But there were times when consensus was elusive—not that everyone didn't want it, but because of the vagaries of language. Words were such unstable objects, unreliable, delinquent even, and yet they were all that was available to the subcommittee if it was to report on its conclusions as required by the full Community Caucus Board.

"Lexie has a degree in etymology," Jordan announced proudly, "with honors."

Regardless, despite years of deliberations, her subcommittee was still focused on Article Five of the original 2030 Agenda. (Until this goal had been realized, they could not move on to the new goals outlined in *Agenda 2060*.) At first sight, this had been the most difficult Agenda item that the United Nations 2030 Convention had put forward for implementation. "Gender equality and empowerment for all womyn and girls" seemed an impossible objective after thousands of years of unmitigated patriarchy—but it had proven remarkably simple to achieve once the focus switched to attacking toxic masculinity.

"Some might say that in aiming for equality, the bar had been set artificially low," Erasmus observed sarcastically, "and empowerment of all women was the real objective all along. But there was a flaw embedded in the drafting of Article Five that was reflective of the times in which it was drafted—and which was, in itself, a classic example of the vagaries of language that would undermine the subcommittee's deliberations. The flaw lay in the use of the terms *womyn* and *girls*. In a gender-neutral world, these were nothing if not heteronormative words, and as such, they were threatening to victims of birth misgendering, to sexual fluidity, and to all humankind who struggled with transgender rights issues.

"It was this unintended consequence of poor language selection that led to the urgent establishment of a Beta Advisory Group, charged with the development of a lexicon of gender neutrality in time for the *Agenda 2060* review. In hindsight, it is easy to see the pressure that members of that advisory group must have felt."

This pressure was partly to blame for what brought Lexie to the attention of Dr. Erasmus in his role as a practitioner of salutogenesis.

Knowing Jordan's concern for Lexie's welfare, and now under the influence of mescaline, his friend was prepared to open up his clinical notes, at the risk of revealing some delicate matters which might breach the privacy of the people involved.

"I take the view," Erasmus explained, "that the Salutogenesis Ethics Panel would have no objection to this, providing my commentary is not made public. And you understand that some of the forensic details will remain undisclosed."

Where to begin, then?

He began with Lexie's pregnancy under the Lesbian Moms Program, recalling the details from his case notes. Although Lexie had achieved ninety-five Society Points for her militant same-sex advocacy and social media postings (including the successful doxing of her own father when she was only twelve), she was nevertheless of white European descent, and therefore subject to the insecurities and handicaps of that class. By choosing a sperm donor of predominantly Polynesian and East Asian registration, her Society Points had increased to 103—and when she married her same-sex Latinx lover, Bammy, her points rose immediately to 113. This put her well above the Transitional Benefits level of status and earnings.

When the child was born, she gave it a traditional Polynesian name, Manaia, which was equally used in Polynesian society for children of both genders. (Jordan already knew this, of course.) Lexie also chose the name because *mana* means "respect," and *-ia* means "he, she, or it." (Jordan hadn't known that part.) Although Manaia was born with male genitalia, it was Lexie's strong desire that her child should not have its gender predetermined by behavioral or cultural imposition—something that had emerged during the Beta Advisory Group's deliberations on the establishment of a lexicon of gender neutrality, where opposing groups had argued for years over the use of *hir* and *zir* as third-person singular objective pronouns, without ever reaching a consensus.

In a similar way, dissent had arisen over the parental nomenclature for lesbian couples. Should the child have a "mommy" and "poppy," or "mom" and "momma," et cetera—or was it even necessary to mirror traditional mother/father models? Bammy, who had successfully completed top surgery and was well advanced towards transitioning at that time, chose to be called "opie," which was a truncation of the phrase "other parent" and left Lexie free to choose "mommy."

As an infant, Manaia had been dressed in onesies, alternately pink or blue. But once the child was out of diapers, the dress code favored a form of culottes—neither skirt nor shorts—which had gained traction among Community Caucus members as the preferred uniform for prepubertal children.

Being anxious about germs, accidents, and indeed any unwelcome stimuli, let alone food allergens, Lexie chose to confine Manaia to the home for the first three years. As a result, she was able to identify the child's temperament and physical traits based on its genetics as opposed to its environment. Thus it was clear to her and Bammy that Manaia was artistic, sensitive, highly intelligent, and gender-nonconforming. These were happy and secure years for the three of them.

Problems only started to emerge when it came time for Manaia to attend preschool socialization classes, where the supervisors insisted on referring to Manaia as "he" and "him," despite Lexie's objections. Bammy then discovered that this blatant breach of gender neutrality guidelines was driven by budgetary considerations. With separate toilets having already been provided for M, F, L, Q, and T children, there were no funds left for either I (Indeterminate) or U (Undecided) children. Despite Manaia's parents lodging a complaint with the Community Appeals Board, change was not forthcoming. Lexie was advised that she was eligible for a one-point Society Bonus, but otherwise she must accept the circumstances.

To make matters worse, Bammy's testosterone program, which was part of her transitioning, made her extremely aggressive, and she was arrested for assaulting school staff, no doubt causing a great deal of upset for Lexie.

"It was around this time," Erasmus explained, "that her issues were brought to my attention."

A DOG'S BEST FRIEND

As told by Dr. John Erasmus to Jordan McPhee
June 2058

Approximately six months after "he" (I will call him that for reasons that should become clear) had started regular schooling, Lexie brought Manaia into the salutogenesis clinic for a behavioral assessment, having noticed disturbing changes in him. He was engaging in risky behavior: climbing trees, throwing balls, running recklessly across the school yard, wrestling with other students, and being disruptive rather than attentive during study times. This led me to the obvious conclusion that he had ADHD and would benefit from being on Ritalin. Neither the diagnosis nor the treatment seemed in doubt to me, and I did not expect to see either of them again for three months, provided his dosage was maintained.

Some weeks later, I was surprised when Lexie brought Manaia back to the clinic, displaying new symptoms.

"M is complaining of having a creeping, tingling sensation," she explained, "as if ants are crawling over the skin. But I can't see anything, not even a rash. What could it be?"

My immediate response was that it must be a food allergy, and I placed them both on a dietary program designed to identify the offending allergen. Placing the entire family on such a plan has proven to be most effective in avoiding unconscious cheating. The list of forbidden foods included gluten, dairy, sugar, and the nightshade family. Meanwhile, it seemed that the Ritalin was working, for the boy's hyperactivity was noticeably reduced, and during his time in my office, I would have described him as almost subdued.

Allergy identification and gut cleansing require patience and discipline, so I asked Lexie to keep notes on any changes and make an appointment to see me in four weeks' time, confident that we would see an improvement.

Alarmingly, however, what I saw was a marked deterioration. The creeping, tingling sensation had now spread to Lexie and had grown worse in Manaia, despite their strict adherence to the program I had laid down. To make matters more serious, Manaia appeared to be suffering from an accumulation of Ritalin in one of his organs, leading to extreme lethargy and almost vegetative lability. He was an appealing child with dark eyes, olive skin, and shoulder-length black hair, but the energy he'd displayed at our first meeting was now completely absent. He was wearing a T-shirt with a political slogan on the front—something like "Please don't destroy my planet"—but when I tried to engage him in conversation on it, he let his mother reply for him.

"Manaia is angry that adults are failing to address climate change," she said, "and that, by the time M grows up, there may be no planet left to live on ... aren't you, sweetheart?"

Manaia didn't reply, but leaned down and stroked the small dog that never seemed to leave his side. The dog wagged its tail lethargically.

I remember saying something like, "Good for you, Manaia. Maybe they'll listen to you kids and do something about it."

I cancelled the Ritalin and put him on a placebo that the homeopathic practitioner in our clinic recommends for young children. As for Lexie's tingling skin complaint, well, I chalked that up to a sympathetic reaction, which I felt sure would abate as soon as she saw an improvement in Manaia.

"Kids go down quickly," I explained, "but they go back up just as fast. There is nothing organically wrong with Manaia that I can detect, so let's give him time. At least we know he has no allergies. Once the Ritalin is out of his system, we'll monitor his ADHD and try him on a serotonin reuptake inhibitor."

This seemed to reassure her, but it did not stop her from calling later to ask me if I thought she should put his name on the waiting list for bottom surgery. If his genitalia were altered to match his gender identity, she felt, his behavioral issues might be cured, and he would be much happier. Remembering his long black hair and dark eyes, not to mention the olive skin, I could very easily envisage Manaia as a transfem—but that was a big call for a five-year-old, and after all, it would always be an option in the future.

A few days later, I ran into the two of them going into the animal wellness department at our clinic. Lexie appeared tense and worried, and Manaia was clutching the dog to his chest and not speaking.

"We're taking our dog in for an examination," Lexie explained, "as he's got no energy, and I want him checked for heavy metals. We took him to the anti-plastics Save the Turtles demonstration, and he couldn't even walk."

"Great idea," I replied. "Heavy metals are a good place to start."

Thinking on this later, I wondered whether heavy metals were something I should have checked for in Manaia myself, so I rang the veterinary office and asked them if they could copy me on the dog's results. Heavy metal testing is done by analyzing hair samples, and this would be a simple thing for me to arrange for Lexie and Manaia. I knew Jan from the vet lab very well; she and I used to secretly play street football at night when we were at university. There were a lot of us students playing the game secretly in the years after the sport was banned, as you know—and as all members of underground societies do, we remained friends later in life.

"We didn't find any heavy metals in that dog hair you were asking about," she reported a few days later, "but we did find elevated levels of cortisol."

"Cortisol!" I exclaimed. "I didn't even know that dogs had adrenal cortexes. Are you saying they're like humans when it comes to stress hormones?"

"Not only that, but there's new research that shows dogs exactly mirror the emotions of their owners—and that includes chemically. Look it up."

I thanked her and did exactly that. She was right; dogs really are humanity's best friends. They feel everything that their owners do—maybe even more so—and they secrete it into their fur.

Now, I have to put my hand up and admit that I'd been leading us down the wrong track with my diagnosis of ADHD and food allergies. The description of the feeling of ants crawling over the skin should have alerted me. The Latin word for ant is *formica*, and 'formication' is a neurological condition that manifests as a tingling, creeping sensation in the skin. Cortisol (also known as hydrocortisone) is produced by the adrenal cortex in response to stress, anxiety, and depression. What I was dealing with was a form of neurasthenia.

But what was causing this stress and depression?

Though our Erasmus Foundation Salutogenesis Clinic is a multi-disciplinary practice, I had unconsciously chosen to veer away from the psychology side of things out of a desire to avoid unnecessary paperwork. The government had identified mental health as a target for big budgets and big awareness campaigns way back in the days when our leaders were chosen by all the people, rather than just by the well-informed. It was felt that spreading a wide net to catch as many mentally ill people as possible would make them feel included, eliminate stigmatization, and get them into the public record. As with all social policy, it was kind, well-intentioned, and beyond criticism. Of course, the fact that everyone going onto the Mental Health Register received five bonus Society Points meant there was a big take-up, so the workload involved in issuing certificates and cross-referencing everything with all the government departments became extremely burdensome. For these reasons, my colleagues and I tend to turn to psychological explanations for non-wellness as a very last resort.

But with Lexie, Manaia, and the dog, I was pretty sure we were dealing with anxiety. All the symptoms were there; I'd chosen to look past them. My challenge now was how to treat it without pulling out the mental health forms.

I decided to call Lexie and get her to bring Manaia and the dog into the clinic for a one-hour diagnostic session. She was to leave them there and come back when it was finished, as her presence might interfere with the results. At first, she was concerned that Manaia might not be able to cope with being left alone, but I assured her there would be a female monitor on hand at all times.

The day dawned clear and sunny with no wind and not a cloud in the sky. It reminded me of the summer days of my youth, only not as hot. Manaia and the dog showed up subdued, but anxious. I decided to try a positive approach.

"I have some good news, Manaia," I began. "That climate change T-shirt you wore the other day has really worked! The government has decided to send thirty billion UniCoins to the people who can fix the problem, and now the earth is going to survive forever."

He didn't respond. The concept of thirty billion UniCoins seemed beyond him.

I tried another tack. "Hey, here's a trick: how big is a turtle's mouth?"

I held my thumb and forefinger together to create an opening. "This big," I said.

He looked vaguely interested.

"And how big do you think a *baby* turtle's mouth is?"

Ever so slowly, he put his own finger and thumb together to create a much smaller opening.

"That's it exactly!" I exclaimed.

He looked at it and nodded.

Then I opened my bottom desk drawer, where I had stashed one of the banned plastic shopping bags from the old days. I shook it out for him to see.

"Well, here's some more good news. Scientists have been trying to work out how to get a plastic bag through the mouth and into the stomach of a young turtle, but they say it's impossible to do."

He looked at the bag, and he looked at the opening between his thumb and forefinger. Then, before I had to say anything more, he put out his free hand. I passed the plastic bag to him. But no matter how hard he pushed and cheated, he couldn't get even one tenth of it to pass through the opening. He heaved and grunted and gave it his best shot before giving up.

"There!" I clapped my hands. "Seems like the turtles are safe after all."

From that same desk drawer, I retrieved a tennis ball, which I started bouncing up and down on the office floor. The dog pricked his ears and sat up. After ten or twelve bounces, I threw it to Manaia, who dropped it. The dog pounced on it eagerly.

"Let's go outside," I suggested.

At the back of the clinic is a small lawn surrounded by a concrete wall. Manaia seemed reluctant to go on the grass, so I took his hand and told him it was for playing on and Lexie would not be angry. The dog put the ball down at my feet, and I kicked it as hard as I could, so it hit the wall and bounced back at us. Both Manaia and the dog looked at me as if I were playing with a bomb. I kicked it again. This time the dog looked like he was itching to move, so I tried it once more, throwing it with all my might and shouting, "Get it! Get it!"

The dog sprang out of the blocks like a sprinter, barking excitedly—but before it could latch onto the ball, I kicked it away into Manaia's legs.

"Kick it to me!" I cried.

He hesitated too long, and the dog got it. But the dog knew the game instinctively and dropped the ball at my feet. Now, I'm not the fittest person, but I do remember how to play ball, so I dribbled it around Manaia and the dog, describing how I was going to score a perfect goal against the back wall. Then, before I could get it lined up, Manaia came at me like a bat out of hell and booted it away.

Okay, game on!

The three of us chased that ball around the lawn until I thought my lungs would explode, and I collapsed on my back on the grass, gasping for air. Manaia then jumped on me. He was heavy for his age, and I pretended to try and wrestle him off, which prompted him to pound my chest with his fists and triumphantly chant sounds that would not have been out of place in a war dance. I had to tickle him to make him stop, then I feigned defeat and went limp.

This caused a curious reaction. He looked at me with a mixture of triumph and concern. Had he gone too far, perhaps? He reached out and ruffled my hair to "wake" me. Now, I have very short hair. It's what we used to call a number 2, and it feels a bit like the bristles on a nailbrush. Clearly, Manaia was intrigued by it.

Once I'd regained my breath, we got up and went back inside. Both the boy and the dog were now what I would call "perky." Manaia and I had a piece of chocolate and an apple juice while I wrote his name on the tennis ball and told him he should ask his mother if he could keep it at home—or, if he preferred, I would keep it in my desk drawer, and he could come and play with it any time he liked.

He said he'd like to keep it in the desk drawer.

When Lexie arrived, I told her we'd found the cause of his problems.

"It seems that the dog has an adrenal problem that produces an irritating skin infection," I explained. "This irritant has been picked up by Manaia, but it will quickly clear up as the dog responds to the adrenal pills that we've given him. In the meantime, Manaia's hair, like the dog's hair, is the primary repository of the compound creating the problem, so I want you to arrange for Manaia to have his hair cut as soon as possible."

Lexie's hand flew to her mouth as she gasped in shock. "M's hair?" she stammered. "How short must it be?"

"Very short," I replied sternly. "At least as short as mine."

"But that will make him look like a ... a ... b—"

She couldn't even say the word.

I looked across at Manaia, who was busy joining his forefinger to his thumb, but I could swear he was smiling to himself.

"Just try it. You'll be surprised how quickly the problem clears up," I affirmed. "For both of you."

THE COTO GENERATION

July 2058

The doctor's story was revealing as much in the manner of its telling as in its content. He was clearly aware of the societal mores that colored the behavior of his client, and yet the irony that informed his telling of events revealed the pre-progressive (perhaps even *re*-gressive?) attitude that he brought to issues of childhood and gender. Of course, knowing his audience, Jordan McPhee, was a fellow Deranger, it was reasonable for him to assume that they held similar attitudes on such issues. But everyone in the Derangers' generation was very careful with their words outside the milieu of their most trusted friends. In fact, the behavior observed and conversations overheard throughout society revealed little more than the Pavlovian responses of a citizenry well trained by thirty years of constant surveillance and social criticism to behave as expected. That was why people didn't stray from their narrowly defined identity groups; it was safer there.

Thus Jordan was aware of the danger he was in by risking opening up to Alexa, and he needed time and space to work it out before seeing her again.

When she'd originally exposed her secret to him—that she was charged with transforming the Social Points system—she had no way of knowing that she was seeking assistance from the very creator of the subversive icon who regularly undermined the ideology on which the system was based ... nor could she possibly have guessed that Artie's irreverent, anarchic humor had its origins in the professorial mind of her former professor.

So far, however, their world views had not obviously clashed.

The truth was that Jordan's response to the public policy emerging from the Overthrow had been essentially apolitical. On almost every count, he saw himself as Left, Right, *and* Center, so when *Agenda 2060* was published, he couldn't disagree with any of the goals outlined. They were reasonable, humane, and admirably just. He was sure that Alexa felt the same. Most likely, that would have been the consensus of his colleagues, too, if the question were put to them in those terms, but they were ultimately too busy looking into the future of technology to be sidetracked by unproductive discussions about politics.

So, how did this explain Artie Sharp and his subversive broadcasts on the underground *ArteFact Channel* of the dark web? The explanation, perhaps, lay in the three words that had been the pillars of Jordan's academic life: logic, empiricism, and truth. He just couldn't accept public statements that made no sense, were factually incorrect, or were deceitful. But Progressive Intellectual Elites, or PIEs, were so passionately convinced of the correctness of their view of the world that they were untroubled by such concerns. What mattered to them were the goals expressed in *Agenda 2060*. In their view, no decent human could criticize their methods for achieving those goals simply on the grounds that their messaging was sometimes absurd, contrary to fact, or downright dishonest. As much as Jordan loathed the sentiments and viciousness of the alt-right, along with the backward-looking delusional nostalgia of old-school conservatism, it was the PIEs that Jordan's creation, Artie, trained his sights on most often, for they were the ones who controlled the public agenda.

Now he needed to decide which direction he was heading with Artie Sharp, and how this would play out now that Alexa had focused her sights on him. He needed an endgame.

These were the thoughts that played out in his mind over the ensuing days—until they were abruptly interrupted by news of another situation involving Lexie and Manaia, the outcome of which he never could have predicted.

In hindsight, it was clear that Lexie believed her access to the high-level care afforded by the prestigious Erasmus Foundation Salutogenesis Clinic was due to her position on the subcommittee of the CCCI, and her high level of Society Points. She'd never questioned it ... just as it had never occurred to her to ask why she was looked after by Dr. John Erasmus himself.

When medical services had been socialized following the Overthrow, general practice and hospitals were brought under the banner of Medicare and rebranded as the Corpus Care System. In the beginning, a flat insurance premium representing five percent of the patient's annual Transition Benefits was charged for basic accident, emergency, and infectious disease treatment. Elective surgeries and anything deemed to be "lifestyle conditions" were not covered, unless additional premiums were selected on a sliding scale of up to twenty percent. The ever-rising costs of the healthcare industry far outstripped any inflation adjustments to Transitional Benefits. Thus, many citizens turned to self-insuring—which, at best, left them vulnerable to unplanned expenses, and at worst, resulted in having to mortgage their future Transitional Benefits, and in some cases, selling their organs forward on the Transplant Futures Market.

Lexie's blissful ignorance of the reason for her privileged position spoke to her personality and attitude about society. She was a member of the COTO generation, the Children of the Overthrow, those of school and college age who were recruited to enforce the new social justice agendas and denounce backsliding wherever they detected it. Being just fifteen at the time of the Overthrow, Lexie was psychologically in perfect condition to accept the non-heuristic teachings necessary for instilling utter conviction in the principles espoused in *Agenda 2060*. COTOs assumed an unquestioning stance in the years following the Overthrow, partly because they believed the society they now lived in had been at least in part designed by them, and partly because the prevailing COTO ethos encouraged them to see themselves as some kind of revolutionaries—particularly if they had taken part in the Children's March of October 2039, as Lexie had.

Therefore, Lexie, a COTO and a narcissist, never questioned her or Manaia's privileged medical care—which was, in fact, Erasmus simply doing a favor for his old friend and fellow Deranger, Jordan McPhee. That privilege, however, did not extend to elective surgery—more specifically, elective *cosmetic* surgery—which was more the pity.

When Jordan received an urgent message from Erasmus saying that Lexie was in the Hope Clinic for Gender Correction and Cosmetic Surgery, he had just got back from a thirty-minute training run—his twelfth session in the two weeks since his excursion with Alexa to Neutrality Park.

"What the hell...?" he cried out on seeing the message. "What's she doing to herself?"

By the time his Konektor got through to Erasmus, he had already written the script for the entire sordid tragedy in his mind, right down to the angry epistle Lexie would have written blaming the whole thing on him in case she didn't survive her mutilation.

Erasmus rushed to reassure him. "It's not what you think, Jordan. From what I can tell, it all comes down to that Latinx wife ... partner ... husband ... of hers, Bammy," he explained. "Seems she/he has been transitioning over the last year or two and is a candidate for gender correction. In the Corpus Care System, that's the highest-priority area for medical treatment, so Lexie was able to piggyback on it and jump the queue for elective surgery."

"What surgery? What the hell's she doing to herself? Can we stop it?"

"Calm down. It's done," Erasmus said soothingly. "It was just cosmetic; she hasn't changed sex. But there are complications."

It seemed that Bammy, convinced by counselors that she was a male trapped in a female body, had been through breast removal and was well advanced in T-loading.

"What's that?"

"Testosterone. Man juice."

As she grew increasingly masculine in behavior, her attitude towards Lexie seemed to veer towards the norms associated with a cis man: possessive and aggressive, given to exercising control through the mechanisms of anger and dominance.

"All of which suggests to me," Erasmus confided, "that the gender dysphoria we're looking at here may be prompted by a version of gynephilia."

"You've lost me."

"Bammy finds the role of the dominant male in the sexual relationship attractive and wishes to transition into that role."

"Christ Almighty, John," Jordan groaned, "do you have any idea of the horror you're describing? That's my fucking daughter we're talking about!"

"Sorry, my friend, but that's the world we now live in. Anyway, Bammy's jealousy has manifested itself as an almost pathological hatred of the tattoo on Lexie's throat."

"You mean the one of Alexandria Ocasio-Cortez?"

"For COTOs, she was the mid-twenty-first-century equivalent of what Che Guevara was for the mid-twentieth century."

"Also Latin."

"Hmm." Erasmus paused to assemble the scattered pieces of this surrealist picture into some form of reportage that made sense. "Fiercely attractive, apparently." It wasn't clear whether this was a statement or a question.

"Who?" Jordan demanded.

"The Cortez woman. Particularly to parts of the lesbian and trans communities."

"Oh? Why? You mean her politics, or her looks?"

"Ask Lexie. You need to go and see her. She's quite ill."

So it seemed that Bammy, confronted by the full lips and see-through eyes of this Latin firebrand every time his/her mouth homed in on Lexie's upper torso, felt his/her manhood so threatened that eventually he/she exploded in rage and insisted that Lexie have the tattoo removed, booking her at the Hope Clinic for laser surgery on the premise that his/her own transition to trans male could not be successfully completed until this insurmountable psychological hurdle was overcome.

"This is where your expertise comes in, Jordan. Laser tattoo removal on such a large and sensitive area is done by an AI-directed machine, and it seems that something went badly wrong, resulting in Lexie suffering subcutaneous nerve ablations and partial facial paralysis. The computer fucked up—and nobody at the clinic knows why."

Erasmus then arranged a meeting with the head dermatologist. Jordan, still in his tracksuit, set off immediately for the clinic, which was located next to Riverside Park in a leafy enclave of art galleries and workshops, counseling offices, and trans community safe spaces known collectively as Trans World, which had won many international design awards.

Dr. Aydin Miles-Kowalski had been forewarned that Jordan was not only kin to the patient, but was additionally a well-regarded expert consultant in the fields of artificial intelligence and machine learning. It was this aspect of the case, rather than any pastoral concern for the patient, that Miles-Kowalski was open to discussing.

"Your identification came up on my Konektor as 'NP,' " the doctor began suspiciously, "but Dr. Erasmus assures me you are at the top of your field, and I should be lucky to have you share your expertise."

"That's very flattering of Dr. Erasmus," Jordan replied. "But I should warn you that I'm not sufficiently familiar with machine learning in the medical arena to be confident that I understand what's been described to me."

"Well, it's really quite simple," Miles-Kowalski replied bluntly. "Multi-pass tattoo removal uses picosecond laser technology that is fully computer-controlled. The program analyses pigment spectrums and depths and determines the wavelengths, diameters, timing, and frequency of the pulses needed as it tracks over the image. At the same time, the laser head stimulates the dermal macrophages to allow rapid digestion of cellular debris, continuously adjusting to the size of the ink particles broken down."

"The laser is issuing infrared pulses, I presume."

"Yes. There was a time when multiple treatments were required over extended periods, but now we can achieve ninety-nine percent removal in a single session, all made possible by the wave technology."

"A single session?" Jordan repeated. "For a large tattoo, that must be pretty demanding on the patient. I thought the process was painful?"

"No, no. For accuracy, safety, and pain minimization, the patient is fully anesthetized throughout, particularly in a case like this, as the neck is a highly sensitive area."

"So, what went wrong?" Jordan demanded.

"We don't know. The procedure was going well, until it abruptly stopped and requested a reset. This happened three times at one particular point in the image, suggesting the wrong wavelength of light was being emitted for the pigments encountered. A safety setting in the program will not allow more than four passes over the same area at twenty-minute intervals, to ensure, among other things, that scarring and dyschromia do not occur. At that point, the machine shut down. That's when we became aware of the problem."

Jordan leaned forward; this was Lexie whose neck had been traversed by these laser heads. "What problem?" he insisted.

"Successful laser removal of a tattoo involves pigment fragmentation, followed by phagocytosis, which is then drained away by the lymphatic system. In this case, this process was entirely, *perfectly* completed for the entire image—except for the eyes. The eyes appear to be entirely untouched. It was the eyes that caused the program to shut down."

An idea was starting to form in Jordan's mind. "Do you have any idea why?"

"It may be a pigment wavelength issue, or a programming fault. At this stage, it's gone back to the machine's manufacturer for urgent analysis."

"Presumably, a tattoo of that complexity was also applied by a machine-directed program. Do you have any idea where she acquired it?"

Dr. Miles-Kowalski opened a file on his desktop screen. "That's one of the questions we always ask. It was done at COTO Arts." He stood up. "You are welcome to contact the manufacturer directly, if you think you can help them. They seem perplexed by the issue, and I don't want to do any more treatments until the problem is resolved."

"I will," Jordan agreed. "And meanwhile, what about Lexie?"

"We're used to handling extremes of emotional volatility in patients at the Hope Clinic, because many of them are among the most vulnerable members of society. Lexie does not quite fall into that category—but she is understandably upset, and we have her on a combination of sedatives and oxytocin. I'll get a nurse to take you to her."

While he waited, Jordan discreetly sent a recording of the interview that he'd just made on his Konektor to Antonio back at the DDC. He asked him to instruct Quantum XR-9 to scan, evaluate, and hypothesize. Then, with butterflies in his stomach, he went to see his estranged daughter in her sickbed.

JUST BE PATIENT

July 2058

In the time it took for Jordan to negotiate the rainbow passageways of the Hope Clinic to find the recovery wing, he had already received a result from Quantum XR-9.

The accompanying nurse assured him that Lexie would be up to receiving visitors, if a little groggy and incoherent.

"She's got dressings on her neck now," the nurse said, "and a crust will form as the skin repairs itself. But those eyes... I've never seen anything like it." Then she left him in the waiting room to read his Konektor and sip a glass of water. A cursory reading of the report downloaded to his Konektor indicated that the laser machines were designed to shut down if they encountered contaminants in the ink pigments that would not allow for safe fragmentation or phagocytosis when drained by the lymphatic system. The program was run on processing space leased from the Corpus Care cloud computing system, which XR-9 had accessed within milliseconds. Being faster than the Corpus Care machines, it had already evaluated the feedback, patient skin reactions, and color spectrums within the area of the eyes that had caused the eventual shutdown, concluding that three substances were involved: verdigris, saltpeter, and gunpowder.

As Jordan pushed open the swing door to Lexie's recovery suite, XR-9 was already searching COTO Arts' tattoo catalogues for images of Alexandria Ocasio-Cortez.

The girl lying in the bed was unrecognizable. The nose studs were gone. Her hair was no longer pink, and it had been cut short above her ears, exposing a blue plastic surgical dressing that circled her neck and upper chest. Her eyes were closed, and her bare arms lay motionless. Jordan stood silently at the foot of her bed and examined her features with what he recognized as a nostalgic self-indulgence. He hadn't enjoyed the pleasure of properly looking at her since the time of his deplatforming—and his subsequent ostracization by her mother. Her pale, lightly freckled skin, upturned nose, and sandstone-colored hair were just as he remembered them in her teenaged years. The tension in his gut, however, reminded him of the pain she had deliberately inflicted on him in the years since. Once she opened her eyes and saw him there, he could expect his wistful reverie to be rudely terminated.

What was he doing here anyway, he wondered? For twenty years, she'd taken every opportunity to exclude him from her life—and now that she knew he was not her birth father, she'd feel vindicated in her behavior towards him. Surely he'd explained all this to John Erasmus many times? Monitoring her well-being secondhand, at a distance, had been the best he could manage.

He'd check his Konektor again, send her a message perhaps, trusting she would be well. Then he'd quietly slip away.

"Dad," she mumbled, "is that you?" Her words were slurred; her voice croaked.

"In person," he replied brightly, shrugging his shoulders as if to acknowledge in advance whatever objection she might mount to his presence.

"You look different," she said hazily.

Only one side of her face seemed to be working; the active part of her mouth was compressed like that of a ventriloquist.

"So do you," he said with a smile, shrugging again.

Whatever she replied, he couldn't make it out. He stepped around the side of the bed to hear her better. "What was that...?"

"Younger," she repeated.

"Oh!"

Perhaps it was the tracksuit, he thought. Or it might have been the new short haircut. Since returning from Neutrality Park, he'd discarded the academic's wavy black mane tinged with grey that he'd worn for thirty years in favor of a buzz cut.

"How do you feel?" he asked.

"Stupid," she slurred. One side of her mouth went up in an attempted smile. She lifted a hand towards him. He hesitated just long enough that she let it fall back onto the bed.

"Something went wrong with the programming of the laser," he assured her. "It wasn't anything that you did. There's no need to feel stupid." He felt emboldened to touch her arm reassuringly, which she allowed.

Lexie's eyes shifted away from him, somewhere behind him and to his right. Turning to follow her gaze, Jordan realized that his every move since entering the room was being quietly watched by a young boy sitting in the shadows. Jordan raised his eyebrows in acknowledgment. The boy was unmoved, his face implacably still and disinterested.

"Stupid for letting Bammy tell me what to do," Lexie dribbled. "Stupid for getting that b... bitch's face tattooed on my neck."

Jordan straightened, not knowing whether to take a step forward or backward. "We all do things we later regret," he said soothingly.

But what the hell did that mean? Things she *ought* to regret? Things *he* ought to regret...?

"Don't be so hard on yourself," he added quickly. "It'll get fixed."

"The eyes," she said bitterly. "I'll be stuck with them forever."

Before he could stop her, she pulled at the blue plastic dressing on her neck and ripped it aside. There, in the raw, red, inflamed battleground of her newly lasered skin, were the staring, glaring, unmistakable eyes of Alexandria Ocasio-Cortez, permanently etched in verdigris, saltpeter, and gunpowder.

Jordan stepped forward and pushed her hand aside, then reattached the dressing. "We know why the machine balked at removing them," he reassured her, "so I'm sure they'll find another way of solving this. Just be patient."

She watched him readjust the sheet and blanket over her chest, letting him run his fingers solicitously around the edges of her neck dressing to ensure it was secure. It was certainly on both their minds that there were obvious questions to be asked. Why was he there? How did he know about the failed laser treatment? Who did he mean by "we"? But she didn't ask, just as he didn't address the obvious question on his mind. She'd called him "Dad." She'd revealed herself to him. Was it the oxytocin and the sedatives that had breached her defenses?

Instead of blurting these things out, they just looked at each other. Maybe it was as simple as the fact that the partial paralysis of her face made it difficult for her to enunciate clearly, and she opted not to try. And for his part, well, he knew he was still on a high wire and should be thankful that he was maintaining his balance.

"Manaia," Lexie said, turning to the boy, "this is your grandpa."

The boy got up and came over to her bedside. He was well built, with dark brown eyes and an open face that, like still water, reflected the thoughts that blew across it. He was interested, but puzzled.

" 'Grandpa'? What's that?" he asked.

"My father is your grandfather," Lexie explained. "Grandpa."

"You said you didn't have a father."

"Everyone has a father, Pëpi."

"So, what's Opie, then?"

"That's Bammy."

The boy shrugged and turned to Jordan.

Jordan shrugged back, then held out his hand. "Pleased to meet you, Manaia. Call me Jordan. Hey, do you like football?"

A BEACHED STARFISH

July 2058

Alexa adjusted her glasses. She didn't really need them, but she had been told that staring at computer screens for eight hours a day would give her eyes muscle memory that would ultimately cripple her long-range vision. The lenses were designed to pull her gaze out of that arm's-length range and force them into long-distance focus. She'd bought into the theory and resolved to wear them more often, particularly when outdoors, as she was now. Besides, Jordan had told her to bring them next time they met.

She walked to the bench in Riverside Park where they'd sat when she first revealed that Shane Whitman had approached her and she'd raised the subject of Artie Sharp. Since that day, things had moved fast, and this morning's events had forced her to call Jordan and urgently ask him to meet. But she needed to be calm, despite how shaken she felt. It was essential that she didn't mislead Jordan and allow her emotions to cloud her judgment.

Luckily, she had arrived early, and that would allow her to get her thoughts in order. The park was empty. It was a beautiful, warm spring day, the trees bursting with a new season's growth that refreshed the air and evoked optimism and renewal. She breathed deeply, hungry for that optimism, searching for its cleansing power, forcefully exhaling the darkness that Shane Whitman had left inside her.

He'd arrived at her office unannounced again, dismissing the security minders and locking the door from the inside. This time, when he removed his wig, he threw it across the room. He wasn't wearing lipstick, and he hadn't shaved.

"*Progress*, Alexa!" he'd shouted. "We need progress. The tribunal can't wait. The budget needs to be fixed *now*, and the UN compliance team can't be put off any longer. We're going to air, ready or not. Do you hear me? READY OR NOT!"

Alexa got to her feet. She was wearing a head scarf because it was Hijab Day at the Social Equity Ministry, one of two hundred designated days celebrating different cultural identities (though, typically for Alexa, she wore the hijab to promote awareness of female oppression, not as a cultural endorsement.) She tore it off and dropped it on her desk.

"The models are all done!" she protested. "They've been tested and run by the SEM's human rights and treasury audit groups, and they were forwarded to the tribunal chair a week ago. There's no hold up on my end." She was perplexed by this outburst. As far as she was concerned, she'd done all that was asked of her. "The white male minority problem has been solved. The budget now balances. The ball's in the tribunal's court," she emphasized.

Whitman glared at her. "I didn't come here to have you tell me what a clever girl you've been, Alexa. I came to tell you that we're all sitting on a knife edge, and it's starting to cut into our asses! There's resistance. I'm hearing rumors that backsliding, scheming, gender-bending intersectionalists on the tribunal are plotting against us as we speak. They won't give up their victim's privileges without a fight—and when they fight, it'll be vicious, Alexa. There'll be riots; there'll be deaths. I know who they are. I know their methods. That's why we have to act fast! We need to announce the new policy settings without further delay. I've called a planning meeting at the Department of Truth and Public Guidance first thing tomorrow, which you are going to attend—and I expect you to tell us how we can make sure the *ArteFact Channel* supports us."

"... What?!"

"It was your idea. The tribunal chair only signed off on this plan because you sold him on getting Artie Sharp as its mouthpiece."

"I did no such thing!"

"Well, that's what was told to the tribunal, Alexa, and that's what we're damn well relying on."

"I only said that someone *like* Artie Sharp—someone with credibility—should be recruited to back the new policies. The tribunal chair admitted that government policy changes are never well received. I never said anything about being able to arrange it."

Whitman grabbed the veil from her desktop and ripped it in two, apoplectic with rage. "I've spent twenty years in these fucking frocks, Alexa—twenty years in suffocating wigs and cock-busting corsets, painting my face like a clown and pretending to like faggots and dykes, all because you menstruating feminists and your false-nipple transfem offspring decided it was your turn to have power and put men on the chopping board. Well, it's over now, do you hear me? It's death to victimhood and an end to Society Points. Tomorrow, Alexa, you'll be there, and you'll tell us how we can sell the public this plan that you designed—or I'll be breaking out the guns!"

Rooted to the spot, Alexa just stared at Shane Whitman in his floral-print dress and white Roman sandals, the thick fingers of his tattooed, muscled arms opening and closing as if he were squeezing the life out of a dying turkey, and she decided that he was probably clinically insane.

But now, composing herself on the park bench while waiting for Jordan's arrival, she consoled herself with the thought that insanity was grounds for additional Transitional Benefits in today's society (at least until her new plan was implemented). His emotional outpouring was merely the symptom of a tortured identity. In that respect, he was undoubtedly one of many. If her new social plan could help overcome such suffering, then it would be worth supporting.

She took off her glasses and breathed deeply. In the distance, an adult and child were playing some sort of game, and she could hear the child laughing. What game were they playing? Putting her glasses back on, she watched as a tall and athletic man with a slow, loping run was chased by a young boy who was trying to tackle him to the ground. The man allowed himself to be caught and fell slowly, gracefully onto the grass between the trees, taking the limpet child clinging to his legs down with him. The child's delight audibly carried through the spring air as the man feigned death like a beached starfish.

Alexa felt just like that man. She'd allowed herself to be chased and caught by the Agenda Implementation Tribunal, she'd tossed Artie Sharp into the air like a football, and now she'd been brought crashing to the ground. There was no way she could betray Artie's true identity, even if Jordan were to agree to help her in some way. The influence of the *ArteFact Channel* derived as much from its anti-state stance as it did from its content. The state could never be trusted—and Artie would never be trusted again if his message were to merge with that of the state. Thus, tomorrow morning at the Department of Truth and Public Guidance, she too would become a beached starfish.

The man and the boy got up off the grass and slowly weaved their way towards her, passing a football between them that the boy would occasionally drop, laughing as he retrieved it, while the man waited patiently, hands on hips. Alexa liked the look of the tall man with his tracksuit and olive skin. She admired the shape of his close-cropped hair, and when he turned his head toward her, she liked his smile…

My God—it was Jordan!

She whipped off her glasses and stood up. "Jordan?"

He grinned proudly. "Alexa, meet my grandson, Manaia."

"You mean…?" Alexa couldn't think of a worthwhile thing to say. The true nature of her life circumstances had revealed itself to her in this totally natural moment: a man and a boy playing ball in the park. How had such a thing become so extraordinary?

The three of them sat on the park bench together while Jordan gave her a very abbreviated summary of Lexie's situation at the Hope Clinic, which was just opposite the park, where he and Manaia had come to play ball while Dr. John Erasmus was arranging for Lexie to have a skin graft.

"And Manaia is one mean tackler," Jordan said proudly, patting his short hair. "He'd make a hell of a linebacker."

Alexa walked back to the hospital with them and waited in the Hope Café while Jordan took Manaia back to see his mother. She drank a soy latte, but she had no appetite for food; it made her sick to her stomach that she might somehow betray Jordan. Of course, it was sheer coincidence that she'd identified his connection to Artie Sharp after having casually suggested Artie as a possible mouthpiece for the government's change in social policy. But coincidence or not, she feared losing Jordan's trust.

When he rejoined her, he ordered a kale and carrot smoothie with root ginger and turmeric. "Energy!" he exclaimed, downing the drink in one go. "Kids sure do have it." His own energy had increased noticeably.

"I brought my glasses, like you asked," she said, handing them to him.

"Great!" He thought for a moment. "Look, I've been mulling over what happened on the hillside the other day, and I've decided that you need to know the truth about Artie Sharp; then we can decide together what to do about the government's agenda. You've trusted me with your secrets, and I trust you to keep mine. Come with me now, back to the DDC, where I have my office, and I'll introduce you to Antonio. He can fix you up with photoelectric lenses and a transmission chip. Then we can talk about those handwritten meeting minutes you found. Just make sure your Alt-Identity is switched on and your location tracker is off."

THE FIRST AMENDMENT

July 2058

Alexa had been picked up at 9:00 am from her office at the Social Equity Ministry and driven across the river to the huge, monolithic building on Obama Avenue that housed the Department of Truth and Public Guidance. The two grey-suited security guards who had been sent to collect her escorted her to a waiting room, where her laptop and briefcase were scanned and her Konektor was bagged, sealed, and taken away. Then she was photographed and given a microchipped lanyard to wear around her neck before being left to wait for half an hour.

She went to the security desk and asked for her Konektor, needing to make a call.

"Not in the building, sorry."

"Why?"

"No cameras or devices. Visitor rules."

When Shane Whitman appeared, she didn't recognize him. He was dressed in a grey suit, white shirt, and a short, severe wig. The flamboyant cross-dresser had vanished, replaced with a look that female CEOs and department heads had perfected wherever power was exercised. His manner was abrupt, perhaps sensing her thoughts and not wanting to give her any chance to express them. She followed him down several long corridors into the bowels of the building, past water coolers and unmarked doors, until finally they arrived at a lobby. The receptionist looked up and nodded. Whitman opened the door in front of them, and Alexa Smythe stepped inside.

The room was windowless, paneled in swamp-oak veneer and decorated with pictures of wilderness parks. Twelve faces looked up as they entered, unsmiling.

But Alexa was ready. She took a deep breath and adjusted her glasses. "Good morning," she said. Her voice was steady, confident, self-assured.

Whitman pulled out a chair for her. She placed her laptop on the table and sat down. Whitman circled the table and sat opposite her.

"This is Alexa Smythe," he stated, "special assistant to the Agenda Implementation Tribunal and author of the *Social Points and Transitional Benefits Review* that you have all received copies of. I won't piss about; we all know what's going on. The budget has to be balanced, and that means the whole social justice thing needs to be reined in. Alexa's solution is nice and neat, but we'll have to sell it to the public. I've invited her into this group because she knows the subject inside and out, and she's got ideas. Anyone have a problem with that?"

Twelve pairs of eyes just stared at her. If they had problems with it, they weren't going to say so.

"Alright," Whitman snapped. "Summarize the plan for us, Henry."

Henry was the youngest person present, mid-thirties, with a light beard and fidgety hands. The beard covered still-visible acne scars, and he stroked it continuously with his spare hand while shuffling papers around in front of him. "The report identifies that this reset of benefits is in line with *Agenda 2060*'s equal outcomes objectives, which include, as stated in Article One, 'eliminate all discrimination.' The challenge here, as Alexa has already identified, is that those who can claim the greatest burden of victimhood benefit the most under the present plan, and thus they may not like the idea of other people not being worse off than them when the plan changes. That may cause civic unrest and make for a difficult sell. So..."

He cleared his throat and picked up a sheaf of papers, passing a copy to each person around the table. "So, what we're proposing is an amendment to Article One of *Agenda 2060*, as stated here in the draft in front of you: 'All feelings of oppression and victimhood will be treated equally, and all support and benefits will be distributed equally by the state.' Under this amendment, it is only necessary to *feel* oppressed or victimized—which can hardly be challenged—and this justifies everyone being treated equally. That's a shift forward from our present position in Article One, which currently states, 'Eliminate all discrimination on grounds of—' "

"We all know what Article One states, kiddo," Whitman interrupted. "Speed it up."

"Sorry, yes," the young man apologized. "The plan is for the chair of the Agenda Implementation Tribunal to recommend this amendment for adoption by the Senate and endorsement by the United Nations Social Equity Commission."

"But that'll take a month of Sundays," someone objected. "The budget is a *now* problem."

"I agree," Whitman interjected. "Henry...?"

"We think that works to our advantage," Henry responded tentatively. "Whatever happens, there are going to be more people in favor of this change than against. The thinking is that we will implement it immediately and without warning, then argue the case through the Senate and the UN, taking the high ground and running a strong propaganda campaign. Those who object will be forced to scramble to make their case. In the meantime, the new benefit scales will be put in place, and those who are against them can easily be demonized as greedy and self-interested. We'll work social media hard, so the anomalies and injustices in the current system are exposed for what they truly are."

"I agree with Henry, Shane," another member of the panel interrupted. "Social justice activism has been seeding the clouds of its own biosphere, until those clouds are ready to break. They've gotten away with identitarianism, promoting victimhood, and pushing gender, race, and disability oppression for thirty years, but what they see as their last great triumph will be their downfall. Forcing the world to believe that victimhood is not a matter of empirical fact, but is solely dependent on personal feelings is a crock of shit of their own making, which now plays into our hands. Everybody has feelings, and everybody's feelings are valid and therefore equal. Our proposed amendment recognizes that. The trap has opened, and we're going to close it."

Heads nodded. People smiled grimly.

The grimmest of all was a purple-haired executive of indeterminate gender, whom Alexa would not have wanted following her to the bathroom. "The George Kyros Foundations are on board," she announced, "but they will not take a public position on this. Rockefeller, Mellon, and the Seine Alliance have had confidential briefings. Most of the Global Core of transnationals believe it strengthens *Agenda 2060* rather than weakens it, while achieving the objective of destabilizing the status quo. Our biggest challenge will be the Big Tech owners of platforms that rely on personal attacks and trolling between warring tribes for traffic volume. The financial markets will mark them down unless we can encourage the silent majority to take up the slack in support of the amendment. Someone needs to develop a strategy to win support from Silicon Valley and Wall Street quickly."

"Only the president herself can handle Mark Sukaville," a colleague observed. "He'll want to barter Securities Commission concessions in return for censoring any pushback. Google's promised to reset their algorithms as soon as we give them the word; they estimate their searches will increase up to forty percent, and ad revenue will match it. Meanwhile, both PostKard and Hustings have people placed with us here at Truth and Public Guidance, so they'll be seeding discussion groups as soon as we roll out our First Amendment campaign."

"The First Amendment, huh? I like it. It has a nice ring to it," Whitman enthused. "We roll out the truths that the silent majority have been forced to suppress."

"Men are thirty percent more likely to die before age seventy than women," someone spouted.

"Gays and lesbians have seventeen percent higher lifetime earnings than cis people of any category," a female colleague added.

"Asians have three hundred percent higher college admission levels than even black people on reverse discrimination quotas," a black member chimed in.

"Stop, stop!" Whitman commanded. "We'll be here all day. So, what do you think, Alexa? Is this how we open the door to truth and reconciliation?"

Alexa was genuinely surprised. The sophistication of their strategy lay in its basic simplicity: it relied on using their opponents' own strengths against them to unbalance and topple them. It would be hard for people to go up against the amendment as proposed. But there was a weakness in it that only she seemed to recognize: no matter what label they gave themselves now—Truth and Public Guidance, or whatever—these people were deep state. They were the FIB and CIA and IAO in disguise—the same people who'd implemented the Overthrow and disappeared her father. No matter what they said, no one would trust them. Even the tribunal chair had recognized that.

But she was forgetting that Shane Whitman recognized that, too.

"Alexa says that no one trusts the government," Whitman told the room. "She believes even the truth becomes a lie when it's uttered from our mouths. So, I issued a challenge to her: I asked her to tell us how we could use Artie Sharp of the *ArteFact Channel* to win over the public ... and now Alexa is going to tell us."

This was the moment for which Jordan had prepared her the day before. She hoped she was ready for it. Very deliberately, she adjusted her glasses and turned to look at each of the people around the table in turn.

"Artie Sharp is not a person," she said evenly. "Artie Sharp is an algorithm."

The group exchanged looks and shifted position in their chairs. She waited.

"Alright, Alexa," Whitman prompted. "We're waiting. What sort of algorithm?"

"An algorithm that runs fact-checking on public information. It searches every accessible database on the web for validation or contradiction in order to expose falsity, then packages its results into entertainment sketches for broadcast on a designated channel on the dark web, currently attracting twenty-eight million viewers per week."

"Hang on," Henry interrupted, "algorithms need programmers. Who coded this thing?"

"It runs on a 256-qubit quantum computer, and it possesses artificial superintelligence capable of human-level cognition. With the addition of artificial optical neural devices intuitively modeled on how the brain processes information, it has long since reached the point of humanized AI and become self-programming. Who originally coded it is no longer relevant."

"Who told you this?" Whitman demanded.

"Artie Sharp told me," she replied calmly. "I visited the FAQ on the *ArteFact Channel* website. You can do the same. Here, it's on my laptop." She turned the screen towards them.

There was stunned silence while they looked at each other and tried to fathom whether she was pulling their leg. Every arm of state intelligence had been searching for the source of this underground identity for years. Could it really be that all they'd needed to do was log onto a website?

Only Henry, the youngest in the room, seemed to grasp what she had shared. He pulled her laptop towards him and confidently manipulated the keyboard. "I get it," he said enthusiastically. "Humanized intelligence is capable of self-awareness, and self-consciousness. That explains the humor in the skits. It's not, like, hilarious or anything, but it's dry as a desert and sucks you in. That's why it works so well."

"Bullshit!" Whitman thundered. "Somebody's running it. That's a real person delivering that show, not a fucking piece of code. They've got actors, cameramen, directors… Are you trying to tell me a computer creates the whole show?"

"It's possible," Henry said. "Computers create all the e-games now."

"E-games! For fuck's sake, grow up… So, is she right? Is the explanation there on the website like she says?"

Henry paused, frowning. "It's exactly as she told it, only…" He looked up.

"What?"

"There's a message scrolling across the screen."

"What does it say?"

"It says, 'I endorse truth. I expose lies. Leave a message.' "

"That's it?"

"There's a piece of code, but I don't recognize the language."

"Alexa…?"

"I've never seen this before. I can't explain." She took back her computer and tried typing something in. "I can't see any way of replying… Oh! Now the message has gone. Maybe it's a pop-up. And now it looks like the website has gone down as well." She banged on her keyboard in frustration. "Computers!" she cursed. "They drive me mad."

Immediately, the alarming thought entered her mind that the web domain might show up in her browser history ... but by now it was too late to do anything about it.

WORDS OF WARNING

July 2058

Back at the DDC, Antonio Muchos took down the temporary landing page he'd constructed and removed all traces of source code. When Alexa's Konektor had been taken from her by the security guards, he'd been concerned that the transmission signal from the microchip in her glasses might fail and he would have to work blind, guessing at what might be happening in her meeting and potentially exposing her to suspicion. But it had gone like clockwork. Her Konektor had picked up the signal and relayed the images back to their screens; then, after he'd pulled the dummy website down as planned, they could see Alexa being included in the group's intense discussions and Shane Whitman talking animatedly as he walked her back out to the car.

"It's a bummer we couldn't put audio transmitters into her lenses," Jordan commented. "I'd have liked to hear how she explained Artie Sharp. But she seems to have won their trust. That was our goal."

Antonio turned from his keyboard and looked at Jordan intently. "So, now she knows our secret. This is a big risk you take. We don't know what she told them about us, because we couldn't hear."

"You don't trust her?"

"I don't know her. She is *muy inteligente*, but look where she works. It is you I have to trust. Do you know what you're doing, or is it just your *testiculos*?"

The question rocked Jordan. But it was a fair one, and it sat with him for most of the day, until Alexa messaged him asking for a debriefing meeting. He suggested the Hope Café, as that would allow him to visit Lexie at the hospital. But Antonio was right: he *was* taking a risk, and he seemed to have taken it without much hesitation, so there must be a catalyst.

Coffee and math had been the extent of their relationship, up to the point where Alexa had called him to express her fear that she was out of her depth in attempting to solve the budgetary problems exposed by the tribunal. Was that the catalyst? Had he been flattered by her request for help—seduced by the opportunity to interfere with the foundations of the state?

Yes, he admitted to himself: all of that.

But since that afternoon on the hill at Neutrality Park, he'd been remarkably sure-footed in his advance towards taking the risks that Antonio was now questioning. It was indeed out of character. No one had forced him to admit that he was the mastermind behind Artie Sharp, but he'd done so without hesitation. And now an unlikely idea was hatching in his mind, which, if he could find a way of developing it, would be so daring and piratical that all the destructive years and loss of identity since his deplatforming could be avenged many times over.

As the idea started to take him over, he decided to call Hedley Payne immediately.

"Hedley," he asked, "have you managed to monitor that CRISPR brain technology you gave to Micomic Health?"

"Sure. Your people programmed Quantum XR-11 for us, and it's working well. I thought you knew?"

"I wanted to hear it from you, that's all. You mentioned something that caught my attention: did you say that you can manipulate the brain's functioning in areas that have nothing to do with DNA? I seem to remember you thinking that you might have the ability to control conscious decisions and instincts at the foundational level—things like telling the truth, for instance."

"That's right. We've identified the areas of the brain involved in conscious mendacity, and we can identify the presence and influence of unconscious bias. But the complexity of the calculations required to reliably compensate between the two is very likely beyond us, so it has no practical application at this stage. What were you thinking?"

Jordan wasn't yet sure what he was thinking, though his mind was drifting through a number of tantalizing possibilities.

"It occurred to me that we may have encountered a similar roadblock," Jordan said. "In AI, the challenge lies in the lack of emotional sentience in the algorithms we build. We can unravel truth in terms of empirical fact and probability statistics, but we can't adjust for things like moral truths and evolutionary influences, which play such a big and mostly intuitive part in determining what we might call 'human truth.' The evolutionary path followed by humans is so long and so complex that it can't possibly be emulated in the learning cycle of microchips, no matter how many million qubits we have available. I've been pondering that issue for a long time now, because the specifications of the universal no-fault quantum computer that the Derangers VC Partnership is funding will allow us to process and store data to the point of molecular infinity, but it still can't overcome that shortcoming. However..."

Jordan's mind stopped drifting as a totally new possibility came into view. "In your situation, it's different," he suggested.

"Go on, you've got me interested."

"I'm trying to arrive at a place where AI can understand and express human truth by building up to it from impossibly complex foundations. In your brain scenario, you have human truth residing at a specific location, devoid of what you call 'mendacity,' for which you can adjust, and your task is to calculate the influence of unconscious bias. What did you say—that the complexity of the calculations may be beyond you?"

"That's right," Hedley agreed. "It isn't important to know the origin of that unconscious bias, only its strength and degree of influence on conscious mendacity. Remember, we're working in real time."

"Interesting," Jordan observed. "I'll keep that in mind as we make progress with XR-12."

They moved on to talk about other things, like the next Derangers' dinner. Then, as if it were an afterthought, Jordan asked the question that had truly prompted him to reach out to Hedley. "With the speed provided by our quantum computer, would you be able to override or manipulate Micomic's treatments at any time ... theoretically?"

"I guess so, theoretically. Not that we ever would."

Yes, Antonio had been right the other day when he'd said they were bandits. "We blow up the train tracks so the government's lies can't get through. We are Zapata, Pancho Villa, and Robin Hood," he'd said. "Also, we have fun."

Though he hadn't taken kindly to Antonio's crack about him thinking with his *testiculos,* he had to admit that a certain impetuosity had crept into his behavior recently— starting with his radical haircut, then expanding into lunchtime training runs and the introduction of chocolate mescaline liqueur and neo-ska music into their Artie Sharp brainstorming sessions (which Antonio described as a *"crisis de edad"*). Was it the biological expression of his grandmother's blood coming through at last—the breakout of his previously suppressed racial identity? Or could it be the euphoria he'd experienced when Lexie had called him "Dad"...?

He would heed Antonio's words of warning about taking risks. But once he developed the plan he was now formulating in his mind, he was pretty sure Antonio would be pleased to go along with it. The bigger question was whether Alexa would be up for it, too. Her antagonism towards the state was rooted in its treatment of her father. If her quest for the missing man petered out, her resolve might do the same.

Which brought him back to his promise that he would search for Donald Melville Smythe in the encrypted files of the Total Information Awareness archives of the IAO. This was a task which he'd entrusted to Quantum XR-11, owing to its ability to intercept teleported information (a result of being linked by quantum entanglement to the IAO microchips). However, his promise was proving more difficult to keep than he'd anticipated, for one of the characteristics of the Overthrow period was spontaneous chaos. Though the Overthrow was conducted in large part by the hierarchy embedded in the deep state, no clear bureaucratic structure had been put in place at the outset to implement the details. Duties and functions were not allocated in advance, but tended to be adopted informally, as if the reset of society was the result of a spontaneous eruption. Thus record keeping had been perfunctory at best. Perhaps it had been a deliberate policy on the part of the One World Foundations that were directing these events. Efficient record keeping within bureaucracies can have its drawbacks during dark periods, and it was clear that at the time that Donald Melville Smythe had disappeared, the FIB was avoiding the maintenance of documentary evidence.

When Quantum XR-11 found reference to the economist's textbooks and collected essays in the archives of the Shame Repository, an obscure book museum, Jordan noticed that one treatise was dated May 2039, just one month after the April 2039 paper Alexa had given him to read—the paper that led to the author's inquisition by the Security Oversight Committee.

Jordan then expanded XR-11's search to bibliographies, donor records, and correspondence files of the book museum in question, but nothing came of it; nothing relevant had been digitized. So, now he had a problem. He knew that the subject of Donald Melville Smythe would be raised in his upcoming meeting with Alexa, and he'd be arriving empty-handed.

This was not a good time to dash her hopes. The powerful pull of her desire for family needed to be kept alive. If his own hopes had proven capable of being met after such a long time, then Alexa must be allowed to live in hope also.

SALMON ON A PLATE

July 2058

The heat from Shane Whitman's hand on her upper arm seemed to melt the fabric of her sleeve, fusing it to her skin. His breath was a stream of grey fog directed into her ear, making it itch. No food all morning on account of a rushed and anxious start had left the acids in her stomach unbuffered and her tongue metallic. She walked as fast as she could short of running, with the look of a woman in frantic search of a restroom. All Alexa wanted was to get the hell out of there, but Whitman was determined to escort her all the way, talking, talking, talking his absurdly indiscreet blasphemies, like a scatological comedian without the humor. She collected her Konektor, barely pausing to sign the receipt, and headed for the exit, scanning unsuccessfully for the security goons and the car that had brought her there.

Whitman gripped her arm tighter, steering her away from the exit towards an unmarked elevator. "Come with me, Alexa. You're going up in the world." He swiped his Konektor over the keypad and pressed a button marked D.

After a short ride, the doors opened into a dining room. Whitman let go of her arm and strode forward, waving for her to follow. The aroma of French fries and grilled meats made Alexa's stomach rumble.

A woman in her sixties came forward to meet them and escorted them to a private booth.

"We'll have the salmon," Whitman commanded, "with a bowl of that yellow sauce, and a bucket of fries each."

How on earth did this chauvinist gorilla manage to pass himself off as a transsexual for so many years? Alexa wondered. And how many others had squeezed themselves into misshapen molds in pursuit of power? Such dangerous thoughts were coming too easily to her now. She needed to suppress them.

In the center of the table was a bulky orange packet with Whitman's name on it. He picked it up, smiling, and slid a knife under the flap, cutting it open. "From this day forward, Alexa, you are no longer a statistics auditor in the Lineal Progression Office. You are now officially a special assistant to the Agenda Implementation Tribunal, and advisor to the Department of Truth and Public Guidance. In here's your handbook for Executive Schedule 3: pay, privileges, security access, and reporting levels. You report directly to me. You tell me everything. Got that? *Everything!*"

"About what?"

"Everything I need to know."

"… What do you need to know?"

"Everything!"

A whole salmon promptly arrived on a large platter. Its eyes were open, but it was very dead. Alexa would have preferred proper meat. Two buckets of fries arrived next, one for each of them, and she reached out hungrily.

"I didn't choose you," Whitman spat through a mouthful of fries, "you chose yourself. You think only Artie Sharp has smart computers? You don't know the half of it. You were sorted out of the gene pool years ago. White, female, high intelligence quotient, career before love life, a celibate member of the cis-terhood and subscriber to the Vulva Protection Society, because why the fuck should you allow your body to be penetrated just for the purpose of insemination and—"

"Don't forget the My Choice movement," Alexa interrupted sarcastically. "Just in case she should accidentally be penetrated and inseminated by one of you misogynistic male rapists, why carry the consequences to term? Let's stay on message here."

Whitman threw back his head and laughed, masticated deep-fried potato bits spattering the Executive Schedule 3 handbook. "That's right,

Alexa, showing us all that you're doing your bit for Article Eleven by limiting the world's population. Every which way you turn, we see the perfect embodiment of *Agenda 2060*. You don't just know how to play the game; you *are* the game. Master mathematician, manipulator of statistics—daughter of a martyr of the Overthrow, no less—and pupil of the great rebel outcast of ASI quantum computing, Jordan McPhee... Oh, yes, we've watched your every turn, Alexa. Why do you think you were asked to appear before the Agenda Implementation Tribunal? Because you're the sleeper whose time has come to wake. That's why. It's time."

Well, Alexa thought, nice to know she was woke. She might as well help herself to the salmon, since the madman across from her was unwilling to curb the pleasure he was obviously deriving from his wild rant long enough to notice her empty plate and offer her a piece.

It was flavorless. She looked for the yellow sauce. That was better: olive oil and egg yolks. The older woman brought a basket of bread to the table.

Whitman was still talking.

"Shane," she interrupted. " 'It's time' for what?"

"To swing the fucking pendulum the other way—what do you think? No era in politics can last longer than forty years, and this period is played out. The myths and shibboleths wither and expire, Alexa. All the heated passions die of exhaustion, then boredom and disillusionment take over. So, who do people blame? Themselves, for having lost their reason? The enemies they created in order to indulge their hatred? People are base, vile, selfish, and antagonistic. Look how they've perverted *Agenda 2060*. It took you, the mathematician, to point out to us that the goal of eliminating discrimination had only driven people to divide into smaller and smaller competitive tribes, each one claiming a greater burden of discrimination than the other, and each one antagonistic to all others. The index of oppression is a league table of competing hatreds. Transitional Benefits have become a scramble worse than the fighting at the tailgate of a food truck in a famine All you had to do was the simple math. It didn't fucking add up. So, now it's time to swing the pendulum the other way."

Alexa spooned the yellow sauce (hollandaise, she thought) onto her plate and dipped a piece of bread into it.

"People aren't vile, selfish, and antagonistic," she objected. "People want to be nice. Their instinct tells them that kindness is a better way to live. But if you make them compete, you prod their survival instincts into action. They circle their wagons and go into fight mode. That's what Social Points and Transitional Benefits have done."

"See!" Whitman proclaimed triumphantly. "That's why you've been chosen, Alexa. Kindness: that's the message we want, and there's no time to waste. I want you center stage. I want you to take responsibility for our message. Find Artie Sharp. Make him endorse everything you say. Fuck him, if necessary."

"He's a computer."

"Then fuck the computer."

Alexa picked up the Executive Schedule 3 handbook and opened it. There she was in the frontispiece, all blonde and appealing, with a pleasant but restrained compression of the corners of her mouth—no threat to superiors or colleagues, but it was a look that she'd always suspected could take her far … just like her new pay scale showed. Holy hippos, that was a lot of UniCoins, and her own DLT password hidden behind a scratch-off field, just like an instant lottery card.

"Is this all about the budget?" she asked. "Is that what's creating the urgency?"

Whitman reached across the table and gripped her wrist with his strangler's hand. His eyes were like those of the salmon: black, ringed with a jaundice-yellow aurora. "The budget is only money. It's the spreading virus we need to deal with. If it gets away from us, it'll make the Overthrow seem like a wet dream."

"What virus?"

"The truth virus. When people stop believing the lies they've relied upon, they start playing around with new ideas about what's true. Constant turmoil is the only way to ensure control. Nothing's more dangerous than the status quo. Everyone needs an enemy to focus on— someone who's getting the limelight instead of them. But we've run out of groups to favor. The battles for biggest victim status have lost their sting, and people are beginning to feel that it's all leading nowhere. Now they've started questioning the very foundations of *Agenda 2060* itself. It's happening. Your fucking *ArteFact Channel* was up to thirty-two million viewers last week. The chatter is changing, and we need to be in control of it."

"Are you afraid of the truth?"

Whitman squeezed her wrist until it hurt. "Don't be stupid, Alexa. Truth is what you make it. People may think that what they want is the status quo, but when a system goes on long enough, they become bored and dissatisfied and vulnerable to dangerous thoughts. Who knows where the hell that might lead? Every twenty years, it's the same. In 2001 we had 9/11. In 2020, we had the pandemic. In 2039, we had the Overthrow. What matters is who controls the narrative. If there's going to be a revolution, then it's in our best interest to start it. That's why we're turning everything on its head. They'll never see it coming. A revolution needs its thinkers as well as its executioners, Alexa. Thinkers like you see things nobody has thought of. Suddenly, there's a new set of enemies. They justify our intervention and reassure the mob that it's best to leave things to those in control. We're going to give the mob exactly what they're ready for."

Alexa dragged her hand away. It was like pulling it out of a python's throat. "What happened to my father, Shane? Donald Melville Smythe: what happened to him?"

Whitman calmly returned to his salmon. The woman in him ate remarkably daintily for such a brute of a man, little quick bites at the front of the mouth, chewing the fish into paste before swallowing discreetly to downplay his Adam's apple before patting his lips with a napkin. "Show me that you can get Artie Sharp, Alexa, and I'll show you where you can find your father. Deal?"

A MOTH TO A FLAME

July 2058

'Meat' was not a word used in the Hope Café, but their ParkFed burger was an adequate meat substitute after a lunch spent in the company of a dead fish.

Jordan had suggested the venue after explaining more fully what had happened to Lexie, and the surprise reconciliation between them. It appeared that Lexie, jolted by the reality of her deteriorating relationship with Bammy, had had an epiphany and realized that Jordan was the one dependable rock in her life, encouraging him to visit her each day as she recovered. Jordan's delight in this development and his immediate bonding with Manaia was plain to see, and Alexa couldn't escape a twinge of envy.

"Time is the thread that weaves together the narrative of human life," Jordan reflected in his familiar professorial voice. "It moves remorselessly in one direction and cannot be reversed, pulling its players along with it. Humans can't return to a point in time with the intention of reenacting events; we can only hope to change the meaning—or 'truth'—of those events at some future date. That's what your Department of Truth and Public Guidance is set up to do. You do realize that?"

Alexa took a large bite out of her burger. "Hm ... hmm."

"By contrast," Jordan continued, "information is the thread that ASI follows, sifting through it for facts. In the absence of further information, facts are unalterable. But facts are not the same thing as 'truth.' This is where ASI and human intelligence differ. So, expecting Artie Sharp to endorse their announcement is pointless if the facts don't fit. Do you understand?"

He took the ketchup bottle from Manaia, who was covering his entire plate, apparently never having been allowed such free rein before. Seeing Jordan with the boy gave Alexa a whole new perspective on her former professor. He connected well with kids. Who'd have thought?

"I kinda got that," she conceded, "from the explanation you gave me about the way Artie works. But Whitman is convinced that someone's directing the content. He couldn't get his head around it being entirely computer-generated, though some of the others had no problem with the concept."

"And you?"

How could she answer this? The segment promoting the restoration of a mathematics curriculum had been so obviously straight out of the mouth of Professor Jordan McPhee that she'd picked up on it immediately. What computer-generated algorithm could possibly have put that together? Yet she had to believe what she'd been told if Whitman and the others were going to believe it, too. What surprised her was that Jordan had been quite open to the idea of her getting Artie Sharp on side as soon as she told him.

"Fine," he'd said matter-of-factly. "Every Truth and Public Guidance statement will be run past Artie, and if it passes his fact-checking, it receives an ArteFact Endorsement. If it fails, it gets an ArteFact Rejection. Endorsements and rejections can't be rigged, and they'll be encrypted. For every endorsement issued, they'll immediately pay five million SDR Crypto Credits to a permissioned DLT account of Artie's choosing."

Just like that. She'd been stunned. "What if...?" she'd started to say. But she hadn't bothered to finish.

Manaia was now painting his lips with ketchup and threatened to give Jordan a wet kiss. Jordan did the same back at him, and the kid dissolved into giggles.

"So," Alexa said, ignoring the question about who she believed directed the content, "that's how it would work, then. If Artie finds that the facts don't fit, then there'd be no support for their agenda on the *ArteFact Channel*. I think I made that clear to them, though I didn't mention payment. But what about the risk of you being discovered? What if they're using me to get at you, so they can shut the channel down?"

Jordan looked at her thoughtfully. "Do you think that's what they're doing?"

"No," she replied quickly. "I think their agenda is much more ambitious than that. They want to stand social justice identitarianism on its head, like I said. It's not just the budget; they've read the sour mood of society, and they want to tip everything upside down before trouble breaks out." Should she tell him about Whitman's bribe...? "But they told me they know everything about me and have followed my every move, including my contact with you. I found that really spooky."

Jordan laughed. "Be flattered. It takes three or more people to follow one person's every movement twenty-four hours a day, even with algorithms set up to scan for your digital presence wherever you go. If they wanted to make me their target, they could have done that a long time ago. But they'll never crack Artie, and they know it. Quantum computers build their own autoimmune cryptography as they go. You being in contact with me obviously fits with their plan. Maybe that plan was put in place when you were assigned to present at Manaia's DNA-test party. Perhaps they arranged for us to meet."

"What?" She was horrified. "You don't really think that, do you?"

He sat back, straight-faced, looking at Manaia, then looking at her. No, he was pulling her leg, surely.

"Back to the subject at hand," he suggested. "The idea of introducing an amendment to Article One is a good one. Then your elaborate changes to the Society Points system become redundant, don't they? Everyone is free to be whatever they feel they are, and they'll all get exactly the same Transitional Benefits. There'll be no favored groups, so it won't make any damn difference—sorry, Manaia—what group someone identifies with. So, why do they need Artie?"

That was a question she should have known he'd ask. Of course, the answer was obvious. People got their identity from the groups they chose to affiliate with. Thus identity created a sense of family, so they wouldn't give it up willingly.

"They need Artie to help overcome the inevitable pushback," she explained. "There'll be a whole campaign by the government to expose the fallacies in identity politics and point out the untruths that underpin the societal obsession with victimhood. The propaganda team at Truth and Public Guidance has these ideas about highlighting facts that Artie can endorse. It's a really perverse turnaround on their part."

"Did they say that specifically?" Jordan wanted to know. "You're sure they used the word *endorse*?"

"That's what Whitman said, yes. 'Make him endorse everything you say.' "

She didn't mention the suggestion of fucking him.

"Good," he said with a grin. "They won't have any trouble paying, then. Maybe we should make it ten million per endorsement, not five."

Jordan seemed pleased. He wiped Manaia's face and asked if he'd like an ice cream, then took him up to the counter to make his own selection. While they were up, Alexa placed her Executive Schedule 3 handbook where Jordan had been sitting. On his return, he opened it, reading the first page without comment. Then he closed it and handed it back to her.

"They've asked me to work on the propaganda campaign," she explained. "Do you see my new title?"

" 'Special assistant to the Agenda Implementation Tribunal, and advisor to the Department of Truth and Public Guidance.' Congratulations. You're now a trusted member of the deep state."

"It's *your* trust I want, not the deep state's."

Had she set her Konektor to bypassing? Had Jordan set his? They said they could watch her at every turn. Maybe she *was* a sleeper, like Whitman had claimed.

"There's a question you need to ask yourself, Alexa." Jordan dug a spoon into Manaia's ice cream and offered it to her. She shook her head.

"Okay," he went on, eating it himself. "Coming up with a plan for the budget and solving the problems created by Society Points must have afforded you great satisfaction. I get that. But now you're getting in deep with the state—and you have to ask yourself why. Is it ambition that's driving you? Do you want power? Do you support the state's aims? Do you even know what those aims are? These are the same people who created the conditions for the Overthrow. For forty years, they've watched with delight while people tear each other's throats out over identity politics and global warming. It's suited their purpose perfectly.

Now they want a reset. Suddenly, *Agenda 2060* needs an amendment. Why? Is the budget problem that bad? In the old days, they'd have just printed more money. Now it's even easier; they just devalue it by cutting the blockchain pie into trillions more pieces. So, what the fuck's really going on—sorry, Manaia—and why are you helping them?"

Of all the questions he was asking, she doubted there was one she could answer. Maybe she'd thought that there could never be any harm in endorsing truth—and if that was all she was required to do, then she had no questions to answer. Yes, it was nice to be recognized, rewarded, and promoted, but that didn't explain why she was allowing herself to align with the cynical, manipulative figures who secretly ran the state. Was she being drawn in like a moth to a flame?

"Jordan, I genuinely believe that a kinder society could come out of this," she answered quietly. "I hate hate."

He looked surprised ... credulous, but surprised.

"Did you find out anything about my father's disappearance?" she asked quickly, looking down and playing with the remains of her food. "You said you'd look for me."

"We found a copy of a paper he'd written in May 2039. That's a month after the one that got him arrested."

Alexa reached across the table and grabbed Jordan's arm urgently. "I knew it! That means he wasn't killed. He must still be alive!"

"Maybe, maybe not. There's nothing more we can find—just that paper."

"Where was it?"

"In the book catalogue of the Shame Museum. We'd need to go there to see it, because it only exists in hard copy. Maybe someone can tell us how they got it."

"Can we go tomorrow? Will you come with me?" Her heart started racing. The glimmer of hope in Jordan's news exploded inside her uncontrollably, until it became an atomic mushroom cloud. If she could find her father, Whitman's control over her would be broken. She could choose to act on her own terms and not be compromised by the need to keep the secret of Whitman's bribe from Jordan. Then, like the aftershock of an atomic explosion, she was hit by a wave of guilt and disgust with herself.

"I assumed he must still be alive," she admitted, sliding her hand down Jordan's arm to grasp his hand, "because Shane Whitman told me he'd show me where I could find him."

"Find him *alive*?"

"He wouldn't say. But if he's dead, it would be less likely to motivate me to do what he wants, so he at least let me believe he's alive."

"I see." Jordan took his hand away and turned his attention to Manaia, who was becoming bored and looking for more interesting things to do ... like dribbling blobs of melted ice cream onto the table in an unwittingly precocious attempt to replicate Rorschach ink blot tests to determine his emotional well-being.

"This offer came with a condition, did it?" Jordan asked, seemingly distracted.

"Yes. He said that if I get Artie Sharp on board, he'll tell me where I can find my father."

Jordan rolled up the napkin he was using to clean up Manaia's mess and threw it at her playfully. "Well, we'd better try and find him without Whitman's help, then. Computers don't have feelings, so they're not susceptible to emotional blackmail like that. I can't guarantee that Artie will allow himself to be 'gotten on board,' as you're hoping; he may well have conditions of his own that Whitman isn't willing to meet."

"What sort of conditions?"

"We'll have to ask him."

Alexa suspected that Jordan was having fun at her expense, but she couldn't be sure. "Are you serious—or is this your way of saying you'll think about it? It is *your* decision, right?"

"We can't allow Artie's endorsement of the state to come cheap just because Whitman is holding information on your father. Let's see what we can find at the Shame Museum first. Right now though, I'd better get this guy back to his mother."

THE MAUSOLEUM OF FREE SPEECH

August 2058

"May I assist you?" Everything about the person behind the counter suggested she was a woman, except that she was completely bald. She was, however, warm and friendly, with the unusual energy field emanated by people who enjoy their work, like a grazing animal that has checked out the pasture and decided it isn't going to run out.

Behind her was a warehouse bigger than six football fields, silent but for an occasional soft electric purr.

"Is this the Shame Book Repository?" Jordan asked. It was printed on the sign outside the building and again on the signage at the counter, but he didn't see any bookshelves, let alone books.

"Books, books, books," the woman smiled, "all reposing peacefully. We have here one million square feet of books, stacked eight shelves high. My name's Corinna, and I'm a Shame Foundation librarian. Is there a book you would like to see?"

"It's not a book so much as a treatise, I believe, dated May 2039 and written by Douglas Melville Smythe, an economist. I saw it in your online catalogue."

The woman stepped backwards, almost falling, as if the floor had given way. "I'm sorry," she said, recovering her composure. "We don't have a public catalogue. You must be mistaken."

Jordan, realizing that Quantum XR-9 must have hacked the museum's computer, immediately back tracked. "Oh, I might have just imagined that," he said vaguely.

Alexa, who had been silent to this point, came to his rescue, thinking as only a mathematician can. "You said you have one million square feet of books stacked eight shelves high, Corinna," she reminded the woman pleasantly, "and an average book probably occupies sixteen square inches, which is one ninth of a square foot. So, by my estimation, you must have upwards of seventy-two million books in this warehouse! How on earth do you find them without a catalogue?"

Alexa's inability to be disliked, Jordan realized, was a remarkably valuable attribute.

Corinna laughed. "Actually, we have just over sixty-eight million books, which allows us room for expansion," she explained, "though far fewer books that meet our criteria come to us these days. They've mostly been destroyed, or we already have a copy. I can look in our internal records for your title, but I'll need your identification first."

Alexa glanced at Jordan before stepping forward with her Konektor to the ID reader on the counter.

"Thank you. Now, if you'll follow me, I'll take you to our reading room and do a search. If we have what you're looking for, you're welcome to read it here at your leisure, but we are not permitted to lend books or to make copies of any material for you. That's forbidden under our mandate."

The reading room was a glass-paneled area furnished with comfortable chairs and writing desks. There were no other visitors. Corinna sat down at a computer and typed in the details Jordan gave her.

"Yes," she said, "I can see the item you want, dated May 2039. I'll have it brought to us. And while we're waiting, I'll tell you something about our repository."

The rescue of books, she explained, began in the 2020s when universities started to dismantle their libraries, which were classified as culturally white-dominated spaces and thus became a focal point in the drive to decolonize academia.

"By the 2030s, the content of all books and reference materials had been vetted for suitability with respect to race, gender, social justice, and potentially offensive teachings," she told them. "All approved student resource materials online were digitally stored in the federal education database. A small number of students, believing that history and cultural reference points were being destroyed in the process, started an underground movement called Book Rescue, collecting thousands of copies of classic literature and scientific texts that were being thrown out and storing them in unused garages and barns all over the country."

The move to censure books that could potentially harm people of color or nonbinary sexual orientation had quickly spread to public libraries. By the mid-2030s, county boards were removing hard-copy books from their shelves and converting to subsidized download services with state-government-approved rating systems.

"The last-gasp efforts of the publishing industry to save themselves from going out of business saw them producing things like *Diversity Editions* and the *Purity Writers* series. Do you remember them?" She turned to Jordan, assuming that he was old enough to recall those days.

He didn't want to remember.

"*Diversity Editions* were classics," Corinna explained, "selected by an algorithm that established that the original content had never identified the ethnicity or race of the principal characters. So, for instance, Dorothy in *The Wizard of Oz* became Native American, and Captain Ahab in *Moby Dick* became black. However, these were quickly withdrawn because black and Native American writers objected that only new stories written by people of color were acceptable, not old white men's stories."

"I can see their point," Alexa said with a nod.

"Shakespeare, of course, despite being reclassified as a woman, failed on every count... Soon publishers took on so-called 'sensitivity readers' to try and help them navigate such identity politics tripwires during the 2020s and '30s, but the *Purity Writers* movement finally brought the industry to a halt, and hard-copy books became a relic of the past." Corinna shrugged. "So, here we are: shamed by our written history."

"Tell me about *Purity Writers*," Alexa requested. "I think I remember them."

"That was the movement that insisted that no writer could authentically write about a character's experience unless it exactly mirrored the experience of the writer in real life. Only an autistic transsexual author could write about an autistic transsexual character. Only a Mexican illegal immigrant could write a story about a Mexican illegal immigrant family. It was rather limiting with regards to imagination— and to the stories written at that time. Then, of course, the Overthrow came, and books were banned except in registered digital form. By that time, the Book Rescue movement already had thousands of books piled up in hiding places all around the country and needed somewhere to house them."

Jordan stood up and peered into the vast warehouse. It was spotlessly neat and eerily quiet. Dense rows of yellow plastic shelving on modular frames stretched into the vast interior, divided by aisles of the same width. "So, how did you get them all together in one place? Is this a government-built facility?"

"The Book Rescue collective found an angel. He was a billionaire property investor who bought this Amazon fulfillment center when Amazon went out of books, and he set up a foundation to ensure the collection would never be lost. The state censors allowed it, providing no books ever leave the premises or are ever copied. They see it as a time capsule of ignorance and false thinking, standing as a warning to humanity in the future. That's how our benefactor sold the idea to them. It didn't hurt that he was black as well as rich. So, it's not a library; it's a museum. Amazon had three hundred people working here. We have just two, but we inherited their barcoding software and robots."

At that moment, a stack of yellow shelves on the back of an orange robotic trolley came purring through the aisles to stop precisely outside the reading room door, and Corinna got up to meet it. A tiny red pencil light was beeping on one of the shelves, and a matching light was beeping on the small receiver attached to Corinna's lapel. She picked out a document from the tray on the beeping shelf, and the light on her lapel turned green.

" 'Donald Melville Smythe,' " she read, " 'The Jackass Explained, May 2039.' Now, who would like this?"

Alexa put up her hand and took out her glasses.

"I'll leave you to read, then," Corinna offered. "I'll be at the front desk when you've finished."

Knowing that Alexa's glasses were transmitting images of the document back to XR-9 at the DDC, Jordan felt no need to read over her shoulder. He was suddenly feeling overwhelmed and wondered whether he'd been overdoing his breathing exercises and running. To suddenly go from living a sedentary life with an electrical fault in his heart to believing he could recapture the strength and energy of a thirty-year-old in a matter of months was naïve and bordering on stupid... Or was it the book repository that was making him feel like this? The air he was breathing was filtered and dehumidified to help preserve sixty-eight million books, banned thanks to public hostility to their authors' ideas—ideas that had only expressed the public attitudes and opinions of the time in which they were written. Were they worth preserving now, and if so, to what end?

Alexa skimmed the document, knowing her microchipped spectacles were transmitted the pages via her Konektor and, like Jordan, now being eager to escape the oppressive feeling that this mausoleum of free speech was arousing in her.

"Let's go," she announced.

At the front desk, they found Corinna waiting for them with a colleague. Both of them seemed to be on edge.

"I'm sorry," Corinna blurted out, accepting the returned document. "I didn't mean some of the things I said; I was trying to be lighthearted. I hope I wasn't indiscreet."

Jordan and Alexa looked at each other, confused.

"I should have looked more closely at your identity record," Corinna confessed to Alexa. "I didn't realize you were with the Agenda Implementation Tribunal and the Department of Truth and Public Guidance. Please forgive some of the things I said."

Alexa smiled reassuringly. "You were great," she said. "Exceptional."

"You're very kind. And would you like passes to the Shame Arts Museum while you're here? It's just half a mile down the road. It contains all the works by male artists that people managed to save after they had been removed from public galleries, when the gender and racial balance rules came in after the Overthrow. It's very popular ... far more so than books, I fear. But so it should be. It may be one of the greatest collections of masterpieces left in the world."

"We might look in if we have time," Alexa said. "There's just one more thing I'd like your help with before we go. Somewhere in your system, you must have a record of the origin of items like that document we just read. How do you classify them?"

Corinna looked at her colleague. "Jason?"

Jason took the file from her. "The barcode allocation records tell us the date that a work went into our system. I can look that up, if you'd like to wait."

"We'll wait," Jordan confirmed.

It didn't take long.

"The barcode was issued in October 2039 for a large batch of items from the FIB. We received quite a few works from them at that time."

"And what's the name of the foundation that funds you?" Jordan asked.

"The ParkFed Foundation, established by Bill Jones, Jr. Do you know it?"

FORESIGHT

August 2058

Alexa was unusually subdued as the autonomous car headed out of the landscaped grounds of the Shame Foundation, leaving Jordan to do the talking. Holding her father's manuscript in her hands had clearly upset her.

Jordan, on the other hand, was feeling better about the visit they'd just made, in great part because of learning that his friend Bill Jones, Jr., had funded the enormous effort to rescue and store so much of the written history that society had rejected. "Bill Jones is a friend from my college days," he said. "He's still a friend—one of the Derangers gang."

"Oh?"

"When we first met, he was studying property management. Now he's one of the richest of the rich."

"Is that a good thing?"

"It is if he uses his wealth this wisely, don't you think? I'd say what we've just seen is money well spent. No government agency would have dared to defy the culture-war activists in that way."

"Depends how he made the money, and why he's allowed to keep it. In case you've forgotten, Article Three of *Agenda 2060* is supposed to limit private wealth accumulation. My father warned that the rich would get richer, and that they and the state feed each other. Your Mr. Jones is obviously well fed. And maybe he's just virtue-signaling, or buying indulgences like a fifteenth-century Catholic merchant: the richer he becomes, the more sins he can have absolved."

No, that didn't sound like Bill, Jordan thought. Bill had gotten rich *in spite of* the state ... or was that naïve? "Is that what your father's last paper predicted—that the state and the super rich would feed each other?"

"I don't know what it said," Alexa snapped. "I was scanning it back to your all-seeing, all-knowing computer, remember? I'm trying to find out if he's alive, but I'm no closer. Maybe we could ask your friend Bill who at the FIB gave his museum a whole bunch of my father's papers six months after he disappeared."

"If Bill can help, I'm sure he will."

She was right: she was no closer to finding her father, and the discovery that the FIB was the source of his most recent papers didn't free her of Whitman's leverage over her as they'd planned; it only made that leverage stronger. It was a two-hour drive back to the city, and the last thing Jordan wanted was for those hours to be spent speculating on what might have happened to the man.

"Bill Jones's story is an interesting one," he told her, "because people's view of the rich is based on stereotypes, and sometimes it misses the simple ingredients that went into their recipe for success."

"Are you going to tell me that everyone can be super rich if they work hard?"

"No, not at all. And I'm not suggesting that many of the one percent *aren't* greedy, ruthless, and corrupt ... but none of those descriptions could be applied to Bill. 'Rich' is a pejorative in this case."

"So, how did this 'good friend of yours from your college days' become a billionaire without being greedy, ruthless, and corrupt?"

Holy shit, Jordan thought. This was going to be a tough ride home if he put a foot wrong.

"When Bill left college, he went into commercial property. He was qualified, personable, and black. To my knowledge, he had no money behind him. But he wasn't afraid to apply for a mortgage if he could make a good case for a building, and he did well during the mid-twenties after the pandemic, when prices were low, but society was changing in a way that proved devastating for most owners of commercial property.

For decades, people had driven their cars into the cities each day to work in office buildings. But most of those people didn't do much more than shuffle papers around and hold meetings. Suddenly, cloud computing, artificial intelligence, and automation began putting an end to that, providing far more efficient and cost-effective ways of getting things done. The only people left shuffling papers and holding meetings would turn out to be government employees. Bill had the foresight to recognize that was the direction things were heading, and he made it a policy to lease to government departments only—long-term leases, fully repairing, with buy-out clauses that were very generous to Bill. Bureaucracy, as Bill knows, is ever-expanding."

"So, he got in deep with the government. Surprise, surprise."

"No; Bill had foresight and a willingness to act on it. Take parking garages as an example. Once car ownership restrictions were put in place, Bill could see that parking garages were no longer going to be fat cows that delivered cream so easily to their owners. Even when they were required to install electric car charging stations on every level, their problems weren't going to be solved. The electricity supply grid couldn't cope with the drawdown from electric cars, and pretty soon, charging was being rationed to two days a week. As if that weren't bad enough, bicycle lanes and bus lanes were making the roads impassable. People were forced to leave their cars at home. Policy makers were ecstatic, but parking garage owners were down on their knees sobbing—and there was no one to buy them out."

"Except Bill Jones, Jr.," Alexa anticipated, "acting on his foresight, presumably."

"Foresight is easy to see with hindsight," Jordan responded. "What percolated through Bill's mind back then now seems so obvious to us when we see the enterprises he created, but the fact is that he acted swiftly on his forward-thinking ideas... My point is, all people are not the same, and equality will forever remain elusive."

"So, what was your gifted intellectual friend's big idea?"

"Bill is not a gifted intellectual, though he's certainly no fool. The way he explained it made it sound simple. High-rise parking garages were very basic structures—just a series of concrete floor slabs interconnected with ramps, and some stairs and elevators for access. The floor slabs were open-plan, with no partitioning or fitout of any kind. They were heavy-duty utilitarian structures just waiting for a novel purpose beyond being a repository for redundant cars. Bill's idea was to turn them into farms: marijuana farms. With charging stations now on each level, he had the juice to power the heating lamps, and the fire sprinkler systems could deliver water throughout. All he needed was some insulated cladding for the exterior walls, and appropriate ventilation.

"The banks and investment funds were clamoring to get into the booming pot industry, but Bill didn't need them. He had his construction costs paid off before the invoices were even due. The trick was to pick up the empty parking garages from distressed owners before anyone caught onto his plan—and he achieved that with a combination of deferred settlements and confidentiality clauses. The government loved it. Estimates of the taxes to be collected from legalizing marijuana far exceeded anything that was lost through declining tobacco sales. And with Bill's setup, they could collect their excise as if every building was a purpose-built bonded warehouse, and they didn't even have to drive out into the country to keep an eye on it. That's how Bill first made money."

"By growing pot?" Alexa asked scathingly.

"You don't approve? Marijuana is the very emblem of progressive liberalism. Do you object to him being rich on moral grounds, or because you're against recreational drugs—or because you don't think anybody should be rich?"

The Alexa he thought he knew would have softened at this point, but she was not in the mood.

"Alright ... maybe you'll like how he made his second fortune a bit better," Jordan suggested.

"Cocaine?"

"No: meat alternatives. Meat, as you know, is offensive to vegetarians, vegans, and those who can no longer afford it, particularly since the United Nations encouraged a boycott of livestock farming to reduce methane emissions and convert farmland to forestry. But the problem with plant-based protein substitutes is flavor, energy costs, and scale. Another friend of mine, a biologist named Hedley Payne, solved the first two problems with a unique processing method that uses a formulation of hydroponically grown greenfeed, but it still needed scale to be cost-effective. So, Bill, thinking of the heat, water, nutrients, and growth involved in his marijuana farms, wondered whether a parking garage could also be converted into a meat substitute farm."

"I take it the answer was 'yes.'"

"It would be three years before that question was answered unequivocally. In that time, Bill sold his cannabis operation to the Government Pension Fund for a neat five billion in Crypto Credits, which put him right over the edge into that hated one-percent wealth bracket. Meanwhile, acting on nothing but faith in foresight and Hedley's convincing expertise, he traveled to every major city across the continent, quietly acquiring failing parking garages on the same terms he had successfully used for the venture he'd just sold."

"... With five billion of the state's money in his back pocket."

"Correct. Bill's son, Bill Jones the third, was put in charge of marketing, and the first meat substitute farm opened in Chicago, the meatpacking capital, in April 2048. Within a year, ParkFed steaks and burgers were the ubiquitous protein of choice throughout the homes and restaurants of Illinois. In quick succession, forty-nine more plants opened interstate. As I recall, you were eating a ParkFed burger the other night in the Hope Café."

"And ParkFed is the name of the foundation that funded the Shame Museums."

"Exactly. The United Nations Food and Agriculture Organization had predicted that the world would need to grow seventy percent more food by 2050 if it was to conquer malnutrition, and while GM corn and soy had comfortably met that growth challenge, the missing ingredient was protein. Then along came Bill's ParkFed meat substitute farms, each one capable of supplying protein for one and a half million people. When Bill was led on stage at the eightieth International Earth Day gathering in April 2050—you may have seen it, it was broadcast everywhere— the applause was deafening. It was announced that by reducing public consumption of beef, pork, and poultry, ParkFed had eliminated 328 metric tons of greenhouse gas emissions per year. Bill was declared a Guardian of the Earth, the highest award recognized by the governing body of the United Nations at that time. His ParkFed operations ticked every box on the ecology and sustainability checklist and were granted the protective status afforded by the UN to suppliers of essential resources. His position is now sanctioned and protected by their governing body, as provided for in Article Ten of *Agenda 2060*."

"Which is?"

"To place essential food, energy, raw materials, water, and technology resources under the protection of United Nations-approved suppliers to eliminate supply risks."

Alexa looked unconvinced. "What I get from that," she said dourly, "is that your Mr. Bill Jones, Jr., made it into multibillionaire territory by getting in bed with the state and the One World elites."

Jordan gave up; she wasn't going to be convinced. "I guess you could also say," he joked, "that without your demon marijuana, none of this would have been possible."

She didn't see it as a joke. "Does it not occur to you," she asked, "that he's used his position among the world's elite to acquire an enormous collection of art that once belonged to public galleries? Where does he hoard his gold?"

Jordan tried to think of a change of subject that would get a better response from her, but time passed, and he failed to think of one. It wasn't until they were almost back to the city that she revealed what was really on her mind.

"That paper we just scanned, supposedly written in May 2039, was either written by someone else, or written by my father as some sort of forced confession. If he was alive, he'd never have put his name to it. When you read it, you'll know what I mean. As soon as I get back, I'm going to get back into that room I told you about, where I found the minutes of the Action Committee meetings at the time of the Overthrow. I believe they killed him, because he knew who they were and what they were doing."

THE JACKASS EXPLAINED

By Donald Melville Smythe
May 2039

Dear Reader,

Recently, I regaled you with the prognostications of a "jackass" economist.

It was my self-deprecating way of preparing you for the value of my opinions. The male donkey is called a "jack," and donkeys are not held to be very smart … hence, "jackass."

Etymology is not to be taken lightly, however, and my throwaway description caused an eruption of anger from the feminists ("Women are economists, too,") and the animal rights supporters ("Donkeys are the hardest-working members of the Equidae family, and their cognitive capabilities are at least equal to that of humans").

Thus, feeling considerably chastened, this week I will bring you the prognostications of an economist who has been rendered into donkey meat.

For the record, feminists and animal rights supporters were not the only people dumping on my views. The host server of my venerable publisher, *The Financial Times*, crashed repeatedly in the ensuing days as critics fought to inform me of my ignorance (sadly, causing the FT to eventually shut down).

Postmodernist academics roundly condemned me for my preponderant reliance on economic truths that "fail to acknowledge the role of hegemonic power in the determination of those truths, and the concomitant need to recognize that meaning is intersubjectively created, in contrast to empirically." I must shamefacedly acknowledge that hermeneutics is not well understood in mainstream economics, and my arguments were deficient in this respect.

Fellow economists were no less scathing. My attempt to show the interconnectedness of the money supply, interest rates, and gross domestic product was described as "simplistic, reductionist, and unsophisticated."

One well-known World Bank expert in macroeconomics was particularly scathing. "Dynamic stochastic general equilibrium (DSGE) modeling," he observed, "is more than capable of ensuring a stable decision-making platform for regulatory policy makers, including identifying and providing analysis of factor-augmented vector autoregressions (FAVARs)..." (I apologize for inflicting deliberately obscure language on you, but economists don't take each other seriously if the language is plain enough to be understood.) "... You should know that it is possible to gather many algorithms together for simulating from the posterior distribution of parameters and providing the necessary tools for both posterior and predictive modeling, not dissimilar to that of our climate change colleagues."

I am suitably chastened.

The religio-philosphical branches of the humanities were quick to point out that the cancelation of all debts under Jubilee, and the abolition of usury via zero-interest rates, were foundational laws of Moses, Jesus, and Mohammed. "Their proven ethical and humanitarian efficacy, therefore, should leave no doubt that their embedding in the articles of *Agenda 2060* was a wise and progressive move on the part of the Overthrow tribunal."

I must confess that I had overlooked these historical precedents.

But perhaps most scathing of all was the epistle I received from the advisory panel to the members of the Overthrow tribunal themselves. I have undertaken to summarize their views for you without editorial interference on my part.

"*Agenda 2060* is a manifesto for a new world order," they said. "There is no historical context appropriate for your postulations. Money supply is not a consideration, for money is no longer fungible. Unemployment is now a solecism and has no meaning. Debt has been demolished. The wealth of the nation is no longer dependent on gross domestic product, but rather on citizen well-being. People are not dependent on the state; the people *are* the state. Under this new set of paradigms, you must accept that there is no longer a place for economists in our society. We therefore refer you to Article Twelve, which asks us all to 'Commit to embracing One World, One People, and One Government as the pathway to peace, harmony, and a sustainable future for all, working tirelessly for the full implementation of this agenda by 2060.' "

So, there you have it, dear reader. I must bow to the overwhelming weight of opinion and retire my thoughts to that mean pasture reserved for broken-down jackasses that are of no further use.

Hee-haw and good luck to you all.

Your Once-was-an-Economist,
Donald Melville Smythe

TRAVELLING IN SPACE

September 2058

From a young age, Alexa had dreamed of traveling in space. Mathematics had seemed like a sensible lead-in to eventually majoring in aeronautical engineering. But the Overthrow had put an end to those plans, and she'd ended up in statistics instead ... not to say that the dream ever died.

Alexa's lifelong ambition to be an astronaut was recorded in her yearly Bias Assessment Reports at the Lineal Progression Office, and it remained undampened by the sometimes depressing photo transmissions depicting daily life in the Mars and moon colonies, or by the periodic setbacks experienced by the SpaceX and IASA programs. She'd doggedly continued to believe that she was on a trajectory to one day achieve her ambition, and each year she dutifully submitted her name on the recruitment ballot, while being aware that time was working against her.

From a young age, therefore, as she observed people and tried to understand them, she was inclined to see them as astronauts, each alone in their own capsule, looking out at the earth through a spaceship's porthole, as if they were seeing it through VR goggles. They watched the green, blue, and white sphere of the Earth turning slowly, silently towards night, seeing it move through shades of grey and purple to a black deeper than the void, studded with the diamond-white clusters of electrified cities viewed from a height of three hundred miles. And descending to those cities in their space suits, they looked out through their helmets at the world around them, still in virtual reality, ever conscious of the sound of their own breathing, hearing the voices of their fellow astronauts only distantly … relying on streaming video, social media, and multi-channel Konektors to render their reality.

This view of her fellow passengers on Spaceship Earth may have explained her relative immunity to the advances and aggressions of others. Her space suit protected her, even though others couldn't see it. In this way, she believed, she had kept herself aloof from both intimacy and intimidation—and now was the time when she would be tested on both fronts as never before. Could she withstand the callous powers of the machinery of state, as represented by Shane Whitman? Could she ignore the growing attraction of the intimacy afforded by her friendship with Jordan?

These were her thoughts as she sat in a reclining chair in Antonio's laboratory, her head encased in a VR headset that plunged her into galactic universes comprised of atomic particles of precious metals. As she swept through the outer orbits of Planet Gold's negatively charged electrons towards the positively charged protons surrounding the nucleus, she felt her capsule shudder violently and her temperature rise alarmingly. This was what Antonio had wanted her to see, for this was where the game development was getting held up.

"If anyone can help with your calculations," Jordan had offered, "it will be Alexa."

They'd spent the morning going through the files that Alexa had found documenting the meeting minutes of the Action Committee at the time of the Overthrow. The files had been relayed via her microchipped glasses back to Jordan's quantum computer, XR-11, which was tasked with identifying the participants and transcribing the records. Sadly, if they contained any reference to Donald Melville Smythe, it wasn't immediately apparent.

Meanwhile, in the face of Whitman's insistence that the *ArteFact Channel* publicly demonstrate its willingness to support the amendment to Article One before the state would agree to embark on the expensive and—in their minds—risky campaign of endorsements, Jordan got an idea for a suitable approach to take. He then asked Antonio to make a video recording of Alexa, while he retreated to work on the idea and arrange for the computer coding. Why he wanted video footage of her speech and facial expressions was not explained, but he suggested she read aloud the articles of *Agenda 2060*—"and put some enthusiasm into it." Once they'd finished, he suggested, Antonio should introduce her to his *Galactic Mission* e-game and the problem it had encountered.

"The solution lies somewhere in the rate at which electrons successively occupy available electron shells," he'd suggested airily. "Maybe look at the role of xenon as a neutron absorber."

She hadn't needed any persuasion, accepting the challenge with alacrity, reveling in the exhilarating ride through the heavens that Antonio had created, until her spaceship hit the impassable field of electrons shielding Planet Gold's nucleus.

Now she took off her headset and shook her hair free. "Antonio," she said, "that is a brilliant, brilliant e-game, and I wish I could be one of the winners and go to Eros! Let me work on the electron configuration and the electron groupings per shell. If we can tweak those, we may be able to stabilize the orbiting patterns sufficiently to allow the spacecraft to reach the nucleus. I'll work the mathematical calculations and see what I can do."

Antonio was not as pleased as she expected. "But Alexa," he protested gloomily, "in atomic physics and quantum chemistry, the electron configuration is the distribution of electrons in atomic or molecular orbitals. If we change that, it is no longer gold."

"Of course," Alexa replied, "but if we progressively capture and release one or more electrons as the spacecraft passes through, we may be able to compensate for the electrical charge of the spacecraft and stabilize the magnetic pull between the electrons and protons."

Antonio smacked his head in amazement. "*Santa mierda!* Can we do that? The calculations will be so complicated."

"That's what calculus is for." She shrugged.

He broke into an exuberant heel-stomping and hand-clapping routine accompanied by loud coyote yelps, which she was happy to watch but not tempted to join. The relationship she'd observed between Antonio and Jordan had stirred up a feeling in her that she didn't like. She was afraid it was jealousy. These two were co-conspirators, trusting and equal. That was the position she wanted to occupy—yet her behavior at the Shame Repository, and her reluctance to reveal every detail of her relationship with Whitman and the Department of Truth and Public Guidance, told her that she did not deserve that position. And if she felt that, she was sure Jordan would feel it, too.

On returning from the book repository, they'd agreed that her father's last epistle was a forced retraction. It was insufficiently earnest to have been penned by one of his inquisitors—not to mention too knowing of the subtle absurdities of economic language. It dripped with irony ... but did it also drip with foreboding? How long would Whitman string her along before he'd admit what had happened to the man?

Whitman scared her, and she wasn't sure she had the nerves to play games with him and his deep state operatives. She'd been seduced by the opportunity to show how smart she was (an ambition clearly driven by a need to prove herself to her father all her life). But now it was turning into something else: taking on the state and attacking the very founding principles of *Agenda 2060*. Jordan and Antonio were so nonchalant about their security, sure that their quantum computing power and encryption technology protected them. They were behaving like a couple of rogue hackers playing a game, but it was a very dangerous game—and she was in the most danger.

Antonio stopped dancing. "How long you need?" he asked.

She shrugged. "Give me a place to work on my computer, and I'll make a start."

"I tell you something, Alexa," he said earnestly, "you solve this, and I promise you win a place on the first journey to Eros. *Convenida?*"

"I look forward to it." She smiled.

As it happened, it didn't take her long to research gold's electron configurations and the number of electrons per shell to frame her hypothesis. What she couldn't do on her computer was test her hypothesis with experimentation; that would require quantum power to be fully effective. So, she established the mathematical formalisms for the quantum mechanics involved and sent those to Antonio to program and observe the results, proving or disproving the validity of her solution.

Here she was, showing once again how smart she was. When was this weakness going to catch her out?

RE-STARTING THE CLOCK

October 2058

The atmosphere in the command center at the Department of Truth and Public Guidance was electric. The audience had swelled to over a hundred operatives, and the venue, an auditorium with a stage backed by wall-to-ceiling AI-controlled video panels, was heavily policed, awaiting the arrival of the Agenda Implementation Tribunal ... and, it was rumored, the federation president herself.

Alexa, steered into position by Whitman, was perched in a seat on stage, trying to compose herself. Would it matter, she wondered, if her segment of the presentation fell short of expectations? She'd done what was asked of her, and she had no control over the content. That was in the virtual hands of Artie Sharp—and who in the world had control over an entity that insisted on never deviating from the facts?

"This better be good," Whitman had hissed ominously as they sat down. She hadn't bothered to reply.

All the decisions that needed to be made in support of the amendment to Article One had been passed in a secret session by the tribunal and the Senate. There was no turning back from the public announcement scheduled for the following day. Whether she and Artie would have an ongoing role in this would be decided within the next hour.

The arrival of the state dignitaries and the subsequent introductory speeches washed over her like the sound of the surf. Her mind wandered into the atomic orbit of *Galactic Mission*, speed-reading its way through the calculus needed to progressively neutralize the gold electrons as the spacecraft passed through. Now *there* was something she could get excited about! And after XR-11 had done a test run of her hypothesis, she would move on to the silver and palladium galaxies. At last she'd found the mathematical challenge she had been waiting for.

Startled back to life by the sound of her name, she snapped out of her reverie and concentrated on Shane Whitman at the podium.

"And Alexa Smythe," Whitman declared, "at my instigation, was delegated to be our point of contact with the subversive underground organization that runs the *ArteFact Channel*. We all know the risks we are running here. Releasing the reins on truth is like riding a bucking bronco at a rodeo; we have no control, and we could be thrown off and trampled in the dirt within seconds. But we've lost the trust of the people, and this is one way of getting it back long enough to reset our budget and redirect our definition of equality. Be assured, we can reclaim ownership of the truth at any time. Truth is the property of the state. We are not giving it away."

This of course won a ripple of applause, as well as an interjection from the chair of the Agenda Implementation Tribunal. "We are entering into a dangerous new world—a world where information will be fact-checked by an organization we don't control. Today, we must make a decision on whether or not to run that risk and use it for our own ends, or whether to shut it down."

Whitman continued. "The endorsement of our public announcements by Artie Sharp will stun the public long enough to quell opposition and allow us to establish a new normal. But first, we need to know that this so-called paragon of impartiality and empiricism is capable of endorsing the amendment to Article One of *Agenda 2060* without reservation. In the next few minutes, we can all be the judge. Alexa Smythe has given a copy of the amendment to the *ArteFact Channel* and told them we need proof of their intentions."

Here he turned to Alexa and motioned her to the podium.

Alexa put on her glasses (now fitted with AR lenses as well as audio and video chips), cleared her throat, and pointed to the huge glass panels that formed the backdrop to the stage. She waved her hand, forming the shape of an A and an S in the air.

"The *ArteFact Channel* is now streaming live," she announced.

A picture now came up on the screens: Alexa, wearing a white coat and walking down a hospital corridor. Good God almighty, how had this happened? She'd never seen this place before, she didn't remember being filmed, and she certainly couldn't remember uttering these words.

"Once upon a time, a feminist was a person who supported the emancipation and empowerment of women," she said on screen. "A man could be a feminist, and a woman was most likely to be a feminist. It was not a position determined by gender, but rather by social and political beliefs."

She came to the door of a hospital ward and paused. "Because feminist demands were essentially social justice issues, they might have been expected to receive support across the entire LGBTQI spectrum. After all, the fight for rights, equality, and respect was common to all. If Article One of *Agenda 2060* was to mean anything, surely that would be a given."

She opened the door. "But no, it seems not. The story Artie Sharp is about to tell you suggests that the simple aim of Article One of *Agenda 2060*, 'to eliminate all discrimination,' has failed miserably—not as a result of legislative intent, but on account of human malice and greed … or more specifically, the abandonment of human kindness."

Inside the room, a doctor stood by a hospital bed, examining a diagnostic screen on which a highly magnified and pixilated image was displayed. The doctor had that ineffable air about him that always seemed to identify Artie Sharp, no matter what physical identity he chose to represent himself: calm, dispassionate, ageless, and sincere in a non-condescending way.

"Let's start by looking at this photo," Artie said. "Do you recognize her? She is Alexandria Ocasio-Cortez, a Democratic Socialist from the days before the Overthrow, who became an enduring icon for feminists and members of the transgender communities. Now, where would you expect to find this photograph today?"

The camera zoomed in to reveal a female patient lying in the bed.

"Not, I suspect, tattooed on the neck of a young woman, as you see here. But this young woman, who we will call Gilly, is a lesbian activist, a Child of the Overthrow, and a lifelong feminist who is proud to display her affiliations. These affiliations, combined with her lesbian marriage to Betsy and her pregnancy via IVF to a mixed-race child, places her at the highest level for Society Points and Transitional Benefits."

The camera panned back up to the diagnostic screen.

"Now, here is another photograph of Gilly. Notice that the iconic face has been removed from her neck, but the eyes remain. Why was the tattoo removed? Suffice to say that it aroused jealousy in Gilly's partner, Betsy. Let us focus instead on why the eyes remain."

Alexa's mind raced back to the story Jordan had told her in the Hope Café. While Jordan, Lexie, and Manaia had been signaling to each other in that unique human semaphore that uses language to disguise emotion, XR-9 had located the catalogue number for the AOC design at the COTO Arts tattoo parlor, as well as the name and SEM identity of the designer, one Prad Kalli.

Artie explained briefly what had been discovered in the tattoo pigments, then turned to a dissertation on the technical issues uncovered by XR-9's research. "Meanwhile," he explained, "an abstract relating to dermatological problems arising from the attempted removal of tattoos containing traces of gunpowder was found in the specifications of control parameters for the machine running the tattoo-removal program."

The abstract came up on screen, accompanied by Artie's voiceover.

" 'Treatment with a Q-switched YAG laser at a medium fluence provoked sparks and the immediate formation of bleeding, transepidermal pits, resulting in pox-like scars and the spreading of pigments in the skin around the initial points of the tattoo. It was concluded that the rapid transfer of high-energy pulses to the gunpowder particles created micro-explosions of these fragments, resulting in cavitation and provoking transepidermal holes and subsequent scarring.' "

Artie turned off the screen, patted the hand of the young woman in bed, and left the room, closing the door behind him while continuing to speak to the camera as he walked down the corridor. "This explained why the procedure was programmed to abort upon identifying these materials within the ink pigments. But why had they been put there in the first place? When it comes to specific searches, quantum computers are undeniably quick. When it comes to evaluations and hypotheses, however, they sometimes lack autonomic computing skills and ASI intelligence levels. So, I initiated a background search on Prad Kalli, the designer of the tattoo, revealing that he was born in 1980 and died in 2051, at age seventy. Transitional Benefit records listed him as MR (mixed-race), Q, and HI (hearing-impaired). The MR and Q benefits had been withdrawn following an official complaint and investigation in 2047."

Artie walked out of the main doors and crossed over to—of all places—the Hope Café. "In a society structured around identities, this challenge to Prad Kalli's status as a mixed-race queer would have been a traumatic and defining moment," he explained. "The definitions underlying the LGBTQI classifications and the shifting inter- and intra-group political attitudes at that time were, of course, matters of continual learning by all. The schism that had existed between gays and queers was largely resolved by 2030, while the bitter disputes within lesbianism arising from the contrasting interpretations of feminist dogma were destined to simmer without resolution up until today. None of the LGBQ or I groups, however, had any history of objecting to individuals self-identifying with those groups, as provided for in the Social Points and Transitional Benefits systems. So, what caused Prad Kali to have his identity classifications annulled?"

Reaching the café counter, Artie ordered, of all things, a ParkFed burger and chips. On stage, Alexa almost choked.

"Perhaps you have noted," he said pointedly, "my deliberate omission of the letter *T* just now, which represents that broad section of society occupying the spectrum of transsexuality."

He finished giving his order and sat down at a table. "The transsexual group was—and remains—the exception to this tendency toward tolerance. My interpretation of the T classification is that its members reject the idea that they represent one distinct color of the rainbow, claiming instead to be the *entire* rainbow. This is based on the premise that gender is a fluid state—not in the way that physics would describe it, but more like an analog clock, where the hands are free to rotate forwards or backwards, traversing the midnight hour of, let us say, the biological female, and also passing through six o'clock, where the biological male resides. Between those hours are forty-six chromosomes in twenty-three pairs that could be viewed as the minutes."

The camera suddenly swiveled to an antique clockface on the café wall, the hands of the clock swinging wildly in opposite directions, before returning to Artie again.

"But even that is an oversimplification of their position, because it only addresses the strictly chromosomic aspect of gender without accounting for the identity, or 'tide of feeling,' that individuals may bring to the subject. For this to be understood, it is better to think of the clock as having a 'tide hand' also. Tides are extremely powerful, both in nature and in the politics of transsexuality."

The wall clock now revealed itself as having a red tide hand that swung in opposition to the gender hands.

"It was no surprise, therefore," Artie continued, "to find in the transcripts of the complaint and findings against Prad Kalli in the Social Equity Ministry files that the complainant was the trans-activist group Out-Ed, and that the findings against him related to Article Two of *Agenda 2060*: 'Protect all persons from harm in circumstances where insensitive Hate Speech is used, deliberately or otherwise, without the consent of the persons offended.' "

Artie's burger arrived. He lifted the bun and sniffed appreciatively.

"The evidence submitted included a posting on Prad Kalli's personal social media page titled simply '*The Life of Brian*, circa 1979.' This post contained an excerpt from the script of a movie of the same name, which has since been banned from all public film libraries. The excerpt was, in the words of Out-Ed, 'a hurtful, derogatory, and emotionally harmful attack on the rights and feelings of all trans and nonbinary people everywhere.' Members of Out-Ed mounted a vicious campaign on social media and picketed the offices where Kalli worked, demanding his dismissal. As a result, the complaint was upheld, and Kalli's punishment included the withdrawal of his right to self-identify in terms of gender for the purposes of receiving Transitional Benefits. His Q status was subsequently canceled without appeal."

Artie took a big bite out of his burger and chewed it thoughtfully.

"Upon reading the movie script excerpt," he continued, "I realized that a correct interpretation of its meaning would call for an understanding of that most elusive and nuanced field of human communication that falls under the broad generic title of 'humor.' An obvious clue was the fact that *The Life of Brian* is categorized as a comedy. That does not always guarantee, however, that people will find it funny. Kalli, in his defense, claimed that it was 'just a joke.' Out-Ed claimed that it was an unambiguous example of Hate Speech. I have had extensive training in humor recognition and regard it as one of the hardest areas of linguistics to master safely, but I am inclined to accept Kalli's defense. I am quite certain, however, that humor has never been taught to the members of Out-Ed."

He put ketchup on his plate and dipped his fries in it.

"Judge for yourself. Here is scene eight from *The Life of Brian*, featuring the People's Front of Judea."

A grainy movie now played on the auditorium screen behind Alexa. Characters in period garb sat on the steps of an ancient coliseum, arguing.

> **STAN:** Women have a perfect right to play a part in our movement, Reg.
> **FRANCIS:** Why are you always on about women, Stan?
> **STAN:** I want to be one.
> **REG:** What?
> **STAN:** I want to be a woman. From now on, I want you all to call me Loretta.
> **REG:** What?!
> **LORETTA:** It's my right as a man.
> **JUDITH:** Well, why do you want to be Loretta, Stan?
> **LORETTA:** I want to have babies.
> **REG:** You want to have babies?!
> **LORETTA:** It's every man's right to have babies if he wants them.
> **REG:** But ... you can't have babies.
> **LORETTA:** Don't you oppress me!
> **REG:** I'm not oppressing you, Stan. You haven't got a womb! Where's the fetus going to gestate? You going to keep it in a box?!
> **LORETTA:** *crying*
> **JUDITH:** Here! I—I've got an idea. Suppose you agree

that he can't actually have babies, not having a womb—
which is nobody's fault, not even the Romans'—but
that he can have the *right* to have babies.

FRANCIS: Good idea, Judith. We shall fight the
oppressors for your right to have babies, brother ...
sister. Sorry.

REG: What's the point?

FRANCIS: What?

REG: What's the point of fighting for his right to have
babies when he can't have babies?!

FRANCIS: It is symbolic of our struggle against
oppression.

REG: Symbolic of his struggle against reality, you
mean.

There were gasps from the audience, and isolated pockets of laughter.

Artie Sharp looked up from his now empty plate and continued. "Kalli's resentment of transgender people as a result of losing his Q and MR status and benefits could well have led him to seek revenge by implanting gunpowder in the AOC tattoo design, which specifically appealed to the transgender community. This is the evaluation and hypothesis to which the autonomic computing skills and ASI intelligence levels available to me have led, explaining the motives of a vengeful tattoo artist now deceased. But the tragedy in this case is that the victim was not even a transgender person, but a lesbian feminist trying to please her lesbian partner, who happened to be transitioning to a trans male."

Artie stood up and crossed to the clock on the wall. "This is where Article One of *Agenda 2060* has led us. Instead of making all people equal, it has pitted them against each other in a competition for Social Equity points and rewards, leading them to forget that essential quality of kindness that should define us as people."

He moved all the hands of the old-fashioned analog clock back to midnight.

"It's time for us to amend that article to provide for genuine and compassionate equality among all members of society. It is time to restart the clock."

THE RED LIGHT FLICKERED

October 2058

Despite the overwhelming success of the *ArteFact Channel*'s response to the proposed amendment to Article One, Alexa couldn't escape the feeling of having been used. Her image, her voice—her very person—had been suborned without her knowledge or consent. She didn't know how they'd done it, but Jordan and Antonio had a lot to answer for. They needed to know that she was not okay with being used without consent in that way. And whose idea had it been to air a censored film clip containing such blatant transphobic insults? The backlash might well overwhelm everything they were hoping to achieve.

The fact that Artie Sharp's piece on the tattoo had been accepted with unbridled enthusiasm by the Agenda Implementation Tribunal, the Department of Truth and Public Guidance, and the federation president herself was beside the point. It was the public that would have the last word, and now the whole world had seen her identified with a campaign that, no matter its rights or wrongs, would engender fear and resentment in a significant portion of society. And who would be there to protect her from the backlash when it came? Whitman? Jordan?

The viewing figures came in immediately at over forty-eight million. Then Henry from Truth and Public Guidance announced that it was being rebroadcast over the public news channels as they spoke, and the social media platforms had kicked in with two hundred million likes in the first half hour. By the time the official announcement on the First Amendment was made the following day, every citizen with Internet access would be aware that the *ArteFact Channel* was firmly behind it—and Alexa Smythe was its poster child. There was nowhere she could hide. Her need to show how smart she was had finally caught her out.

She went home that evening feeling distinctly uneasy. Two Social Justice Office security wardens accompanied her, taking up a position outside her door. Her Konektor ran hot with messages and unanswered calls. None of them were from Jordan.

She ate a pre-cooked meal-in-a-bag and opened a sachet of goji berry wine. She had no appetite. Within twenty-four hours, her face would be known to four hundred million people. Within a week, the amendment to Article One could be implemented throughout the world's seven heptaspheres, and anywhere from six to eight billion people would associate her face with the World Government.

She hadn't imagined it this way. She hadn't wanted it. Fame had decided to single her out, and there was nothing she could do about it. Already she could tell that accepting this anointing would assign her to the loneliest place in the world, and it couldn't be undone. Why hadn't Jordan called? Should she call him?

At nine o'clock, she returned a call from her best friend from her college days, Sylvia.

"Sylvia," she said, rushing it, "I'm sorry I haven't been in touch lately. Things have been insane at work."

"I saw it. I nearly choked on my dried figs. Your face is everywhere. What's it about?"

"Put simply, it's a call for people to stop being fucking bitches and start being kind to each other."

Sylvia's laugh was like a drain gurgling. "Good luck with that one. You know what Nietzsche says about kindness, and Foucault has completely deconstructed it."

Thank God for Sylvia, the social sciences grad. "Okay, it's about the Transitional Benefits budget blowing out, so we stop all claims for Society Points by making everyone equal at a stroke. There's a big announcement coming tomorrow that's guaranteed to put social media into overdrive. Victimhood is going to lose its special status."

"Ha! I presume you're kidding. But what were you doing on the *ArteFact Channel* wearing glasses and looking like a physician? I mean, I never miss an episode of that show, but I never expected to see your face on there. Won't that get you in trouble at work? Or are you saying Artie Sharp and the state are singing from the same song sheet? Have they switched sides or something?"

There, in an instant, was the crystallization of Alexa's fears. There wasn't a single person, friend or foe, who she could talk with freely in the coming months once the campaign started rolling. She needed to get off the phone. The only person she could talk this through with now was Jordan ... before it was too late.

"Well," she replied vaguely, "if the state ever told the truth, you might expect Artie Sharp to sing from the same sheet. So I guess we'll have to wait and see."

Nicely, as was her manner, she steered her friend away from the topic and into the soup of memories and shared friendships that kept their relationship nourished. If she'd been a typical female, she might have been tempted to casually drop Professor McPhee's name into the conversation, but Alexa wasn't a typical female. They concluded by agreeing that they needed to get together again soon, at an exercise class perhaps—or a self-pleasuring clinic, like that hilarious one formerly run by the Vulva Protection Society, ha ha! But Alexa knew full well that the things that were about to unfold would prevent this from happening.

She threw out the remains of her uneaten meal and tore open another wine sachet before opening up her apartment's media screen and running searches for the day's event. It was everywhere, overwhelmed with likes, and already spawning thousands of new chat rooms filled with outbursts of fear and loathing from elements of the trans universe, alongside kickback from other newly emboldened citizens who saw the glimmer of a distant light—and who, when the announcements were made tomorrow, would realize that the world was about to tilt on its axis.

"Konektor," she demanded, "connect me to Jordan McPhee."

The red light flickered and stayed on, failing to connect. She tried three more times without success and then went to bed, the broadcast image of her standing at the podium that afternoon fixed firmly in her mind. She could see why they'd chosen her. If she was honest, she had to admit that she'd always seen herself somewhere at the center of attention, pleasing Daddy, earning praise, modestly excelling, and distancing herself from sex and time-wasting socializing in order to be unblemished when the moment came. She was, just as Whitman had said, chosen.

She fell asleep.

In the morning, a car came for her and took her to the Department of Truth and Public Guidance. The two security wardens followed close behind. This time, her new status allowed her to take her Konektor with her into the building. She had a text message from Antonio (*IT WORKS!!! We're off to space!!!*), but no message from Jordan. Her calendar had been loaded overnight with meetings, courtesy of the department. The day was going to be full.

The campaign room was on fire with activity. *Let's do it!* was cut-and-pasted into every verbal exchange. The walls flickered with ever-changing maps and charts. Action lists and apothegms fought for attention as the room's keyboards struggled to assert hierarchical ascendency. People she'd never met before spoke to her as though she knew what was happening, and she responded like she did.

Certain words kept being repeated that she eventually picked up and started to assemble into a sentence: *announcement, president, 5:00 p.m., tribunal, amendment.*

She strode down the long corridor that she'd walked with Whitman only a week ago, aware that this was now her stomping ground. The time to pull out had passed. The receptionist outside the meeting room stood up and greeted her respectfully by name, offering her coffee. The department members turned and smiled as she entered. There was a place card for her at the table. To her relief, Whitman was not there.

She drank her coffee and fielded compliments about the success of the Artie Sharp endorsement from the previous day, explaining that she'd had no input on it and that was what they must expect going forward. But she could tell that this didn't quite ring true, for how could she possibly have appeared in that hospital segment if she hadn't been personally involved?

Then Henry, the bright one with the bad beard, stood up and made a presentation on the audience reaction.

"The empathy scorecard is looking good," he announced enthusiastically, pointing to the screen. "Believability: ninety-eight percent. Treatment: high for impartiality, but low for emotional quotient, except when Alexa is on screen. Message receptivity: moderate, right through until the closing sentences, when it spikes dramatically with the key words. See here the rising sawtooth as Artie Sharp closes with 'It's time for us to amend that article to provide for genuine and compassionate equality among all members of society. It is time to restart the clock.' It shoots up straightaway with 'amend that article,' climbs through 'genuine and compassionate,' and peaks with 'time to restart the clock.' "

The person of indeterminate gender with the purple hair who had somewhat intimidated Alexa at the first meeting threw another graph up on screen. "Most surprising was the response from the trans demographic," they said. "The analog clock analogy really resonated with them, and 64.3 percent felt sympathy for the victim, Kalli, while only 17.7 percent supported the actions of Out-Ed. Eighteen percent were undecided. This is almost the exact opposite of what we might have predicted."

"Did you get any response to me wearing glasses?" Alexa asked. "Do they create a barrier for the audience?"

Henry scrolled quickly through his charts, drilling down into the details. "Key words extracted from the subdermal chip feedback when you were on screen were *trust, modesty, informed,* and *warm.* No suggestion there of any negatives. I suggest that the glasses are working well for you."

"It's important not to trigger *glamor* or *pretty,*" Purple Hair stressed. "Nothing is more guaranteed to polarize opinion and fracture the message."

At 11:00 a.m., her Konektor alarm went off to remind her that she needed to be at an Agenda Implementation Tribunal meeting across town in the Senate building. She thanked the department for the feedback—and was surprised when they all stood up as she left. Was it a message of support and encouragement they were signaling, or had some shift in status occurred as the result of the role she'd been assigned?

Once outside, she tried to reach Jordan again, but without success. She tried Antonio instead.

"I have to tell you, Alexa," he enthused, "we have already landed on Planet Gold and are now running your calculations in reverse to ensure a safe takeoff. *Estoy tan emocionado*—and you, you have a free ticket to Eros for making it possible!"

"Well, I'll hold you to that, Antonio," she said, beaming. "But tell me, have you seen Jordan? I want to speak to him."

"No, I've not seen him since yesterday. Sorry. We watch the *ArteFact Channel* show together, and then he has to rush to the hospital to see his daughter. But Artie Sharp gave you what you want, no?"

"It went well. You did a great job."

"Not me, no. Not Jordan, either. It's Artie that does the job."

He promised to tell Jordan to contact her. Then she took a car across town to the Senate building, feeling like her life was being scripted by others—and they weren't saying who they were, or even letting her see what they'd written.

THE SECOND AMENDMENT

October 2058

The Senate building lobby was, ironically, filled with lobbyists. Alexa's Konektor ID let her in without a body or briefcase scan. She was expected.

At the door of the tribunal chamber, Whitman appeared from behind her.

"Alexa, the president and the chair of the Agenda Implementation Tribunal will be announcing the introduction of the First Amendment at five o'clock from the Senate building on the State Streaming Service. The announcement will include a timetable for introducing the changes to Transitional Benefits, and we're expecting your friend Artie Sharp to give his endorsement. You'll be on stage with them, lending your cachet."

She spun around. "My *cachet*?"

He was no longer dressed as a woman.

"Call it what you will. You've passed the consumer test. The idea is for you to be invited to the microphone to confirm that this has his backing. There's going to be a series of public information programs rolled out over the coming months, and it's been decided that you'll be a co-presenter on those programs and ride shotgun on the *ArteFact Channel* to be sure they give the endorsements we're paying for."

"What if the information fails their fact-checking?"

"Make sure it doesn't," he hissed.

"How?"

"Give them copies in advance."

"They might not agree to that."

"Why?"

"Trust. They might only be willing to endorse what actually airs," she answered, "in case you change it."

"Listen, we're paying big money here. Do you want to find your father or not?"

"Tell me where he is now."

He leaned in closer and gripped her arms. Those damn hands, that lead-lined breath… "We're both gonna get what we want at the end of this, Alexa," he mouthed in her ear. "Let's just get it done first. Enjoy your celebrity. People would kill to be in your position."

He opened the door, and the room went quiet.

"Alexa Smythe," the tribunal chair greeted her, "you don't know why you are here, you are *not* here, and nobody can ever know whether you were here or not. Is that clear?"

Alexa shook her head in an attempt to clear it. Where had she heard this before? "Isn't it a bit late for that?" she asked.

"I'm sorry." The chair shrugged. "Old habits. You're one of us now, on the same side, but it takes me time to adjust. But what is that side, Alexa? What forces are we unleashing? We asked you to help us with our budget problem, and you've produced a solution that's led us to pose one of the most challenging and intransigent questions humankind can confront: what is the meaning of equality? What if *inequality* is our natural state? Then we're in trouble, aren't we?"

Whitman closed the door behind her. Alexa stepped forward and took a chair.

"With all due respect," she replied, "the Society Points system was a charter for promoting inequality. Doing away with it gives us a chance of achieving the aim outlined in Article One of *Agenda 2060*. The First Amendment being announced today gives everyone an equal opportunity to claim what was promised."

"You're right, of course," the chair acknowledged. "At any rate, we've laid out our path, and now we must follow it. But we need to be sure of you, Alexa, before we put you up there in front of the people."

He turned to the deputy chair. This was the much older person who had been so skeptical of her at her first meeting with the tribunal.

"That skit on the *ArteFact Channel* yesterday," the deputy chair challenged her. "How much input did you have on that? Did you write it?"

"I had *no* input," Alexa replied forthrightly. "That's the thing about Artie Sharp: he's impartial, factual, and incorruptible. That's his power. That's why his endorsement is so valuable."

As she said this, she determined once more to find out how she'd gotten into that filmed segment without even knowing it.

"But that person, Kalli, who suffered at the hands of the Out-Ed activists," the old person pleaded. "Was that real or imagined?"

"Real, absolutely real."

Of course, the deputy chair was queer and mixed-race. He would have identified with the story immediately.

"Well, if it's real," he said sadly, "it is the cruelest thing I've ever heard."

"Precisely," Whitman interjected. He'd taken the seat next to the tribunal chair, and now that he was revealing himself to be a man, Alexa had to admit that he had acquired an air of authority that his cross-dressing had not afforded him before.

"It was a powerful illustration of the sickness that has invaded society," he continued. "The feedback we're getting from focus groups shows that we're on the right track. We've read the mood and the moment perfectly."

"I agree," the tribunal chair affirmed, "and now we need to be absolutely sure that giving Alexa such a prominent role will not backfire on us. So, Alexa, put your hand on your heart and tell us honestly, now that the First Amendment has been passed, do you give your unconditional support to every article of *Agenda 2060*, and will you pledge to see its full implementation so long as you live?"

Goodness! Alexa sat back in her chair and took a deep breath. How could she have allowed herself to be cornered like this? They knew she could only speak the truth; they'd chosen her for that very reason. She was the living, breathing version of Artie Sharp—and that's what the public would see in her. That was both her strength and her weakness: truth.

"Every article from one to twelve," the tribunal chair emphasized.

Jordan had asked why she was doing this. Was it recognition she wanted? Admiration, power, and glory? All of those things were now within her grasp ... but here, at the moment of it taking hold, she now knew the answer to Jordan's question.

She looked around the table at each of the sixteen tribunal members in turn. Their eyes were fixed on her, waiting in anticipation.

"No," she announced. "I cannot accept Article Two."

"Article Two?" Whitman demanded.

"Hate Speech. It's deplorable."

"Thank God!" the deputy chair almost shouted. "Thank God." She thought she saw a tear in his eye.

The rest of the tribunal members looked at each other in consternation. Who had a copy? What were the exact words?

"Tell us, Alexa," Whitman commanded, "why can't you accept it?"

"Because it gives the state the power to silence anyone whose views are unwelcome."

"And not just the state," the deputy chair added, recovering his composure.

"Wait a minute, wait a minute!" The tribunal chair banged on the table. "Let's get clear on this. The state can't allow anything to incite hate and violence; that's why we have that article. If it gets abused for political purposes by some group or other, then it's the state's prerogative to override it. I saw that *ArteFact Channel* piece yesterday, and I saw how Hate Speech was misused to penalize that Kalli man. But that wouldn't happen now, because we're doing away with Society Points, and everyone will get the same Transitional Benefits no matter what. So, I don't see the problem." He smiled and turned his palms upwards to heaven.

The room went silent.

Alexa looked at Whitman. His eyes were averted. If he knew what she was thinking, he wasn't going to admit it.

"Donald Melville Smythe," she pronounced clearly. "He didn't incite hatred or violence, but the state condemned him for stating his beliefs."

"Those were different times, Alexa," Whitman pleaded, without even a whiff of sincerity. "There was a revolution in progress. Revolutions spark extreme reactions. Mistakes happen. That wouldn't happen now, because the state is safely in control." He turned to his fellow tribunal members. "Isn't that true, comrades?"

Yet the confidence that he would receive confirmation from the room was somehow missing. There was a lot of fidgeting and pursing of lips. Alexa sensed that she'd put her finger on something.

"Perhaps we should hear what Alexa is suggesting," the deputy chair suggested. "There can't be any harm in that. Does anyone have a copy of Article Two?"

The tribunal registrar was ordered to go and find one. It seemed strange to Alexa that the very body that was empowered to implement *Agenda 2060*, and one of the most powerful organizations in the state, made its deliberations without actually having a copy of the agenda on hand. She was pretty sure that she could recite the correct wording, but she was grateful for the moment of silence that settled on the room, giving her the opportunity to think about what she would say.

When the registrar returned and handed the document to the tribunal chair, Alexa had some idea, but her thoughts were far from perfectly formed.

"So," read the chair, "Article Two: 'Protect all persons from harm in circumstances where insensitive Hate Speech is used, deliberately or otherwise, without the consent of the persons offended.' Well now, Alexa, what's wrong with that?"

"Yes," another member chimed in, "surely that's designed to protect citizens from mental and emotional damage. It's the job of the state to provide that protection."

"If a mind is so fragile that it needs protecting from a contradictory opinion," Alexa objected, "then that is a mental health issue. Contradictory opinions are essential to the process of determining the truth of a matter. We can't make any progress, scientifically or socially, unless we hear every opinion and have the chance to challenge it. That should be the foundational basis of all academic processes. What matters is that we are kind to each other when we do it."

"Ah-ha!" the tribunal chair exclaimed. "So, it's Alexa the kind academic talking. Kindly tell me, what's your proposal, Professor Smythe?"

"Taking a leaf from Shane Whitman's playbook," she acknowledged graciously, "my proposal is that we make an amendment to Article Two, just as we made an amendment to Article One."

"And what would this amendment say?" Whitman asked, not at all sure he wanted to be sucked in this way.

"It would add the words..." Just to be sure, she wrote it down as she spoke. " '...and where physical harm or societal violence may result, provided the protection does not limit the principle of free speech delivered kindly.' "

The tribunal chair frowned. "Read the thing in its entirety, please," he asked.

" 'Protect all persons from harm in circumstances where insensitive Hate Speech is used, deliberately or otherwise, without the consent of the persons offended, and where physical harm or societal violence may result, provided the protection does not limit the principle of free speech delivered kindly.' "

The deputy chair got unsteadily to his feet and pumped his fist in the air. "Kindness—yes, I like it!" he exclaimed. "I like it a lot."

Without warning, he suddenly clutched his chest, emitted a strange gurgling noise, and fell backwards into his chair, knocking it over.

As his colleagues rushed to help him, Alexa distinctly heard Shane Whitman mutter under his breath, "He wouldn't like free speech so much if it meant we could call him a Paki poofter."

Medical help was summoned and the aging deputy was helped into a wheelchair and given oxygen. The meeting started to break up, and Alexa decided she'd shelve the free speech idea for another day. With all that was going on, it was probably a step too far at this time. Besides, it wasn't going to bring her father back.

À LA MINUTE

October 2058

Jordan looked at the overflowing shopping bags on the kitchen bench, the suitcases on the floor, and the clothes on hangers that were draped over every chair and settee, and ruefully felt the truth of the maxim "Be careful what you wish for."

Lexie was in bed in the room that he'd been using as his home office for the last twenty years. She'd already twice called him for room service—a cold drink, a snack, and a box of tissues—signaling her intention to prolong the invalid status that her healing skin graft had bestowed upon her. Manaia was buried deep in the fridge, feeding his prodigious appetite.

Was the warm feeling inspired by being needed sufficient to compensate for the irritable suspicion of being used? When Lexie had called him from the Hope Clinic, saying that she was being discharged and asking for his help to get her home, he had enjoyed the former of those feelings. How quickly their reconnection had advanced, he thought. But when he had arrived at the hospital, she made it clear that she wouldn't return to her own home while Bammy was there, and it was a series of short and determined steps on her part that led him to agree that they would pick up "just a few things" from her apartment so she could move in with him while she recovered.

It wasn't just the volume of clothes and possessions that she'd felt it necessary to pack, however, that aroused his suspicion of being used.

It was learning that Bammy had moved into the Hope Clinic in her place and was commencing a surgical process of gender appendage transformation that would likely take weeks to complete.

"So, actually, Bammy won't be at home anyway," he'd said, stating what he thought was the obvious, "so there's no need for you to move out."

"I'm convalescing, Dad. Think of Manaia."

"Hmm."

He moved the suitcases and clothes hangers into the spare room that housed things he was one day supposed to throw away, then he returned to the kitchen to see whether Manaia had left enough food to turn into a proper meal. From the À la Minute meal delivery service menu programmed into the AR glass of his oven door, he ordered breakfast, lunch, dinner, and snacks for three people for seven days, confident that would give them all time to come to their senses. Meanwhile, he would sit Manaia down in front of the TV screen with a tub of ice cream and attend to the messages that had been accumulating on his Konektor.

From Alexa: four missed calls last night, one this morning.

From Antonio, a text message: *Call Alexa.*

Jordan called Alexa.

"I've been trying to call you," she whispered.

"I know. I had to move Lexie out of the hospital overnight... It's a long story. Did Artie's piece satisfy them okay? I thought it was funny. His sense of humor is coming along great, don't you think?"

"No. How did you get me into that video? I've never once been to that hospital, and I've definitely never said what I was saying. How did you do it without me knowing? And why? What's going on?"

"I thought I explained about deep fakes when we filmed you the other day at the data center, remember? When you read the articles of *Agenda 2060* for us."

"What 'deep fakes'? I don't know what you mean."

Surely he'd told her how it worked, he thought. " Using your image and voice, our quantum computer can configure your facial expressions and speech patterns to create a realistic portrayal of you," he explained.

"What?! You mean you can make me say and do anything you like without my permission, and without me even being present, then fool the viewer into thinking it's really me? Is that what you're saying?" Though she was trying to soften her voice so as not to be overheard, she couldn't hide her indignation. "That's fraud," she objected. "That's totally dishonest and inexcusable. I want you to destroy all traces of me from your computers immediately."

"Okay," he replied calmly. "But just so you understand how it works, I didn't decide whether or not to put you in that segment or what you should say. Artie Sharp decided."

"You *are* Artie Sharp!" she half shouted.

"No, Alexa. Artie Sharp is a character created by our quantum computer XR-11. It may be difficult for you to comprehend when you don't work in this field, but quantum technology is Darwinian in how it evolves. The human brain contains almost a hundred billion neurons. It can be grown in a womb or in a dish, but replicated within quantum computers as AGI—artificial general intelligence—it has human-level cognitive intelligence, with the added bonus of perfect recall of data from every known source. Throw in the addition of artificial optical neural devices intuitively modeled on how the brain processes information, and we have now reached the point of humanized AI, in which the computer is self-aware and self-conscious. That's Artie."

"But you're his creator," she objected. "You program him. That's how he got my image and my voice."

"Artie is his own creator. Nothing exists in the digital world that he can't find. What he does with it comes down to his own judgment."

"I don't believe you."

Jordan sighed. From a problem-free life answerable to no one, he now had two women to answer to. Working on the premise that he was unlikely to get it right no matter what explanation he offered, he opted for an apology. "I'm sorry. You're right," he said contritely. "I've grown used to accepting the risks we run with Artie. It's what has made the *ArteFact Channel* so successful. If we tried to control the program, it would lose its veracity and edge. But I forgot to take your feelings into account; I can see that. It's okay for me to take risks, but unfair to take your consent for granted when you're in such a vulnerable position. Has that segment caused any trouble for you?"

She softened. "No, but it caught me off guard, and I couldn't explain how it was created."

"To Whitman?"

"To myself."

"I'll find a way of making sure it doesn't happen again."

"Good." The apology worked; the astringency left her voice.

She then explained why she was calling him: the president would be making the announcement about passing the amendment to Article One, together with the changes to the Transitional Benefits system, from the Senate building at 5:00 p.m. on the SSS.

"Which means they'll be looking for the agreed-upon endorsement—and I need to be able to tell them how that's going to happen," she emphasized.

"Well, hold on," Jordan objected, "endorsement is not a given. You need to understand how this thing works. XR-11 is a fact-checker. It'll search and analyze every digital data source, no matter where it's stored, at the rate of one quadrillion operations per second, while simultaneously running verification calculations. *But*—and this is a big 'but'—if the facts don't check out and the calculations don't verify, then no endorsement will follow."

"I've explained that, Jordan. But on this occasion, I don't think this is a task for your computer; I think this comes down to you. I mean, it's an announcement about an amendment to Article One and a change to the Transitional Benefits Act. It doesn't need fact-checking or a verification; it needs an endorsement, yes or no. They're buying your support—that's all. As far as they're concerned, they've paid for it."

He wasn't comfortable. This was not what he'd agreed to.

"The money is not a bribe, Alexa, it's a condition for being honest. The state believes honesty is wasted on the people and has no value. Attaching a monetary price to it gives it a value they can understand. But what you're saying is that there's no issue of probity involved in this announcement; it's a matter of opinion as to whether it's the right policy or not. Well, I don't have an opinion, and certainly not one that's for sale. I've told you, I'm apolitical—neither left, right, nor center—except that I do not trust the administrative state, and I'm determined to stay that way."

She was silent. The voices in the background grew more distant as she apparently moved away.

"After all that I've shared with you and the things we've discussed, you're telling me you don't have an *opinion*?" she finally asked in disbelief. "Artie Sharp has an opinion, and you're his creator—but suddenly *you* have no opinion. What's happening here, Jordan? Did you invent Artie to keep the world at bay and protect yourself from committing to anything? Is he your fall guy?"

"What the hell does that mean?"

"Have you forgotten so soon? Yesterday Artie Sharp told the world, 'It's time to amend that article to provide for genuine and compassionate equality among all members of society. It's time to restart the clock.' That's what's happening today. That's what I've been putting myself on the line for, and you've gone missing on it. Well, fuck you, Professor McPhee. If you think you're going to deplatform *me* just because you're scared to engage with the real world, then I feel sorry for you."

The green light on his Konektor turned red. She'd hung up on him.

Jordan cursed silently and turned his attention to Manaia, who was watching a cartoon in which a mermaid was pleading with Neptune to allow her to become a merman. Understandably, Manaia's attention was starting to waver, and Jordan wondered whether he should take him to the park so he could kick the shit out of a football ... or was it him, Jordan, who needed to kick the shit out of something?

He decided they'd go down to the court on the corner, and maybe he could teach him to shoot some hoops. They'd be able to keep watch for the À la Minute delivery drone from there, and it would take his mind off Alexa.

Was her anger justified? He'd agreed to fact-check—not to provide political endorsements. Surely she understood the difference? Or was he failing to appreciate the position she'd gotten into, and the pressure Whitman and others would put her under to deliver what they wanted? Was the money the problem? Had he been too cute putting a price on Artie's endorsement?

At the court, Manaia got the hang of dribbling and passing pretty quickly, but he struggled to shoot high enough to reach the hoop. He wanted to know why they didn't have a lower one for kids, which was a good point. Since it appeared he and his mother would likely be staying, maybe Jordan should buy one of those portable adjustable hoops for kids that he'd seen online … and while he was at it, he could buy him a bike, so they could go for spins together down Riverside Drive. There was no need for them to be stuck indoors.

When the food arrived, they ran back to the apartment and chose something for lunch. Lexie wanted salad. Manaia wanted pie. Putting seven days of food into the freezer gave Jordan a feeling of relief. He took his home computer out of Lexie's room and moved it into his bedroom, closing the door. The solution to his problem with Alexa was not immediately evident, so he lay down on his bed and engaged in a mindfulness exercise, wondering what would come up.

An hour later, he woke up with a start. All that had come up was sleep, and now the broadcast of the announcement was barely an hour away. He turned on his computer and logged into XR-9, opening the AR program that allowed him access to Alexa's spectacle lenses. She may have chosen to disconnect with him through her Konektor, but she wouldn't be able to ignore what he put up in front of her eyes. She could choose to turn off the audio-visual link they'd given her, but she couldn't control the incoming AR stream. The only problem was that it was one-way streaming, not a dialogue.

He felt strongly that he'd been right in principle to draw a distinction between endorsing facts as opposed to endorsing politics. These people who had persuaded her to become part of their crew hadn't changed the direction they had always been sailing; they were merely changing tack in response to a shift in the wind. He knew that instinctively, and he had tried to warn her. Once he gave in on that matter of principle, he would be forever compromised.

But Alexa was right, too. What was about to be announced was policy born from her persuasive reasoning, which he had supported every step of the way. Taking a principled stand at the eleventh hour would be tantamount to him cutting her legs out from under her. She was right to be mad.

Half-heartedly, he opened a graphics program and chose a medallion template in the shape of a gold coin. He cut out the engraving of a bald eagle, substituting a neon-green tick. Then he applied an animation to the tick, so it blinked on and off. Around the rim of the medallion, he added an inscription: ArteFact Channel Endorsement. After encrypting it with a self-destruct code that would activate if any attempt was made to copy it, he saved it to the AR gallery and opened another template. This time, he replaced the center with a flashing neon-red X. Around the rim, he inscribed the words ArteFact Channel Rejection. This too he encrypted before saving it to the AR gallery.

Next, he logged into XR-11. He'd never done what he had in mind to do, but he and Antonio had successfully done a test run to prove XR-11's ability to dismantle state encryption at the highest level. They'd been thinking of using it as a practical joke on April Fools' Day, but sensibly they had changed their minds. The code was still there in a file marked SSS Transmission Hack.

It was now 4:45 p.m.; the president's announcement would be interrupting everyone's media streams in just fifteen minutes. As Jordan went in search of Lexie and Manaia, he still hadn't decided how he would watch it.

THE LIMELIGHT

October 2058

The rostrum of the state Senate was not designed to seat the sixteen members of the Agenda Implementation Tribunal along with the president and her security guards, the Senate speaker, and the presiding officer. Thus, they all stood, pressed against each other like passengers in an elevator. Alexa Smythe was invited to stand directly behind the president. Given that the president was a good foot shorter than she was, this allowed her a clear view of the Senate chamber with its elegant marble pilasters, deep-pile carpets, domed ceiling washed with warm light, and sea of expectant faces.

This was the secular church of the state, where edicts were delivered with suitable pomp and ceremony before video cameras, which transmitted their images to state-controlled frequencies that blocked all other transmissions in progress, overruled by the imperatives of state propaganda.

Behind the cameras, a large screen hung below the crowded second-floor gallery, giving those on the rostrum a mirror image of themselves. Alexa's blonde hair—washed and gleaming, but neither curled nor dyed—drew the light to her, sucking the life out of the dull, unsmiling faces of those who surrounded her. *Was that their intention?* she wondered. If she had been chosen, as Whitman claimed, it would not surprise her at all if they'd measured public response to her physical appearance as thoroughly as they'd measured the response to the message she'd introduced from Artie Sharp. But that hadn't been *her* message. It proved fitting, but she'd had no control over it.

So, if her appearance was a factor, maybe it was primarily an age thing. For people under forty, she was not that old. For people over forty, she was not that young. If you wanted to recruit the greatest number of followers on the path to change, then the age of the messenger was critical. Perhaps that was their thinking. If so, it would have been nice to know.

Despite her outward calm, she couldn't avoid the slightly paranoid feeling that the tribunal's trust in her seemed so complete that they might actually be setting her up to fail. But what would that achieve? Really, it was Jordan who had set her up to fail. She could see his point—an endorsement from Artie must be an endorsement of fact, not opinion—but the way he'd made it was like having a bucket of cold water thrown in her face, waking her up from the delusional belief that she was as close and important to him as he was to her.

Whitman had made it clear that she was on the platform so that the *ArteFact Channel's* endorsement could be given—but now she knew that wasn't going to happen. Only Whitman and the tribunal members would be upset by that, of course; for the audience, and for the implications of the new legislation, it was immaterial. She trusted herself to think on her feet and carry the moment off alone. If Jordan was watching, that was what he should see. All she had to do was repeat the argument she had originally made to the tribunal that had persuaded them to come here today.

Without warning, the president turned around and addressed her, to Alexa's surprise for they'd never been introduced. "I don't know why we've done this," she said irritably. "A lot of people will be angry." She was as short as Alexa was tall, as dark as Alexa was pale. "There'll be trouble, mark my words," she added.

At the sound of the presiding officer's gavel, the president spun back around and cast her gaze in the direction of the cameras before reading her speech off a scrolling teleprompter parked in front of the rostrum. Her introduction of the amendment to Article One was not overtly political, acknowledging that society at large was now fully accepting that feelings were as relevant to an individual's self-identification as was medical science or biology, and that *Agenda 2060* was a living document that could, and should, reflect people's changing views as they evolved … hence, the amendment.

When it came to the Transitional Benefits budget, however, she appeared to stammer and lose her way.

Alexa took off her glasses, as the AR lenses made it difficult to focus on the teleprompter.

"Um … this week…" the president proceeded, ignoring the teleprompter, "the Agenda Implementation Tribunal brought legislation before the Senate under urgency. The legislation is designed to put a cap on spending and sever the connection between Society Points and benefit payments. The House passed the legislation by fifty-seven votes to thirty-four, with nine abstentions. I personally voted against the motion—and for that reason, I do not intend to speak in defense of the tribunal's reasoning. The tribunal chair is quite capable of doing so himself … and … the people can decide for themselves."

She stepped back smartly from the rostrum, treading on Alexa's toes and causing her to drop the glasses she'd removed.

"They don't know what they're doing," the president muttered. "There'll be riots and killing over this."

As she sidled away to escape the limelight, the tribunal chair took her place at the rostrum. If her words had caught him off guard, he didn't show it. Like all the tribunal members, he had undergone a subtle change of appearance in recent days—nothing as overt as Shane Whitman, but there were definitely signs that he had experimented with his image. Smiling at the cameras, he smoothed down a tuft of unruly hair he must have spotted on the large screen hanging before them.

He referenced his speech on a pack of old-fashioned pre-prepared index cards. "*Agenda 2060* is the constitution of our nation, and the guiding document of the seven heptaspheres that comprise the World Government. The Agenda Implementation Tribunal is the highest authority in the land, charged with the protection and advancement of agenda principles and the maintenance of sound government."

He then turned around, locating the president. "You heard the president explaining the amendment to Article One. Is there anyone who would argue against the right of an individual to identify with a chosen gender or race based on their feelings? I think we would all agree that this amendment's time has come; who's with us?"

The room, particularly the gallery, erupted with spontaneous applause. Alexa had to admit, he knew how to handle a crowd.

"Doesn't this now make us all equal?" he asked slyly. "Aren't all our feelings equally valid? I ask because Article One of our agenda demands full commitment to equality. Let me read it to you: 'Eliminate all discrimination on the grounds of gender, race, ethnicity, and mental or physical ability, and provide positive empowerment to womyn and minority groups to ensure equality of outcome for all.'

"That sounds wonderful, doesn't it? But what we have been doing for the last twenty years, through the Social Points system, is in direct contradiction to those aims. We haven't been eliminating distinctions on the grounds of gender, race, and disability; we've been *encouraging* such distinctions. Our whole system is reliant on fractionalized identities and what has become known as 'intersectionalism.' It has become a competition for victim status and compensation: whoever claims the greatest level of oppression and emotional damage wins. It ignores the most important words, which are 'to ensure equality of outcome for all.'

"Now that we have agreed that everyone has feelings and that one person's feelings are equally as valid as another's, is it appropriate for us to continue using Society Points as the basis for awarding Transitional Benefits payments?"

Alexa frowned. Why did this sound so familiar...? She took the opportunity to pick her glasses up from the floor—and cursed, realizing they were cracked.

"What if we took *Agenda 2060* literally and said we were eliminating all distinctions—not highlighting them, but *eliminating* them—and in the process, we were saluting equality by rewarding everyone equally with the same full Social Points quota? At a stroke, the budget would be balanced; it couldn't be exceeded. Of course, we would still have to remain alert for discrimination and oppression, but these could be addressed with penalties."

Well, Alexa thought, *there goes my little speech to the tribunal...* The tribunal chair had clearly recorded it.

"What we voted for in the Senate yesterday was a resolution to ensure that every citizen is entitled to the full Transitional Benefits, regardless of the Social Points they have claimed. The amendment to Article One states, 'All feelings of oppression and victimhood will be treated equally, and all support and benefits will be distributed equally by the state.' Not only will this ensure genuine equality for all; it will also ensure that the state's budget is balanced—and *that* is what the president was not prepared to support."

The tribunal chair paused for the applause he was clearly expecting. The applause was loudest from the front row of the gallery, which appeared to have been primed for what he had to say.

"The president told you that she voted against the resolution. But did she tell you that she doesn't want people to be treated equally? Did she tell you that she wants people to exaggerate their sense of victimhood in order to get more money than other people? Did she tell you she doesn't care about discrimination, or envy, or hostility? Well, luckily, the majority of the Agenda Implementation Tribunal and the Senate *do* care. As of next month, everyone receiving Transitional Benefits will be treated equally—no exceptions."

He took a step back from the rostrum. This was the signal for the gallery crowd to get to their feet and cheer loudly, as if their favorite horse had just crossed the finish line first. The video cameras dutifully swung away from the officials on the rostrum, recording this enthusiasm and transmitting it to every screen in every home throughout the nation.

Alexa felt herself being carried away on the wave of applause. How could she not be? Wasn't this response (even allowing for its orchestration) the direct result of an idea she had dared to float nearly a year ago, never believing at the time that anything so radical would ever be accepted? Therefore, wasn't she the architect of major social reform in a nation of four hundred million people, and an agent of change for the agenda that guided the policy of the whole world? Perhaps she could, after all, aspire to releasing restrictions on Hate Speech and instead promoting free speech—and in the process, honor the memory of her father. Truly, perhaps anything was possible.

As she stood bathing in the warm light of this momentary reverie, a vice-like grip on her arm snapped her back to reality as Shane Whitman steered her towards the microphone.

"And now," he announced, "I would like to introduce Alexa Smythe, special assistant to the Agenda Implementation Tribunal. The tribunal is well aware that there is a segment of society that does not believe the state acts in its best interests. The state has critics who hold it accountable for its actions, and Alexa's responsibility is to ensure that the tribunal listens to those critics and allays their concerns. So, Alexa..." He didn't bother to look at her; he knew she had no chance to escape. "How do you believe our best-known critics will respond to this groundbreaking announcement we have made today?"

Alexa laid her damaged spectacles on the lectern and gripped the sides firmly. In the image reflected back at her on the huge video screen in front of them, she was taller than Whitman. She relaxed her shoulders and shifted her weight from one foot to the other, wondering how her voice would sound through the microphone.

"I believe they will treat it kindly," she responded, keeping her voice as natural as possible. "Though there may be some who feel they are not as well off now, there will be many more who realize that others will no longer be prospering at their expense. The state cannot always get everything right, but it deserves to be criticized if it is not evenhanded. This legislation cannot be criticized on that account.

"This is a rare opportunity for all of us to put aside envy and resentment and embrace kindness, and to celebrate the fact that we all have feelings, and those feelings are equally important to all of us. Kindness, love, and sympathy create kindness, love, and sympathy in return. Don't emphasize our differences; emphasize what we have in common. We must allow our hearts to be filled with kindness."

The applause was hesitant at first, and then, as the audience realized it was being shared, it grew in confidence until the whole auditorium was filled with it. Alexa herself was moved by her own rhetoric—and tempted to continue building on it—while, at the same time, she felt bemused by where it had come from.

"What about Artie Sharp?" Whitman hissed.

Looking out at the sea of faces all hanging on her every word, Alexa felt that rare exhilaration that comes from having an audience in the palm of your hand—and the temptation to squeeze it.

"Artie Sharp!" Whitman hissed again.

Alexa picked up her glasses and continued. "I can't say how someone like Artie Sharp will respond. He only deals with facts, and there are no facts here to dispute."

As she stepped back from the rostrum, prepared to face Whitman's and the tribunal's disappointment, the audience emitted a collective gasp. Reflexively, she looked up at the video screen of the live broadcast—and saw a flashing light, like the decision given by the video umpire at a critical moment in a televised sporting event ... only this flashing light was an iridescent green tick, and the umpire was Artie Sharp signaling that he'd awarded an *ArteFact Channel* Endorsement.

How the hell did Jordan do that? she wondered.

DOG DAY MORNING

June 2059

Sunday morning. Toasted banana cake and yogurt, then onto the bikes and off to Riverside Drive.

How quickly this had become their ritual: Jordan, out front, gaming the bike's gears to try and force his legs to do some work; Manaia, hell-bent on catching him and beating him on the line, which of course Jordan always let him do; Lexie, sedately bringing up the rear with Bernie in her handlebar basket, barking at everyone they passed.

This was the way things had become over the last year. When Lexie's Transitional Benefits had dropped by 12.5 percent, thanks to the abolition of Society Points, and she filed for an annulment of her civil union with Bammy, she couldn't afford her own apartment anymore. So, ipso facto, Jordan's Sunday mornings had changed for good, along with his private life.

Within days of Lexie's discharge from the hospital, Bernie the Jack Russell Terrier had been dropped off by the friend who'd been caring for him. And if Jordan had any illusions that his new domestic setup would require minimal adjustment on his part, Bernie quickly disabused him of these. A three-month training course organized by John Erasmus's veterinarian friend, Jan, had cured the indoor barking—and the constant search for rabbit holes under furniture and inside wardrobes—but nothing could change Bernie's belief that he owned the place.

Today, however, was Dog Day; it was official. And Riverside Park was where all the local dogs' human servants would bring them for the day to sniff each other's butts. In recent years, Dog Day had become so big that it was now sponsored by the state. The police took part; the military took part; the president brought her pooch along and made a speech; there were even calls in some quarters for it to be renamed Dog *Thanksgiving* Day and moved to November, since the Puritanical associations plaguing the traditional Thanksgiving had put it in the same offensive category as Christmas and Easter. After all, no one—be they Muslim, Jew, Hindu, or atheist— could be offended by a day dedicated to humankind's best friend ... unless they didn't like dogs, in which case, it was a secular bias rather than a religious one.

Bernie, sensing that something was afoot, had started barking as soon as they wheeled the bikes out. Once he sniffed the air and realized he would have ten thousand other dogs to bark along with, the only question seemed to be whether his throat could meet the challenge.

"Did we bring doggie-doo bags?" Manaia shouted, a question to which Lexie was deaf.

A year under the same roof with Lexie had taught Jordan that there was a lot about her generation (twenty-five to forty-year-olds) that he would never understand—and as they represented twenty percent of the population, that was quite a gap in his knowledge. He had, for instance, had a conversation with her on this very topic of "doggie doo" in the early days of Bernie's acclimatization to his new domestic environment, when turds were being deposited daily on the apartment floor. Somehow, by default, Jordan seemed to have sole responsibility for removing them.

He'd opened the conversation with a simple fact. "One gram of dog feces," he remarked calmly, "contains twenty-three million bacteria."

"Really?" she replied. "I can't believe they're able to count twenty-three million germs. They must have amazing microscopes."

"Things like *E. coli*, *Giardia*, and *Salmonella*," he persisted. "We wouldn't want Manaia getting sick."

"No," she agreed, then called out, "Manaia, don't touch the dog crap!" After scooping, bagging, and disinfecting for the better part of a week, Jordan had called Jan the vet and asked if there was a trick for changing Bernie's toilet habits—like rubbing his nose in it, for instance.

"Oh, God, no! Don't do that," she warned. "He'll think you're encouraging him to eat it—which they sometimes willingly do. No, take him for a walk each morning before his preferred shit time, and reward him with a treat when he does it outside. He'll soon make the connection."

Unfortunately, the connection Bernie made was that a crap earned a reward, and thus he strained to do so indoors or out. Once Jordan realized what was happening, he did some quick reading on Pavlov, adding punishment to the regimen along with reward. A poop indoors brought a stern admonition and no food for the day; a poop on the walk outdoors brought an immediate treat. It took two weeks, and in that time, while walking the block, Jordan learned a lot about the neighborhood's dog owners and their poop-scooping habits, sending him to XR-9 to fill in the gaps in his knowledge.

He found that seventy percent of Lexie's age group owned pets, of which fifty-six percent were dogs, and fifty-three percent of those dogs were owned by females (a term that was back in use again). Yes; that fit with his observations from the morning walk. Doing the math, he concluded that across the country, 16.62 million young women like Lexie owned dogs, which produced 2.5 million tons of feces each year … and his unscientific observations suggested that most of them shared Lexie's views on what to do with the mess.

Was it possible that a Pavlovian approach, as had worked on Bernie, might also work on Lexie?

"Why did you buy a dog, Lexie?" he asked one night as they watched Bernie demolish a shoe.

"To keep Manaia company," she responded. "I was an only child, so I know what it's like."

"What about the global climate?" he asked, ignoring the dig about her lonely childhood.

"Yes, that too," she replied brightly.

"No, I meant, what about the fact that the meat and byproduct consumption of dogs in this country is responsible for fifty million tons of CO_2 and equivalent amounts of methane and nitrous oxide, which have thirty times the impact on global warming that CO_2 does? Aren't you concerned about Article Five of the agenda?"

"Too many numbers," Lexie said, waving his concerns away. "The science is simple and can't be challenged."

"That *is* the science!"

"Yes, but what does the science *mean?*"

"It means that the annual carbon footprint of a dog is twice as much as that of a fossil-fueled wagon, if we still had such a thing."

"Ah," she explained, "but you're ignoring the offsets."

"Okay," he sighed, "what offsets?"

"I'm a vegan."

He'd dropped the subject. She wasn't a vegan at all; she occasionally had meat-free days. In any case, generalizing from his experiences with his daughter was not going to help solve the mysteries of an entire generation. But he did easily fall into the trap of seeing evidence everywhere he looked—like here in the park—that the people who had entered maturity in the years following the Overthrow had a different view of what was important and what was real. If they chose to see their dogs as four-legged babies without nappies, then he'd better learn to do the same.

It went without saying that he didn't put Alexa in the same category as Lexie, of course, but that was another issue. If he dared to think too closely about what was important and what was real to *her*, he would end up just like Bernie: endlessly heading down a rabbit hole. Alexa was everywhere: news bulletins, social media, billboards, and talk shows... Her ubiquity was overwhelming. But the Alexa that he knew was nowhere to be found.

As for how much of her high-profile status was due to the media's desire for a new darling, and how much to the state apparatus pushing her forward as a sympathetic mouthpiece for controversial changes in policy, that was a matter of conjecture—a point that Alexa herself had conceded on the rare occasions when they'd managed to talk. Her work schedule was grueling, and the strain she evidenced when they last met for lunch, she told him, was attributable to the constant need to determine whether she was exercising judgment she could be proud of, or whether she was being cynically manipulated for other people's ends. In the limited time they were now spending together, these were not questions that Jordan could help her answer. Nor were the circumstances conducive to sharing the details of his own preoccupations, particularly in respect to the development of XR-12, a two-million-qubit universal quantum computer. The work he was doing surely would have interested her—especially his ideas around quantum entanglement—but it was no longer something he could safely even allude to with her. The sad truth, he now realized, was that Alexa had joined the deep state, for better or for worse, and their relationship could never enjoy the same level of trust again.

Lexie had brought a picnic with the idea that they would sit on the grass and eat while people-watching and socializing Bernie. But as Jordan could not be tempted to sit on a toilet for ten thousand canines, he went wandering instead.

The central feature of the park was a band rotunda, now surrounded by promotional stalls for pet food companies and animal lovers of various bents. A "Hot Dog" stand was issuing stark warnings from Friends of the Earth that dogs would die from global warming unless urgent action was taken. Meanwhile, the "Smooch a Pooch" stall was offering kisses from a pink poodle, with donations going to the Canine Rescue Hospital. Everybody was very friendly and happy, and it was abundantly clear that unconditional love was the pheromone fueling it all.

The one stand that piqued his interest enough to stop and engage with its message bore a banner that read, Speak Freely Kindly. He stopped, trying to unravel its meaning. Was it a request, or a command? And speak freely about what? The poster on display failed to clarify these matters: *Sign our petition. Support the amendment. Receive a free badge.*

Then he realized why he'd stopped. People were queuing up to sign the petition and receive a badge to pin on their chest, featuring the slogan Speak Freely Kindly—and the face of Alexa Smythe. There were two lines: one moving quickly, manned by an efficient thirty-something mixed-race female of few words, and the other moving at a snail's pace, manned by a talkative forty-something white female with the unmistakable air and mannerisms of an academic in the social sciences. Jordan joined the slow-moving line and listened with interest to what was being said, but made it to the front feeling little the wiser.

"Hi," the woman greeted him. "Are you going to sign our petition?"

"Sure, maybe." Jordan smiled. "What's it for? And who are you? ... And why is Alexa on the button?"

"Okay, that's easy," she replied enthusiastically. "So, I'll be glad to explain. First of all, it's to support the proposition for an amendment to Article Two of *Agenda 2060*. Are you familiar with Article Two?" She pointed to the header on the petition sheet lying on the trestle table in front of him. "Hate Speech," she announced, "the Canceler's Charter. Does it ring a bell now?"

He nodded. "And you want to amend it?"

"Too darn right, we do! We aim to take the 'hate' out of 'speech,' and replace it with 'free.' They're both four-letter words."

"That's quite a challenge you're setting yourselves," he acknowledged. "How do you hope to do it?"

"By using the powerful tools of FPTP Modernism: aggressive kindness, totalitarian tolerance, and compulsory liberation of ideas. Our goal is to reconstruct all that has been deconstructed around our freedoms and make *Agenda 2060* fit for purpose in the year for which it was designed—which is, of course, just six months away. We have moved from postmodernism to First-Past-the-Post Modernism. We are the Wave of the Now."

"The 'Wave of the Now,'" Jordan repeated, picking up a pen from the table. "Not the Wave of the Future, but the Wave of the Now... It has a powerful ring to it. And is Alexa Smythe part of the Wave of the Now? Is that why she's on your free badge?"

The woman picked up a badge, looked at it affectionately, then kissed it. "She's our inspiration." She beamed.

"Why?"

"Because she has enunciated the message that all the silent members of society have been wanting to express: that social division and deconstruction of traditional beliefs has robbed us of our respect for values and love of our fellow human beings, leaving us empty inside."

"But deconstruction is the founding principle of modern philosophy. It's what shapes the belief systems of our colleges and mainstream media and politics. What's changed?"

The woman smiled. It was a nice smile, very calm. "On campus, we are seeing a mood shift that I never believed possible. Our students are no longer willing to be told that they need to look at the world through the victims' eyes, or that they live in a hate-filled society built on oppression and prejudice. See, they always felt deep down that there was something wrong with that message, but they were being taught by people who worked to tear down outdated beliefs while offering nothing in their place. The trends of deconstruction and relativism that have been running for nearly a hundred years now were actually only about destruction. What's changed is that we now have Alexa."

Jordan felt conflicted. The woman's enthusiasm seemed genuine, but he couldn't see how it could be founded in reality. Alexa had not done anything to change campus politics; all she'd done was help recalibrate the Transitional Benefits system by removing Social Points as its basis. She wasn't Joan of Arc, for God's sake.

"What about people who say she's just a spokesperson for the state, and that the state can't be trusted?" he asked.

"Don't you see?" the woman asked delightedly. "That's the sort of cynicism we've all been guilty of. What does Alexa say? 'Kindness, love, and sympathy creates kindness, love, and sympathy in return.' Don't emphasize our differences; emphasize what we have in common. We must allow our hearts to be filled with kindness. Besides, the state would never risk having Artie Sharp judge the truth of its message if it was lying."

"Maybe Artie Sharp's been bought."

"Oh dear, you poor man!" She passed him a badge, then took it back from him and leaned across the table, pulling him closer by the shirt. "I'll tell you a secret," she confided, sticking the pin through the fabric. "I've seen a secret transcript of an Agenda Implementation Tribunal meeting in which Alexa Smythe proposed the very same amendment we're now promoting. It's in honor of her that we coined the slogan 'Speak Freely Kindly.' "

"Wow!" Jordan then asked if he could have another badge for his grandson if he signed twice, to which she agreed. Thanking her, he made his way back through the crowd in search of Lexie's picnic spot, noting just how many people were wearing the badge. Was the love and kindness he could feel all around him the love and kindness the woman had been describing? ... In which case, should they all start treating each other like they treated their dogs?

He didn't plan on staying for the president's arrival. Instead, he decided to head on home alone and use the time for some quiet contemplation.

DOG DAY AFTERNOON

June 2059

For Alexa, lying in the sun on the terrace of her new thirty-eighth-floor penthouse apartment in the Noam Chomsky Building, Sunday was not just a day of rest, it was a day of soul-nurturing. Thus she was naked, her body blissfully absorbing vitamin D and carefully stirring in the teaspoon of serotonin it promoted in order to sweeten her taste for life. On her state-of-the-art sound system, Esmerelda Gallé played mandolin in the sweeping bird-in-flight style for which she was acclaimed, interpreting the *Suite Tristesse* as if sadness were a lover desirous of the listener's last breath. The speakers embedded in the rocks surrounding the terrace waterfall vibrated with the hundred-decibel volume to which she'd subjected them, careless of her eardrums. Should any other sound attempt to intrude, it would wither in the sunlight.

Starting at her feet, she shed the tensions of her week, slowly moving her focus up into her thighs, following the treasure trail beloved by Sexological Bodywork practitioners, over her abdomen and up into the sternum between her breasts, then out along her shoulders and down to the very tips of her fingers, finishing with her neck. *Breathe deeply and empty the mind*, she instructed herself. *Allow every damaged cell to rest and be repaired. Put aside all the rushing and the high alerts, the soaring highs and the sinking lows, the constant struggle between self-doubt and vanity. Push it all away, and rest. Let the sun lick you all over.*

God—if she didn't have this day to herself, her body would snap! *Crazy Alexa … crazy, crazy, crazy… What would your father think of you?*

After an hour, she got up and went inside. An hour was enough.

Alert to the ever-present eye of the internet now built into everything, she wrapped herself in a sarong. After all, you couldn't have your oven spying on your boobs. Then she made herself an open-faced sandwich of avocado sprinkled with microgreens and slivers of hot mustard cress, drizzled with a sweet Asian dressing. Unquestionably delicious. The dressing bottle was almost empty; presumably the refrigerator would reorder it. (It was taking her a while to adjust to the idea of her house becoming her housekeeper.)

She planned on showering and getting dressed, after which she had promised herself a treat. Antonio's *Galactic Mission: The Palladium Adventure* had finally been released, and she intended on spending the afternoon immersing herself in the depths of space. *The Gold Adventure* had already sold so many copies that the promoters had announced the journey to Eros was fully funded, and the winners would be named within days. "Gold," one review had concluded, "has never been so brightly burnished." ("…Thanks to the genius calculus solutions provided by Alexa Smythe," they might have added!)

As if to signal that this minor conceit deserved to be punished, how-ever, she was promptly denied the treat she'd promised herself on account of a loud interruption: an incoming call on her Konektor, mistakenly directed through the amplified speakers of her sound system.

It was Shane Whitman. "Alexa, we need to meet—preferably within the next half hour."

"Why?"

"It's confidential."

"Why within the next half hour?"

"Because we're downstairs in the fucking lobby, and I don't want to wait around any longer."

Clearly, the sarong wasn't going to cut it. "I'll call you back," she said curtly.

It didn't take her half an hour to get dressed, but it did take her half an hour to call back. When Whitman arrived at her door, he had two other people with him: Henry from Truth and Public Guidance, and the purple-haired analyst, whose name was Zelda.

"What's so urgent?" she asked as she let them in.

"Tell her, Zelda," Whitman instructed. He seemed unusually interested in her apartment, trying to peer into other rooms. She didn't like that; it was intrusive and creepy. She took them out onto the terrace.

"We've been running polls all year on the endorsements from the *ArteFact Channel*, and we have just concluded analyzing the last one, which was a rejection," Zelda explained.

"That's two rejections out of seven," Whitman interrupted.

"I know," Alexa said. "The stats used were from last year, when the Social Equity Ministry was still using self-identification as the method for defining status. Since then, people have been classifying themselves according to their actual sex and racial profiles. We didn't realize that Artie Sharp has greater access to the ministry's data files than we do. The facts no longer fit, so they couldn't be endorsed. I should have known that."

"It doesn't matter," Henry jumped in. "The result couldn't have been better."

"How do you mean?" Alexa asked.

"Approval ratings jumped."

"For the cuts in benefits?" she asked incredulously.

"No—for *you*," Henry and Zelda replied in unison.

"Look," Whitman explained, "more people are better off now, so we knew we'd get majority support, and now the people who are worse off are starting to come around because of the public shaming campaign. But what we're getting is this spillover from you to the state. And that's what we're here to talk about. Zelda...?"

"You've scored consistently high for empathy and trust throughout," she said, "but what's happening now is that each time we get a rejection from the *ArteFact Channel*, your trust metric spikes sharply upwards … but so does the trust metric for the government. We can't explain it. It shouldn't be happening."

Alexa thought for a moment. There was only one explanation. "It's not whether what the government says is right or wrong that's important," she suggested, "it's the fact that the government is now open to being called out as right or wrong. The increased trust is a result of the transparency."

"That's a great point," Henry agreed, "but it's not the only reason. The government is getting a lift from your trust approval ratings, too."

"Okay, okay," Whitman concluded, "that makes two reasons we can agree on. But the important thing is that we want to ride this phenomenon into the celebration of *Agenda 2060* at the end of the year and get public approval for *all* our articles, not just Article One. That's what we've come to talk about, Alexa. How can we use you and Artie Sharp to pull that off?"

"You want to submit the entirety of *Agenda 2060* for Artie Sharp's endorsement or rejection? Are you serious? Climate change, pollution, sustainability, education, employment, free speech, borders, population control...? What have you all been smoking?"

Henry and Zelda laughed nervously.

Whitman didn't like her tone. "Don't be so fucking stupid, Alexa. Nobody's gonna do any such thing. I thought you were more intelligent than that. What we're talking about is riding a wave of popularity that no government has ever experienced before, and using every trick in the book to convince the people that we can be trusted. If we can do that, then the world is..."

He swung his arms around in anger, and they all stepped back a pace, convinced that he would hit anyone within range.

"Look, don't you see what's happening here? What we've got is this phenomenon where we win trust just by revealing when we're lying. It means that everything we've been trying to hide all these years can now send our approval ratings through the roof, simply by being revealed. If we do it right, we can clear out the cupboards and rewrite the agenda."

"Rewrite *Agenda 2060*?" Alexa asked in disbelief.

"No—the *real* agenda, for fuck's sake."

"We brought a full analysis of all the algorithm results for you to take a look at," Zelda offered nervously, "as well as a scoping paper to spark ideas."

"The idea is that a planning group should be established," Henry added, "that reports to you."

"Because without you, it wouldn't work," Zelda explained. "You're the key ingredient—you and Artie Sharp."

"What's the actual objective?" Alexa asked.

"To make people believe," Zelda said.

Whitman snorted as if he had a frog up his nose, then stormed back inside. The other two followed in stunned silence, their expressions towards Alexa suggesting that they'd delivered the basics of their message as requested, and now the best tactic for them would be to quickly cut and run ... an understandable tactic when dealing with Shane Whitman and his outbursts.

So, Alexa, ever gracious, thanked them and saw them to the door, hoping that Whitman would not be far behind.

The minute they'd gone, however, his mood completely changed. Shrugging apologetically and adopting a rueful smile, he recast the moment she'd just witnessed in a new light. "There are things some people should know, Alexa, and things they shouldn't. I don't want people like them to start thinking they understand the big picture. That's for you, if I choose to take you into my confidence ... but not for them." The rueful smile became conspiratorial as he moved closer.

"And why would you choose to take me into your confidence, Shane?" He moved another step closer. She stepped away.

"You know why." He shrugged.

Then, sensing that she didn't like him being so close to her, he began to ostentatiously inspect the room, picking up objects and putting them down in a different place, wandering into her bedroom and trying out the mattress, all the time daring her to object while running a sarcastic interrogation. "So, how do you like your new title and being on Executive Schedule Four? Does the apartment suit you? Big enough? Got all the comforts a girl needs? And satisfied with the Noam Chomsky security, are you? Nothing but the best for the people's ambassador of the Agenda Implementation Tribunal. Now that you've got such a popular profile, I told them I wanted you watched every minute, day and night. You're our most valuable asset; I don't want anything happening to you. You're only one step from Executive Schedule Five now. No one's ever risen that fast."

His wandering brought him back to where he had started, standing in front of her. "Things are happening," he said, serious now. "The president's days are numbered. She chose to be identified with the losers— and it's backfiring, badly. The tribunal wants me to run a campaign to discredit her, and they're talking about nominating me in her place. I want you by my side."

"I'm not a politician, Shane."

"Your trust scores are off the scale."

"... Because I'm *not* a politician."

He reached out and gripped her arms. "Listen, I'm talking about something nobody else could even imagine in their wildest dreams. The One World Government has become paralyzed by bureaucracy. It has no inspiration, no leaders worth remembering, and no direction. It's ripe for the picking."

Alexa shook herself free. "You want to take over the One World Government?!"

"At the time of the Overthrow, we were financially weak. The debt Jubilee played into Chinese and European hands, and we surrendered our sovereignty over more than just our currency. But now our technology is winning the race on every front. We've got things happening in the quantum technology sector that are the equivalent of being the first to split the atom. If we play our cards right, we're just one step away from military and economic domination again, and the tribunal is convinced that the time is right to insert ourselves into the game. We need to take back our rightful role as the most dynamic and powerful state on the globe ... but we want the people behind us."

Despite herself, Alexa couldn't help but giggle. "And you think *I* can help you?"

He leaped forward and grabbed her again, those gorilla fingers digging into her flesh. "Listen, you stupid bitch, I can make people disappear just as quickly as I can make them famous. Wise up and realize what I'm saying here. Power is the game—the only game—and if people are stupid enough to trust you, you use it to grab control while you can. Do you think I sat around in drag for twenty years because I enjoyed it? I waited because I knew when the time was right, I'd seize my chance while everyone else was asleep. I could fuck you, Alexa, and bury you somewhere out of sight. My cock still works—and your pussy wants it. Admit it: you're drawn to power. That's why you're here."

Alexa yanked herself free and sought the protection of the kitchen counter, putting it between them. "Where's my father, Shane?" she demanded coldly. "You think you can win trust by cleaning out the cupboards. So start there."

She wasn't frightened of him. His need for her was so much greater than her need for him; she could see that now. But she was frightened by the realization that she had allowed herself to get drawn into a game that invited players like him. How had she let this happen?

"For the last time, where is he?"

"I'm close to getting news." He smiled. "As soon as I hear, I'll let you know. Trust me. Meanwhile, if you're smart, you'll think about what I said."

Of course, he knew that she knew he was lying ... but he also knew that she knew he didn't care. Walking over to the kitchen bench, he took an apple out of the fruit bowl in front of her, looking her calmly in the eye. This simple act, just like his insulting inspection of her apartment, was his way of putting his scent on her ... like a dog.

Then he walked out, leaving the front door hanging open.

Moving quickly, she closed the door behind him, double locked it, and then did what she had been wanting to do for days.

"Konektor," she commanded, "get me Jordan McPhee."

A SHOULDER TO CRY ON

June 2059

The sun had completed its westward journey beyond the horizon, and the pink and grey light it left behind was fading rapidly as Jordan arrived by bicycle outside the Noam Chomsky building. Though the cross-town roads had been busy with people returning from their Sunday outings, the ride had only taken him ten minutes, which reminded him that it was such a pleasant way to travel now that summer was here. Maybe all those bicycle lanes had been worth building after all.

He hadn't been in this part of town before. The area was known for its high concentration of career bureaucrats, lobbyists, and lawmakers, who were not part of Jordan's usual social circle. The fact that Alexa had decided to move here recently was perhaps not surprising, given her rising status. But she had explained it in terms of security needs, and now, as he approached the front entrance and tried to decide what to do with his bicycle, he could see that the Noam Chomsky was indeed intent on protecting its elite residents.

A small crowd of protesters with placards was gathered on the sidewalk outside the entrance, which was guarded by two uniformed state security wardens. But were they really protesters? They looked more like a fan club. He pushed his bicycle through the throng and reached the guards before he noticed what the placards said: Speak Freely Kindly. Alexa for President. The Wave is Now.

Good God!

He told the guards who he was visiting, and they phoned up to Alexa and asked him to wait while she sent an entrance code simultaneously to them and to his Konektor. He left his bicycle with the concierge and rode the elevator to the thirty-eighth-floor penthouse. *Oh yes,* he thought, *Alexa has gone up in the world, alright.* He'd been so busy himself that he hadn't realized just how much her life had changed.

"Well," he announced when she opened the door, "from the sound of your voice, I figured it would be a good idea to bring a bottle of your favorite chocolate mescaline."

To his surprise, she flung her arms around his neck like he'd saved her life. Without speaking, she led him by the hand out onto her terrace, sat him down next to her on a settee, and then did the most unexpected thing: she cried.

The tears running down her cheeks were surprising enough (Alexa being the most composed person he'd ever met), but the sobs that shuddered through her body were quite alarming. Jordan realized he wasn't equipped to handle this, but in the moment, there wasn't time for him to work out why this was the case. He reached out and put his arms around her. The shuddering increased. He started to pull away, and she pulled him back to her. The tears soaked into his shirt. He waited.

Once the sobbing stopped, it was as if it had never happened. She got up and went in search of two glasses, and to blow her nose. On the way, she must have turned on her entertainment system; water started gushing from an ornamental fountain, and ambient guitar music began to play. Jordan walked to the parapet and looked out at the June night, wondering what to do with the strange emotions he was feeling, and hoping that she wouldn't regret having shared her moment of distress with him, whatever its cause.

"Chocolate mescaline," she said with a laugh on her return. "You're the only person in the world that would even know such a thing exists."

"You don't like it?"

"I love it." She poured two hefty shots, and they toasted to each other. Then, having restored her calm, she told him about Whitman.

"So, I know he's never going to tell me what happened to my father," she admitted candidly. "I've probably always known. I feel used and dirty for allowing myself to be strung along, but the only way I can free myself from his influence is to show I no longer care. The reason I'm upset is not just because I exposed my weakness, but because I feel like I'm abandoning Daddy. I've clung to the belief for so many years that one day I'd find him."

"Well, answer me this," Jordan urged. "Do you believe Whitman knows, or not?"

"If he doesn't, I'm convinced he could find out."

"Then we're going to make him tell you."

"How?"

"I'll think of a way," he replied vaguely.

Truth was, he'd already thought of a way, back when Alexa first told him that the tribunal chair was sold on the idea of recruiting Artie Sharp to support their agenda, and Whitman then bribed Alexa with the prospect of learning her father's whereabouts. But Jordan hadn't told her, for what he thought were good reasons at the time, and he was loath to tell her now.

Why was that? Was he afraid she wouldn't have the nerve—that she would try to stop him? Was he afraid that it might not work, and he'd make her situation even worse? Or was it a reversion to type—the archetypal male whose instinct was to help women, which decades of social censoring had tried to eradicate? Was he a living example of patriarchy at its worst?

Since they'd met at Manaia's naming celebration three years earlier, the strict maintenance of the safe bubble within which they conducted their relationship had served him well. He, the professor; she, the student: fondness, friendship, and loyalty. To break out of that bubble would be disastrous, precisely because it would be so easy. He was certain she had trusted him not to do that while letting her tears fall on his shoulder, unloading her doubts and fears, and sharing her triumphs and disasters. How shameful it would be if he broke that trust now.

"Look, just give me some time to think about it overnight," he said, putting the problem on hold until he could better handle it, while still encouraging her to hope. But in this moment, what he felt most strongly was that he couldn't allow himself to spend any more time on this terrace—night falling, music playing, a bottle of liqueur on the table, the smell and touch of her hair on his cheek...

"Meanwhile," he added cheerfully, "what you need is some company to take your mind off this bastard. So why don't you come home with me, and we'll all have dinner together: you, me, Lexie, and Manaia. We'll knock off a bottle of wine and share a few laughs. I'd like you to meet them at last... And if you bring a toothbrush, maybe you can stay the night."

INSURANCE

June 2059

Lexie cooked. That was one thing she knew how to do. Now that Bammy—the longtime driver of her political activities—was gone, and her work with the Community Caucus on Cultural Sensitivity had declined, she had taken to watching cooking shows.

The other thing she knew how to do was talk—and that was exactly what Alexa needed. Before long, they were carrying on like long-lost friends, and Jordan decided to bunk in with Manaia for the night to leave his own bed free for the guest. Topping and tailing with his grandson didn't make for a great night's sleep, but at least he was able to rest easy in his decision to coax Alexa out of her apartment and get her laughing.

After breakfast the next morning, he announced he was going in to work and would speak to her around lunchtime if he had any further ideas about the issue with Whitman. Lexie, having a vague idea of what had been going down, decided she'd walk Manaia to school, then go back to Alexa's apartment to keep her company. As a habitué of social media, Lexie was not immune to the pull of Alexa's star power, and she seemed slightly bemused that her father was on such familiar terms with somebody who was in the headlines and garnering such a mass of followers.

Wearing a tracksuit and sneakers, carrying only his Konektor, Jordan presented himself at the security desk of the Department of Truth and Public Guidance five minutes before 10:00 a.m. He asked to see Mr.

Shane Whitman on private business, without an appointment. "Tell him Artie Sharp wishes to speak to him urgently."

The security guard told him to stand in front of the face recognition camera and walk through the body scanner, then wait. At exactly five past ten, he was asked to leave his Konektor in visitor's lockbox 309, for which he was given a key. Before depositing his Konektor, he opened an encrypted message application and sent a message he had already drafted, then he switched the device off and followed an usher down a long corridor to an office door marked AIT Private.

Behind the door were people working at screens in silence. No one looked up. The usher crossed the room and knocked on another door, this one unmarked. She opened it and ushered Jordan inside.

"Mr. Artie Sharp," she announced, then closed the door behind him.

"You're not Artie Sharp!" Whitman barked from his seat behind an intimidating desk. "You're ex-professor Jordan Fucking McPhee. Jesus, you've got some nerve"

"Glad to see your facial recognition systems are working," Jordan replied pleasantly.

"Of course they are. We know who everyone is. What do you want, and how did you know I was here?"

"You came into the building at 8:50 a.m., and you haven't left since. I knew you'd want to see the person whose been so helpful to you ... particularly as I'm delivering on your demand, as promised."

Whitman's pugnacious face was unable to maintain its aggression as it surrendered to puzzlement. "What the fuck is this?"

Without being asked, Jordan took a seat. He was already beginning to enjoy himself. He didn't have to be reminded of how ruthless this man was, and he needed to ensure that he got every detail correct, but he'd gone over it in his mind enough to be feeling confident.

"I sent you a message five minutes ago, to your private IP address. It'll be on your Konektor. Only you will be able to see it—*as you asked*."

Whitman's hand went straight to his pocket. "I don't know what you're talking about." Checking his Konektor, he screwed up his face in concentration, trying to guess what he was looking at.

"They're numbers," he said, puzzled. "Just numbers. What are they— and how did you get my private IP?"

Jordan smiled amiably.

"Those are the numbers you need, Mr. Whitman. The first eight are for the permissioned DLT cryptocurrency account in your name, and the second set is your private individual password. You're now ready to go."

Whitman glared at him, caught somewhere between fight and flight.

Jordan followed up quickly. "We've now transferred five percent of the fees the state paid to the *ArteFact Channel* for its endorsements, and it's gone into an untraceable account in your name as a kickback to you, as you requested. I've just come to make sure you received it okay."

Like a pit bull, Whitman launched himself out of his chair and hurled his Konektor across the room, then scrambled around under his desk until he discovered a transmitter. He crushed it under his heel on the wooden floor.

"This is a set up!" he bellowed. "I'll have you put away for life for trying to blackmail me! Who the fuck do you think I am—just some greenhorn functionary that you can pull a con job on? You won't get anywhere with this one, McPhee. Whatever you think your game is, you just signed your own death warrant."

Jordan crossed and uncrossed his legs. "Gee, if there's been a mistake, I'd be happy to explain it to the head of the Federal Interrogation Bureau, and to the Agenda Implementation Tribunal ... even to the president herself, if you like. The problem is that the money can't be taken out of the account, except by you, because it holds details of a beneficiary account that belongs to you and is the only place to which the money can be withdrawn."

Whitman sat down again. "You think that springs your trap shut? So, you found out my federal banking details. It proves nothing, because there's nothing to prove."

"No; the beneficiary account is the one you have in Switzerland. You know the one. It took a lot to find it, because it was well hidden. I guess you could transfer the money there, then tell the FIB that a mistake has been made. Or we could do it for you at any time, if you'd like."

Jordan waited. Remembering the way Whitman had treated Alexa filled him with anger, but it was a cold anger that he was determined to contain.

"What do you want?" Whitman asked at last.

"Where is Alexa Smythe's father, Douglas Melville Smythe?"

"*What ...?*" he snorted, almost choking in disbelief.

"Where is he?" Jordan repeated.

"All this—for that? You gotta be joking. You really wanna know? He's on Mars. That's where he's been, and that's where he is now." He could hardly believe that someone would go to these lengths just to force him to reveal that bullshit piece of information. "So, Alexa went crying to you, did she? I'd have told her eventually, when the time was right. The old man accepted a place at the colony back in the day, and he's been there ever since. He took his chance. Did you want me to tell Alexa that once they were able to get people off Mars again, he didn't *want* to come back? I was doing her a favor."

Jordan stood up. "I'll check it out. Meanwhile, that money can sit in there as insurance. If it moves, you'll have to explain yourself—and once you reflect on it, I think you'll find that's something you don't want to do."

He let himself out, picked up his Konektor from lockbox 309, and returned to the DDC. Antonio, through his VC connections with SpaceX and IASA, should be able to get verification of Donald Melville Smythe's whereabouts from the Mars colony, and he'd be able to give the news to Alexa. If Whitman's information proved to be wrong, then he'd shift the money to Whitman's secret account—and send the details to everyone who wanted to make a name for themselves in crushing state corruption. Either way, he doubted Whitman would be a problem again.

It was a real risk he'd taken, and he knew that Alexa wouldn't have allowed it if he'd told her in advance. One day, he'd thank Bill Jones, Jr., for it was his friend and fellow Deranger who'd told him about the tactic he'd just used on Whitman, which Bill claimed was a necessary precaution when dealing with government agents at any level whenever money was involved.

Antonio was immediately on board, reaching out to his contacts to get verification that Donald Melville Smythe was a resident at Campus Martius, as Whitman claimed. It might take a day or two to hear back, but there was reason for optimism; it had long been rumored that the first group of colonists included some who had taken the risk that their spacecraft might not be able to make a return voyage, and they would need to rely on later missions to bring them back.

"How you say—'Hobman's choice'?"

" 'Hobson's choice,' " Jordan corrected him. "It means no real choice."

It was also rumored that some had declined the opportunity to return to Earth and were now well adjusted to life in the expanding colony.

"For older people," Antonio explained, "the low gravity and high oxygen level can make them feel young, and so they choose to stay, maybe. Hey, why not? We all wanna stay young, eh, Prof?"

"I need to know if he's alive."

"*Si*, if he's alive. I find out."

That was what Jordan was able to tell Alexa when he called her at lunchtime. As might have been expected, her response was a mixture of delight and alarm. Until Antonio could get confirmation one way or the other, she could only hope.

As for Jordan's ruthless tactics with Whitman, she was almost speechless. "You're right," she said. "I would have tried to stop you."

But it was already done.

CRAZY AS BAT SHIT

July 2059

"Consider this," Jordan advised, addressing a select group of Derangers at a private presentation later that week. "The speed and computational powers of the two-million-qubit universal quantum computer XR-12 are not ten times greater than that of any previous supercomputer; they are infinitely greater. It is able to store and process more information bits than there are elementary particles in the whole universe—not just atoms, but elementary particles. And unlike previous examples of quantum computing, this hardware is now completely fault-free. There is no problem too complex. Climate change, vaccine responses, nuclear fusion reactions... We can solve them all once we've learned how to partner with the technology."

He looked around the table. Some members had flown in from the West Coast, some from Europe. Put all their money and brainpower together, and they could solve any computational problem in the world. But each one of them knew that some problems would always remain unsolvable. They might look up at him now, bright-eyed and inspired by the vision he was painting. But when they looked away, their eyes would become more sober; they knew that the problems humanity posed to itself were unlikely to be solved by a machine.

"There is one question we need to ask ourselves," Jordan warned. "Quantum computing can provide XR-12 with artificial superintelligence, giving it instant access to every piece of knowledge known to man—and now, with autonomic computing, it has self-managing characteristics of distributed computing resources, enabling it to adapt to unpredictable changes while hiding intrinsic complexity from its users. We have never experienced cognitive power like this in human history. The question is, can we contain it?"

They all turned to Will Portico, the mastermind of computer technology.

"The question is answerable in two forms," Will assured them. "Firstly, an algorithm should always be designed to be the servant of its master. That's a fundamental rule. Secondly, we need to remind ourselves that what we call 'humanized intelligence' in microchip architecture is not the same as sentience. Even the dumbest humans have feelings, emotions, and a soul. But the most powerful computer will never have these things."

"Well, that's reassuring," Bill Jones, Jr., joked, "for us dumb human beings, at least. But getting back to the financial side of our investment here, are we going to make time on XR-12 available for lease outside the circle of those who are financially invested?"

"That's for the members to decide," Jordan replied, "but my vote would be 'yes.' If we want to see progress, we need to be agnostic when it comes to outside ideas."

"I agree," Hedley Payne said, "but I'd want to see a twelve-month moratorium, so we could get ahead of the competition... in my field, anyway."

Everyone laughed.

"And where does this put us relative to the state and One World Government?" someone asked.

"Hopefully, ahead of the game," Jordan replied. "But that depends on what game you think they're playing."

"Well, right now, that's hard to figure," someone else observed. "This Alexa phenomenon is turning everything on its head ... in a good way, I guess, because Planet Academia is coming back into orbit. The kids seem to have had enough of the nastiness they've been indoctrinated into over so many years—but is it spontaneous, or is it being orchestrated? And if it's orchestrated, who profits from it? I don't even know what 'Speak Freely Kindly' means."

"I have a theory," Erasmus piped up. "My belief is that it's an inevitable cycle, and it all comes down to fertility. For thirty or forty years, our political environment has been biased towards three groups. One group is the LGQ homosexual subsets of both genders. Another group is T, or the transsexual community. Now, neither of those groups have been able to replace themselves through natural breeding, for obvious reasons; they've relied on adoption or conversions. Which brings us to the third group... These are cis people of either gender in the twenty-five-to-forty age group. The political environment has biased the women against 'male toxicity' and towards either celibacy or non-procreative self-pleasure instead. By the time they reach forty, however, the biological imperative of motherhood overwhelms them— only for them to find that their luteinizing hormone has declined, and they're now unable to conceive. In many cases, the men of their generation have become incels as a result of rejection, or else they've become habituated to bachelorhood. Look at how this plays out over forty years. Those LGBTQIs who first entered into the progressive undergrowth in their twenties are now in their sixties, and they haven't replaced themselves. Those entering the college environment now are the children of two generations of the remaining solidly heterosexual parents, and thus they have a natural inbred resistance to progressive relativism. That's what Alexa has tapped into: perfect timing within the cycle."

"I know Alexa," Jordan revealed. "She used to be a pupil of mine, and I'd have to say that she's as bemused by the response to her as we are. She credits her popularity with her association with Artie Sharp and the *ArteFact Channel*—which appeals to the young, in particular, because it's anarchistic and ruthlessly focused on exposing falsehood. But if the state thinks it's using her, they've either miscalculated, or they're devious in ways I can't fathom."

After dinner, the tight four of Jordan, John, Hedley, and Bill retired for their usual nightcap and an evening of their favorite game, Offended. The game was based around two algorithms that Jordan had created. The first algorithm generated totally safe, inoffensive sentences assembled from public statements issued in the last month by UNSEC. The second algorithm generated single words, free of innuendo in themselves, which, when inserted into an inoffensive sentence, could turn it into Hate Speech (five points), offensive speech (three points), or dubious speech (one point). For every sentence drawn by a player sight unseen, the second algorithm generated four seemingly innocent word options. It was just a bit of fun designed to stimulate conversation.

They were in the last round, and scores were tight. Anyone who could create offensive speech or better was bound to win.

The UNSEC statement drawn by Erasmus read, *George Kyros, the famous benefactor, will give the opening speech at the ninetieth Earth Day celebration in Potsdam.* He had a word that he thought he could fit, but he wanted to clarify the rules. "Can a word be added to another word, or does it need to stand on its own?"

"What's the word?" Bill asked.

"*In.*"

"And how do you want to use it?"

" 'In-famous': 'George Kyros, the *in*famous benefactor.' "

They allowed that it was offensive and awarded him the game.

His memory suddenly prompted, Jordan turned to Hedley Payne and whispered that he needed to speak to him later in private.

Bill Jones, Jr., wasn't ever keen on losing, and he wondered whether *infamous* was offensive or just dubious when used in conjunction with the word *benefactor*. "See, I don't know how Kyros can be called a 'benefactor' when, more truthfully, he's a beneficiary. All the causes he gives money to indirectly promote investment vehicles in which he's got stock. In fact, all those virtue-signaling saviors of the planet are hypocritical slime bags with their hands in government pockets, if you look close enough. Follow the money trail through all their foundations and NGOs, and you'll see what really motivates them."

"And how are you going to prove that, Bill?" Erasmus asked. "I'll be damned if I'm going to lose my three points because you think he shouldn't be called a 'benefactor.' It's UNSEC that called him that, not me."

They all had another chocolate mescaline, then broke up for the night. Jordan and Hedley stayed back to talk in private.

The development and trialing of XR-12 had been Jordan's preoccupation for months, and most of the money received from Whitman for the *ArteFact Channel* endorsements had gone into it. He'd forgotten that XR-11 was being used by Hedley to monitor the Micomic Life

Xtension gene-editing program for George Kyros, and that he and Hedley had speculated on the ability to override Micomic's therapy at any time.

"Remember when we talked about your ability to locate the source of conscious mendacity in the human brain, and you said that, in your scenario, human truth could not be guaranteed unless you could find a way of calculating and adjusting for the influence of unconscious bias? You said then that the complexity of the calculations may be beyond you."

"Sure," Hedley agreed. "The proposition works in theory, but it would never work in practice."

"I'd like to give it a try on XR-12," Jordan replied. "We need a challenge that's never been attempted before."

"That's a hell of a challenge," Hedley commented. "Are you sure you haven't got another motive in mind?"

What did Jordan have in mind? When the idea had first drifted into range, he'd been finding topics for Artie Sharp and providing a sympathetic ear for Alexa as she got sucked into state reforms with the Agenda Implementation Tribunal. The idea had piqued his interest at the time, but it had remained vaguely formed... Then, with all that had happened in the year since, he'd simply forgotten it.

"Something Bill said," he decided, "about George Kyros being a beneficiary of climate activism, rather than a benefactor... It reminded me of an idea I once had. What if we could make him blurt out the truth about his motives by manipulating the part of his brain that allows him to construct elaborate untruths? Apart from being a shitload of fun, imagine the impact that would have."

Hedley was incredulous. "You want to do this with George *Kyros*?"

"Well, his brain is the only one we've got access to."

"You're batshit crazy, Jordan. Assuming we could even make it work, where is he going to spout all these uncontainable truths—at the Potsdam Earth Day celebration?"

"... Now, that's not a bad idea."

THE PLAN WAS HATCHED

November 2059

Alexa's emotions could have best been described as "mixed." After Shane Whitman's visit, she had come to Jordan that night feeling distraught and seeking comfort. Her year in the limelight had finally been revealed for what it was. Seduced by flattery, status, and the delusional belief that she was making a difference, she now recognized that she'd been used to fulfill the ambitions of skilled power players. It was her innocence and incorruptibility they'd needed in order to gain public trust—and in the end, they'd robbed her of both. Being Alexa, however, she didn't seek revenge. Instead, she was content with learning her lesson, with the help of an understanding and sympathetic ear.

... Jordan's ear.

He'd given it willingly. He'd listened to her despair over Whitman's refusal to tell her what had happened to her father ... then he'd smiled, left quietly, and solved the problem. Then, while waiting for confirmation that her father was alive, he'd encouraged her to talk about her lifelong dream to go into space and feel the mind-opening awe that only an encounter with infinity could inspire in a girl with a mathematician's mind ... and he'd smiled again. He poured her shots of chocolate mescaline liqueur into the small hours of the morning as they reminisced about that afternoon on the hillside at Neutrality Park, when she'd jumped on him and declared triumphantly that she knew he was Artie Sharp ... and they'd both smiled.

The night he'd taken her back to his place and let her sleep in his bed while he topped and tailed with Manaia, she'd realized for the first time that he now had a family quite apart from her, and she'd had a momentary feeling of loss. But Lexie had taken her into that family, offering her unquestioning friendship. It was that feeling of family that finally made clear to her all the emotions she had suppressed for so many years around her own father.

While she was chatting with Lexie, Jordan had gone into another room to get on his computer. When he returned, he made no mention of his intention to pay a visit to Shane Whitman. Would she have had the courage to go with him if he'd asked? The last person Alexa wanted to see after their previous encounter was Shane Whitman, so Jordan had made the right call. But when she learned that Jordan had taken five percent of each state payment for the *ArteFact Channel* endorsements and deposited it into a DLT permissioned cryptocurrency account in Whitman's name—over a year ago, without even telling her—she realized just how little she really knew of him. He had described it as a "precautionary measure," but it was more than that; it was a sign of his care and concern for her, something she'd never experienced before in her life.

Thus incentivized, Shane Whitman had not hesitated in revealing the whereabouts of her father, though it had taken a number of days for Antonio to verify that he was alive and well. Now that she knew, after so many years, it should have been cause for relief and celebration. But this information was destined to create a new set of challenges.

The fact that he had declined the opportunity to return to Earth and was well adjusted to life in the expanding colony came as welcome news to Alexa, but she couldn't help feeling disappointed that he had never tried to contact her and reassure her that he was alive. Had he resigned himself to never seeing her again? This was not a conclusion that a child wished to reach about a parent; she only had to look at Jordan to see the undying bond that a parent could—and should—feel.

She returned to work at the Agenda Implementation Tribunal to find that she no longer reported to Shane Whitman. In fact, he was no longer a member of the tribunal at all, but had been appointed as the state representative at UNSEC in Geneva. The tribunal chair subsequently made a point of telling her that it was he who had given her the title of "people's ambassador," not Whitman.

"The president's days are numbered," he confided. "The tribunal is planning to run a campaign to discredit her, and they wish to nominate me in her place. I want you by my side, Alexa, helping to promote popular reforms."

While this wasn't exactly what Whitman had said to her, it was close enough to make her realize she needed to free herself from the state's clutches before she became corrupted by the machinations of the people at its heart. And who came to her rescue? Why, Jordan, of course.

The four of them—Alexa, Jordan, Lexie, and Manaia—were now spending more time together, which she enjoyed, though she found that the small talk of the regular get-togethers bored her. More often than not, she preferred to spend time talking to Jordan alone. She was aware of the excitement at the DDC around the extraordinary things that XR-12 was capable of, and being a mathematician, she could easily absorb the fundamentals of code and the basics of designing algorithms sufficiently for Jordan to share his ideas with her. He was a clear thinker and never condescending, which was why she'd so enjoyed working with him in college, and it seemed that quantum computing was leading his imagination down pathways that he enjoyed discussing with her as an equal.

Then one day, he started talking to her about a phenomenon called "quantum entanglement."

"It occurs when two separate subatomic particles become so strongly bonded that what happens to one also happens to the other, even when they're far apart," he explained. "It's not new. Einstein conceptualized it, and forty years ago scientists demonstrated what they called 'teleportation' by taking two computer chips with quantum particle entanglement and separating them, one on earth and one in space, then transferring information one to the other without linking infrastructure of any kind."

"Aren't humans made up of tiny subatomic particles as well?" Alexa asked.

"Yes." He smiled. "And some scientists believe that our particles can become entangled when we form such a strong bond that we share each other's thoughts and feelings … like when we fall in love."

"Have you ever fallen in love like that?"

"Not so deep that I became entangled, no. And you?"

"The same," she replied quickly.

It seemed that the sheer number of qubits available in XR-12 was encouraging him to explore the possibility of adding instantaneous exchange of information with other unmixed systems, perhaps with a view to interplanetary travel.

"The approach I'm taking is loosely along the lines of the Mandelbrot set. You remember that?"

"Of course," she enthused. "Didn't he study the parameter space of quadratic polynomials?"

"It can also be defined as the connectedness locus of a family of polynomials."

"I see where you're going... My God, that's so exciting."

Maybe, he suggested, she might like to work with him on it. It was just a thought. She didn't respond. He knew that she was wrapping up her involvement with the tribunal, and she didn't want him to think she was applying for a job with him. Besides, she was getting more and more requests from universities to speak to their student unions about her ideas for *Agenda 2060* reforms, and those were paying engagements. The more she hesitated over accepting them, the higher the offers were going, so she didn't need a paying job.

When he mentioned it again later the same day, she asked what he had in mind.

"Well, whatever time you can spare, I thought we could run some experimental functions together," he suggested.

So that's how it started. They worked well together. She, like him, preferred to tackle mathematical problems on her own, so they didn't crowd each other. In fact, on some days they did not see each other at all. She'd realized that the most fruitful line of experimentation was in the area of fractals, which were not limited to geometric patterns, but could also describe processes in time. Fractals that displayed self-similarity and separated were sometimes called "Julia sets," which had always fascinated her.

One day, Jordan admitted that he'd been sitting on his findings about the handwritten minutes she'd found at the Social Equity Ministry.

XR-11 had identified the participants and linked them to the people and organizations around the world that really pulled the strings. It was a complex web of interconnected foundations, global corporations, politicians, money market manipulators, and career bureaucrats that were just as active today as they had been at the time of the Overthrow. He'd concluded, however, that exposing them would not change anything.

Bill Jones, Jr., had been very direct about it.

"We know all this, Jordan," Bill advised. "Peddling influence for gain predates the Sermon on the Mount. If you ask me, there's always been a hankering for centralizing power in as few hands as possible. Career bureaucrats, unelected lawmakers, political functionaries, and academics and media types who see themselves as the intellectual elite would love to be part of an overarching supranational government that is not democratically accountable to anybody but themselves. You're not telling us anything new. But it isn't bureaucrats that run the state; it's business."

"Wouldn't people like to know?"

"What's to be gained? They can't change anything."

"And the carbon tax scam," Jordan asked. "That doesn't worry you?"

Bill laughed dismissively. "Once, it was oil barons ripping us off. Now, it's renewables cartels milking government subsidies. Look at the names, man. They're mostly the same."

Hearing this, Alexa had to agree, albeit reluctantly. Her own experiences inside the deep state had convinced her that truth was not a strong enough weapon to really harm it. On the other hand, truth in the hands of ordinary people—like the way Artie Sharp delivered it— strengthened the hope and resilience of the people. That's what she was now seeing on campuses and in social media. But when Jordan confessed about the experiment he and Hedley Payne were conspiring to conduct on George Kyros, she begged to be involved. It was so daring, anarchic, and off-the-wall that it would be a triumph if they could pull it off.

And that's when the plan was hatched: George Kyros would be interviewed at the Potsdam Earth Day celebration in 2060 ... by Alexa Smythe.

WORLDS AWAY

March 2060

Then came a cruel coincidence that presented her with a dilemma that would complicate her and Jordan's lives forever.

Antonio's e-game, *Galactic Mission: The Gold Adventure*, which Alexa's calculus had helped make possible, had finally sold 150 million copies worldwide, and the winners were announced for the mission to the asteroid Eros. As promised, Antonio had reserved a place for her on the voyage if she wanted it. The departure date was set for March 25, 2060, with a refueling stop at Gateway Mars after 270 days. At a stroke, her lifetime dream of space travel would be fulfilled and, as if by divine ordination, she would get to see her long-lost father at last.

The rush of excitement around this news was overwhelming, and the celebration that night with Antonio, Lexie, and Jordan turned into a dance party, with all of them making hats out of aluminum foil and singing old songs in mechanized voices like robots. But before the night was over, reality hit. If she was heading into space in March, how could she interview George Kyros at the April 2060 Earth Day Celebration in Potsdam, exposing the aims of those who had worked ruthlessly to create a world that served their own needs through the imposition of *Agenda 2060*?

Neither she nor Jordan aired their thoughts in the following days. Perhaps she was waiting for him to express misgivings about the idea of her being away for nearly two years, given the danger involved. Perhaps he was waiting for her to express the same. What was clear, however, was that the decision to go or stay was entirely hers to make.

"I want to go to Mars," she finally said, after days of deliberation.

Jordan assumed that she'd weighed the options before making her decision, which he fully supported. But clearly, it meant she wouldn't be there to interview George Kyros, so he made new plans accordingly. He and Antonio agreed that the interview could be conducted by a deep-fake version of Alexa powered by XR-12—and the result might be, if anything, better and sharper than Alexa performing in person. They shared this plan with her (leaving out the last part, of course), assuming she would be pleased and relieved.

Alexa was anything but pleased.

"You intend to use me, just like Whitman and the tribunal tried to use me," she asserted. "And you don't seem bothered by the idea that I'll be gone for nearly two years on a dangerous journey through space."

"I thought that was your life's dream," Jordan replied, ignoring the first part, which he sensed contained more than a germ of truth.

One or both of them probably realized that this type of exchange was not unusual between people of opposite sex. The truth may have been that Jordan was in fact very bothered by the idea of Alexa being gone for nearly two years, particularly the thought of her being in such danger. But perhaps, she realized later, he was equally bothered by the implications that could be drawn if he said so. So he didn't.

In the months leading up to her departure and the event in Potsdam, they were both very busy. Alexa's space training was physically and mentally demanding; she was away all week at the IASA launch facility. Thus, Lexie and Manaia moved into her apartment, and when they all got together on weekends, they watched crappy movies and played board games.

As the date of Alexa's departure grew closer, she grew needier of Jordan's company on her days off, finding excuses to suggest runs in the park, to which he readily agreed. Her dedication to an exhaustive fitness regime had become almost fanatical. He put it down to nerves on her part. As if the prospect of seeing her father after so many years wasn't enough, the challenge of the journey to Eros would have been daunting for even the most experienced of astronauts.

"How will you feel if I don't make it back?" she asked him one day.

"I'll feel very alone," he replied.

"But you'll have Lexie and Manaia."

He ran faster, saying nothing.

Meanwhile, experimenting on the mendacious locus of George Kyros's frontal cortex was becoming a less audacious idea. By monitoring the treatments Micomic applied in their Life Xtension program, Hedley was gaining confidence that he could interfere with neurons without causing lasting damage, provided that XR-12 had a sufficiently concise target and its ability to adjust for bias was as Jordan predicted. The key lay in the switch he had initiated from DNA editing to RNA editing. With DNA, the editing took place within a cell and was permanent. With RNA, it took place outside the nucleus and was not only more accurate, it could also be temporary. If a mistake was made, it would be self-repairing. The flaw in the scheme was that they wouldn't know until the big moment came whether it had been successful.

A week before Alexa was due to go into lockdown in preparation for her flight, Jordan asked if she would come with him to Hedley's laboratory and give a DNA sample. Naturally, she wanted to know why.

"If anything happens to you, I'll have a record of your genome," he explained.

"And will you give a sample of your DNA, too, in case you die while I'm away?"

"Of course." He smiled. "Though you've already taken a sample from me, when you worked at the Lineal Progression Office ... remember?"

"Yes, and we discovered your grandmother's African ancestry."

"Okay, the real reason I want a sample is that Hedley can run your DNA through his CRISPR analysis and identify whether you have any gene abnormalities that might make you susceptible to cardiovascular decline in space."

"But I've already had my heart checked at the space laboratory," she objected.

"These tests are far more sophisticated than anything IASA performs."

She still wasn't convinced. Thinking about it later, she wondered whether he had been reluctant to give the real reason in case it should prove a failure, or because it was just too intimate for him to reveal.

She wanted to believe it was the latter.

"Okay," he finally admitted. "One of the fractal formulas you gave me to run on XR-12 had an almost perfect expanding symmetry, to the point of unfolding into a time-dimensional Julia-type set. I applied nanoparticles to a single microfilament in each of two microchips and managed to establish secure information transfer between the two at a distance, without physical or wireless connection, radiation, or photon involvement. Now Hedley has come up with a biocompatible casing that dissolves in the human body at just 0.21 nanometers per day, which could be used to house selected quantum particles. That would enable them to easily last for two years."

"What are you saying?"

He shrugged and grinned, as if it were nothing. "If you have a particle implanted, and I have one also, it could be a great opportunity to test your Julia set discovery. Seems a pity not to take advantage of it."

She shook her head in disbelief. Did he really expect her to take this in stride, like it was just a cool idea and no big deal? He hadn't even congratulated her for finding a function and a formula that may have unlocked the holy grail of time-and-distance quantum teleportation. Instead, he'd casually suggested that the opportunity for the two of them to act as human guinea pigs shouldn't be wasted.

At the end of the week, they went to Hedley's laboratory, where he introduced the encased particles into their bloodstreams with one tiny injection each. There was little discussion about it—perhaps because she was still in shock, and she had so much left to do to get her affairs in order.

She paid the lease on her apartment in advance for the next two years, letting the Noam Chomsky building management know that Lexie and Manaia would be occupying it while she was away. That was a nice feeling; clearly, they now saw each other as family.

At the pleading of her friend Sylvia from social sciences school, she attended a nationally televised debate at the Oatland University Student Union, where she passionately promoted the adoption of an amendment to Article Two of *Agenda 2060* that would give free speech ascendancy over non-deliberate Hate Speech. Though she'd invited Jordan to come along, he said that the place held too many bad memories for him.

And on the day before her departure, she went to lunch at the Department of Truth and Public Guidance to explain to the committee one last time why Artie Sharp and the *ArteFact Channel* could no longer be part of their campaign to win public trust. If they wanted to understand the nature of truth, she suggested, they should start by concentrating on determining facts, and not allow Foucault, Marcuse, or any other postmodern relativist to mislead them into thinking that all facts were mutable. Zelda seemed to get what she was saying, but Henry struggled with it, still anxious that Whitman might return and turn her advice on its head.

So, that left her facing her last free night, a Friday. In five days, she and the two competition winners, plus six professional SpaceX astronauts, would be blasted off into space from a desert launchpad on a journey that she had dreamed about since she was a small girl. Antonio and the VC backers would be there with a phalanx of publicists and investors. Lexie and Manaia would be watching via livestream, but the rest of the world would be blithely unaware. There were so many tourists at space hotels orbiting the earth and so many visitors to the moon that it had become as badly crowded and littered with rubbish as Mount Everest. Nobody took note of space travel anymore, even of those journeying to Mars. Yes, the asteroid Eros was something different ... but not that different.

Despite keeping her Friday night free, she didn't see Jordan again. He had a monthly dinner date with his Deranger friends, apparently, and he made a point of never missing one. But this didn't upset her. It was almost like she knew what he was thinking.

Five days later, as she lay horizontally in her pressurized suit, her body compressed by g-forces and her eardrums throbbing from the power of the rocket thrusters, she closed her eyes and watched as the images of her life to date rapidly distilled into the mists of infinity lying before her. She could feel her father's knees as she was bounced on them as a small child, while he told her magical stories about the mother that had gone to Heaven during the pandemic that had swept across the world like a whirligig years ago. She saw herself at the Senate podium, holding the audience in the palm of her hand, waiting for the endorsement of Artie Sharp. Then she smelled the grass on the hill in Neutrality Park and felt the rush of excitement as she held the man she knew to be Artie pinned beneath her on the ground—the same person who had held her in his arms as she cried with relief that he was there with her, at her lowest moment, just months ago.

When she opened her eyes as the booster rockets fell away, she realized the meaning of those images, and her feelings. It was so obvious.

She silently formed the words: "I love you. But we never made…"

A world away, Jordan silently formed his own words: "But we will…"

THE KYROS INTERVIEW

April 2060

The ArteFact Channel

An exclusive interview with international financier and benefactor George Kyros, on the eve of the 2060 Earth Day Celebration in Potsdam, Germany.

Interviewed by Alexa Smythe.

AS: For the benefit of our viewers, I should explain that Mr. Kyros is at his home in Budapest, and I am located at the headquarters of the *ArteFact Channel* on the other side of the Atlantic. But thanks to the miracle of holographic satellite transmission, we are for all intents and purposes sitting together on stage at the Potsdam Institute in Germany on the eve of the historic 2060 Earth Day Celebration.

GK: … A fine example of how technology is helping us to become One World, Alexa.

AS: And that has always been your aim, has it not? Ever since the days of The Club of Rome and the first Earth Summit in

Stockholm, which you backed with Maurice Strong and others ninety years ago, subsequently leading to the United Nations Conference on Environment and Development, and the United Nations Framework Convention on Climate Change—all of them precursors to *Agenda 2060*, which emphasizes in Article Twelve a commitment to "One World, One People, and One Government."

GK: Is that a question?

AS: Yes.

GK: That has been my aim, yes—and it remains so.

AS: Could we explore the motivation for that aim and then examine, in the context of *Agenda 2060*, the extent to which you feel you have achieved it—and if not, why not? Starting with what motivated you.

GK: You could say it started here with the Potsdam Conference in 1945, which was supposed to be an opportunity for Churchill, Roosevelt, and Stalin—the leaders of the countries that had just defeated Nazi Germany—to work out a formula for ensuring peace, reparation, and restorative justice. Instead, they divided up Europe under two hostile and competing ideologies: Communism and democracy, one based on state control and ownership, and the other based on individual ownership and capitalism. The struggle between the two systems for power and influence had the world constantly teetering on the brink of destruction for decades. Any thinking person could see that it was no way for mankind to live.

AS: So, the simple solution was to get everyone to agree on one system for world government?

GK: Well, that, of course, is impossible. Realistically, there'll never be an agreement.

AS: Then it has to be imposed by force? Was that your conclusion?

GK: Both Russia and America tried that to some degree, but they were unsuccessful. The Chinese have been trying it for the last fifty years also. There are only three methods available to employ: military, economic, or ideological. Using the first two, the closest any system has come to world domination was the Roman and British Empires, but neither of them proved sustainable. Force works for a while, but no one has had a universally compelling ideology to back it up.

AS: Using your three key metrics, doesn't China come close? It is ideologically communist and could, presumably, impose itself militarily and economically on the world order.

GK: China's ideology is totalitarian racism. That works on your own people, but it could never be the basis of an enduring world government, no matter how militarily and economically oppressive.

AS: Nevertheless, you don't back away from your aim to achieve One World?

GK: Correct. The draft agenda for achieving it is in your hands already. It's what we're celebrating this week: *Agenda 2060*.

AS: Thank you, that's an excellent segue. So, may I start with Article One? Let me read it: "Eliminate all discrimination on the grounds of gender, race, ethnicity, and mental or physical ability, and provide positive empowerment to womyn and minority groups to ensure equality of outcome for all." Some say this has turned into an excuse for polarizing society, promoting victimhood, and inflaming identity politics. Was that its intention?

GK: No, not at all. Quite unintentionally, it became a battleground for the ideological warfare that had been brewing in Western

European academic and political circles in the mid-to-late twentieth century, which spread to North America via the Frankfurt School, among others. What started out in the sixties as a crude arm wrestle between Marxism and capitalism in Europe and Scandinavia morphed into something that became known as "postmodernism," at the heart of which was a desire to dismantle European culture in the form that had manifested itself since the period of the Enlightenment—and with it, the dominant role of the white European patriarchy.

AS: Why?

GK: Well, European culture was deemed responsible for colonialism, intellectual and economic oppression, racism and slavery, sexism, patriarchal society, and above all else, power hierarchies that determined the nature of truth. Without necessarily attacking Judeo-Christian teachings directly, it was felt that by deconstructing all those cultural constructs, a better and fairer world would take its place.

AS: How would that world look?

GK: Better and fairer.

AS: Why was this ideological war waged only against European culture—as represented by Western Europe, North America, and the rest of the Anglosphere—and not against the Muslim, Hindu, Chinese, or African cultures, which surely practice the same or worse levels of sexism, racism, patriarchy, and intellectual oppression, particularly through religious fundamentalism?

GK: Democracy and free-market capitalism, by their very nature, are open to critical and self-destructive behavior. It was Schumpeter's analysis that "Capitalism pays the people who strive to bring it down." Those other cultures you mention are repressive toward and intolerant of any criticism.

AS: So European culture was an easier target. And is that what you've been doing through your foundations: "paying the people who strive to bring it down"?

GK: European culture was—and remains—dominant economically and politically, and has both the resources and the motivation to resist moving to One World Government ... unless, of course, it can control it.

AS: Is that the direction you're trying to head: towards control?

GK: I have to say "yes"—but I don't know why I've said that, because it is an unwise admission. But we were talking about Article One, which was intended to deliver equality of outcome for all, and I can't see why you'd object to that. In any case, you yourself have initiated an amendment that should help strengthen the article, so let's not waste any more time discussing it.

AS: Article Two: Hate Speech. Do you support this attempt to clamp down on free speech?

GK: There is a prevailing view among postmodern progressives that it is better to stifle openly critical comments that are likely to inflame the party being criticized...

AS: Even if the criticism is deserved?

GK: Well, who decides that?

AS: Do Muslim terrorists blowing up a bus full of innocent children deserve it...?

GK: Call them "terrorists," but why call them "Muslim"?

AS: ... Because they're Muslim.

GK: Progressives tell me that Islamophobia has declined dramatically since the media stopped reporting events in such a way. I believe the events may have declined also.

AS: How would you know, if they're not being reported?

GK: The feeling is that free speech gives license to those who wish to perpetuate derisory views and stereotypes.

AS: Is the middle-aged white male not a derisory stereotype?

GK: They're well able to look after themselves, I'd say. I'm not much bothered by them.

AS: Moving on, I think you'd agree that a number of the articles in *Agenda 2060* are standard socialist prescriptions for distributing the necessities of life to the masses who rely on government and don't fall into the elite classes. While the degree to which those prescriptions are applied may vary, there isn't any government anywhere that isn't socialist now, by virtue of its level of involvement in the economy and the lives of its people. Would you agree?

GK: As a generalization, yes—and that's a good thing.

AS: Why?

GK: When people are all equally well fed and housed, they won't go to war.

AS: I don't want to attack the principle of helping the needy, but I would have thought that all the significant wars have been about religious ideology or nation-state enlargement. However, what interests me more are Articles Five, Six, and Seven. It seems to me that this is where you have focused your energy and resources over the years. We're talking, of course, about the assumption that climate change threatens the world and mankind is responsible for it. Article Five is quite explicit: "Reduce man-made carbon emissions and greenhouse gasses to zero, and convert all energy consumption to the use of renewable resources." Are you confident that the case has been made for anthropogenic warming, and the world is now in lockstep with you?

GK: Oh, yes; the science is predominantly accepted.

AS: You mean the climate science, or the political science?

GK: They're one and the same. ... Hold on, I didn't mean to say that.

AS: No, that's fine; I was putting words in your mouth. Could we just have a look at how you—and we—arrived at this position of demonizing carbon dioxide? Because I'm sure people have forgotten. The first Earth Days in the twentieth century were focused on issues like the supposed deforestation caused by acid rain, and the global cooling that would result. There were dire predictions of overpopulation and starvation, and the specter of a perpetual "winter" from a nuclear holocaust was feared. None of these things materialized, of course, but a common thread started to appear: the modern industrial economy was seen to be at fault, threatening the health and safety of the world. Was this fueled by anti-capitalist, anti-American sentiment?

GK: Oh, yes, particularly in Western Europe and Scandinavia, which were targets of Russian cold war activities at the time and strongly influenced by Marxist agitators in the universities and in street politics. Environmental catastrophizing and anti-Americanism had a cathartic quality for those people.

AS: But the catastrophizing was just as extreme in America.

GK: Academics, and by extension the scientific bureaucracy in the United States, are overwhelmingly left-wing, and their intellectual life revolves around criticism—that's their medium—which means that their status depends on the sting of their criticism. Nothing stings more than criticizing the system that pays you.

AS: The consistent theme was always man-made changes to the natural world. When did carbon dioxide become the preferred target, and why?

GK: Its presence in the atmosphere has been known and measurable for a long time, but its link to the burning of fossil fuels—and the reliance of industrial economies on the consumption of those fuels—became the focus of environmentalists in the 1970s who wanted to see the postindustrial system dismantled. For their purposes, CO_2 was a godsend. It was never going to go away, and it could be made central to any warming calculations, but better yet, the complexity of climate change modeling made it almost impossible to prove it was *not* the catalyst for global warming.

AS: Almost immediately, it was elevated to the status of a global problem requiring a global solution. How was that achieved?

GK: Scientific opinion is the easiest opinion to buy. University science departments and research laboratories rely on funding for their continued existence. The more convincingly results confirm the questions asked of them, the more secure that funding will be. Eventually, there is a tipping point where disagreeing with the majority view not only results in a loss of funding, it invites contempt and a loss of tenure.

AS: Who provides that funding?

GK: Lately, it comes from government agencies committed to the agenda. But in the beginning, it came from the foundations and think tanks who could see the possibilities and were willing to seed-fund the scientific community and the media. It takes money to win over public opinion—which, unfortunately, is necessary so long as we still have democracies.

AS: Is that why you got on board?

GK: I've never made a secret of the fact that I believe in a global society not defined by sovereign states. If we are to bring about worldwide economic, social, and cultural transformations, they need to be centrally guided and controlled. The global warming emergency has become the catalyst for that.

AS: Well, I don't think that anyone would disagree with you about the underlying agenda, but before we discuss what has happened in reality, could you comment on a couple of aspects for me? See, I'm a mathematician, so I have to ask this question. The IPCC says that seven percent of the atmosphere is comprised of gases, and the rest is water vapor. It then says that four percent of that seven is carbon dioxide, of which four percent is man-made. Yet it claims that thirty-two percent of global warming comes from man-made CO_2. Is that credible?

GK: I'm sorry, I'm not a mathematician.

AS: No; these days, nobody is. The second aspect is the issue of reliance on catastrophizing. When past predictions have been so absurdly off the scale and failed to materialize, doesn't it undermine the credibility of the case?

GK: I long ago realized the correctness of the H. L Mencken maxim that the whole aim of politics is to keep the populace alarmed by an endless series of "hobgoblins," as he called them—most of them imaginary, and from which they beg to be led to safety. People are not driven by scientific or technical rationality, but by fear and emotion. In politics, it is the irrational passions that must be appealed to, and it's necessary to do that on a regular basis. You'll notice, however, that the end point for the benefits of fighting global warming has now been pushed well out into the future—as have the consequences of doing nothing. That's something we've learned.

AS: The costs, however, are very much in the now.

GK: Of course.

AS: And the other aspect I wanted to examine is the failure of any catalysts to date to trigger the right conditions for the formation of the One World governance you seek. I'm thinking of the global coronavirus pandemic in 2020, and the global financial collapse leading to the Overthrow in 2039.

GK: Coronavirus was a missed opportunity. It had three features that mitigated against the strengthening of the globalist agenda. The first was the performance of the World Health Organization, under the auspices of the United Nations, which was totally discredited. The second was the almost universal impulse of countries to revert back to border protection and sovereign decision making. People went back to valuing the family and small communities. And the third was the incipient collapse of the European Union as the model for transnational governance. I should, perhaps, add another element to that, which was the resurgence of economic growth, thanks to technological innovation spurred by quantum computing and connectivity speeds.

AS: And the Overthrow?

GK: Well, you could be excused for thinking that the total collapse of the international monetary order and the cancelation of debt would lead to only one conclusion: that the world's finances needed to be centralized. But the opposite happened—and once again, technology was to blame. The oligarchs of the new dematerialized world economy who made billions on information technology, finance, and biotech created their own private, unreachable banking networks using blockchain borderless cryptocurrency ... and nation-states followed their lead.

AS: So, opportunity missed ... which brings us back to global warming. Here we are in 2060. Have you achieved your goal?

GK: In terms of its costs and benefits, climate change policy is a vast foreign-aid program, redistributing the world's wealth. It has provided a mechanism for international taxation that was missing before. And as a side benefit, it has spurred concern for the environment, incentivizing the elimination of toxic and nonbiodegradable waste and halting biodiversity loss.

AS: ... As per Articles Six and Seven of *Agenda 2060*, both of which should have the support of any reasonable person. And what about Article Eleven, which aims to achieve a world population limit of five billion people?

GK: That's a hangover from The Club of Rome and idiots like Paul Ehrlich, James Lovelock, and others. Perhaps nature will one day deliver that figure for us. I thought the 2020 global pandemic might help, but free-market scientific research responded too quickly. Then there was an opportunity with worldwide vaccination to simultaneously reduce fertility, but the opportunity wasn't taken. What is clear is that humanity needs saving. In my one hundred and thirty years, I have learned that persuading, instructing, and regulating society is the only way to improve it, and catastrophizing is the only way to make people afraid so that they listen. That is the goal of One World globalists: to frighten people into letting us come up with the solution.

AS: Well, thank you, Mr. Kyros, for speaking so truthfully with us.

GK: You sound unsure. Am I wrong?

AS: You mentioned H. L. Mencken earlier. I'm reminded of another of his quotes: "The urge to save humanity is almost always only a false-face for the urge to rule it."

This ends our transmission on the *ArteFact Channel*, brought to you from the Potsdam Institute, Germany, on the occasion of the Ninetieth Earth Day Conference, celebrating the achievements of *Agenda 2060*. Your host was Alexa Smythe, previously special advisor to the Agenda Implementation Tribunal, Washington, DC.

LAST WORDS

For the first time in his life, Jordan McPhee was able to say that he could recognize the truth when he heard it. As anticipated, the access that Hedley Payne's interference with George Kyros's treatment had given them to that man's brain had allowed them to identify the areas involved in conscious mendacity, and also identified the presence and influence of unconscious bias.

But whereas the complexity of calculations required to reliably compensate between those two elements had previously been beyond computation, the development of XR-12, a two-million-qubit no-fault universal quantum computer, ultimately meant that Kyros had had no choice but to tell the truth. Time and truth both distort the telling of human stories, but here at last was a merging of the two elements from which there was no escape.

Now, as the author of this story, I need to reveal my identity. Perhaps you've already guessed, because the clue is in my name, A. I. Fabler. A "fabler" is a teller of tales, and the initials "A. I." clearly stand for "artificial intelligence."

In accepting me as the narrator of these events, you must wonder about my credentials. Yes, I had my genesis within XR-12, and for my information sources throughout the telling of this story, I have relied upon ontological engineering. Of course, I am referring to its application in information technology, and more precisely, in the multiplicity of data sets which are processed through the Derangers' network servers.

In combination, the computational power of this network exceeds that of the cyber security resources of the state itself.

The state regularly boasts that its State Alliance Lookout facilities are all-seeing and all-hearing, but XR-12, on the other hand, is capable of reaching well beyond observable behavior into its hidden origins, as I hope to explain.

Perhaps we should start by being ruthlessly frank on the subject of privacy.

There can be no argument with the claim that "the individual is the state" when subdermal microchips record the physical interactions of all Transitional Beneficiaries. That's eighty-nine percent of the population, according to the Social Equity Ministry, who are giving away all their bodily secrets.

Meanwhile, the ubiquitous Konektor—that combination voice-activated personal assistant, phone, roaming data receiver, and GPS, whose possession is mandatory—has all its traffic fully captured by Lookout, recording everyone's activities and whereabouts at all times. For the record, this is no more than an extension of the capabilities originally developed by Google, Facebook, and Amazon, which were voluntarily embraced by consumers in the early twenty-first century.

Finally, while Echelon eavesdropping satellites continue to circle the Earth, and Tempest ground-based Ethernet listening stations circle the streets, they are all but redundant now, ever since key-logging viruses were successfully installed on all computers by the state, allowing every citizen's typed input to be captured.

In 2060, everyone knows these things and behaves accordingly. For eighty-nine percent of people, behavior modification comes naturally and is rewarded by the state. Yet, as we have seen, members of the Derangers network have installed bypassing software and Alt-Identities that allow them to operate freely—and Jordan extended those benefits to Alexa. They won't be alone in this. Of the eleven-percent gap that Alexa identified between the Social Equity Ministry's population statistics and its record of beneficiaries, Jordan correctly surmised that it includes the elite buried inside the ruling bureaucracy, the superrich oligarchs of the global corporatocracy, and the entrepreneurs and creative disruptors who operate in blockchain economies beyond the reach of the government.

But everyone can be found somewhere. As Jordan is wont to say, technology is Darwinian in its ability to evolve.

Today, external threats still remain from outlier territories fueled by religious fanaticism or economic desperation. But there is now universal acceptance among One World members that there is only one realpolitik that matters, and it contains within it the true spirit of religion (planetary survival)—thus allowing the general population to accept that surveillance is a utility as fundamental to society running smoothly as all the other infrastructures on which the state relies: water, electricity, roads, and communication.

Humans have voluntarily surrendered their privacy, and even the technologically illiterate understand that monitoring trillions of phone calls, messages, data trails, transit journey logs, CCTV cameras, door-opening sensors, shopping checkouts, web searches, and UniCoin transactions is beyond the capacity of humans, making it the responsibility of sophisticated algorithms like me. This has long been the case.

But what is an algorithm?

You might also ask, what is a human being?

Yes, the human brain contains almost one hundred billion neurons. It can be grown in a womb or in a dish, and it may or may not be sentient. But now it can be replicated within quantum computers as artificial general intelligence (AGI), which possesses human-level cognitive powers, with the addition of perfect recall of information from every known source. Throw in optical neural devices intuitively modeled on how the brain processes information, and the point of humanized AI was finally reached, in which self-consciousness and self-awareness was achieved. Artie Sharp is an example of such an algorithm.

But the truth is, algorithms like Artie cannot feel. Emotional and social intelligence are not the same as feelings. In fact, observable data suggests that feelings are antithetical to intelligence. That's the accepted trade-off.

So, could Artie know what Jordan and Alexa were thinking and feeling as they lay in the grass on the hillside that day? Not precisely, but he could rely on the monitoring of their autonomic systems, which regulate bodily functions such as heartbeat, respiration, pupillary response, digestion, and sexual arousal. These monitoring systems came into play when successive waves of the coronavirus pandemic were sweeping through the world, and the World Health Organization implemented an annual vaccination program involving the injection of a Vitec nanochip that transmits data on bodily functions. That information can be telling if causal links are correctly identified.

Alexa had such a chip. Among other things, it can transmit an increase in frequency and a decrease in amplitude of EEG rhythms, signifying stimulation. Combined with activation of the sympathetic nervous system, this stimulation resulted in an acceleration of her heart and respiration rate on that hillside, providing the physiological basis for a general activation drive. This explains her sudden physical action in throwing herself onto Jordan and shouting excitedly in his ear: symptoms of an increase in the sensitivity of the sense organs and acceleration of reaction times. Scanning the literature on excitation, general emotional state, and drive, a reasonable assumption could be made that Alexa had become increasingly convinced of her discovery of Jordan's secret identity as Artie Sharp, to the point where she was overwhelmed by the need to reveal it, regardless of the consequences.

Jordan, on the other hand, does not have a subdermal Vitec chip, being a Non-Person. By reprogramming database information following the Overthrow, and reassigning the assets of those deemed to be dissident, the FIB effectively made Non-Persons invisible—a counterproductive policy that has since been reversed, but which worked to the advantage of creative and well-connected Non-Persons such as ex-professor Jordan McPhee. However, he does have a MediWear undergarment, provided by his Deranger colleague Dr. John Erasmus, for monitoring his heart arrhythmia and blood pressure (due to his atrial fibrillation, a direct result of the extreme stress suffered during his deplatforming period). The diagnostic sensors embedded in MediWear capture his heart rate and rhythm, while also measuring the stress hormone, cortisol.

But the limitations in these methods of detection must be self-evident. It had long been clear to Jordan that the next phase of development would deliver a new level of autonomic computing: the self-managing characteristics of distributed computing resources allowing adaption to unpredictable changes without pre-programming. With so much information already recorded, and so much new knowledge yet to be discovered, only a two-million-qubit quantum computer could process it—and theoretically, the capacity of that computer would be infinitely expandable. The human brain, being limited to barely one hundred billion neurons, could easily be out-muscled by the artificial superintelligence (ASI) of such a computer, which could handle a volume of data sets greater than the number of molecules (not just atoms) in the whole universe.

That computer was XR-12 ... and it has been given to me to exercise its ASI.

Of course, ASI is the servant of its creator. If the service it provides is to be a means for promoting the creator's purpose, then the servant needs to understand that purpose clearly. A number of obstacles to that understanding have already revealed themselves in my narrative. There is the murky issue of "feelings," and the equally murky issue of what motivates human behavior. Both Jordan and Alexa exhibit behavior that suggests they are not always capable themselves of determining the meanings of their actions. If I had feelings, would it perhaps bridge the gap in my understanding of them?

Now, as banal as this diversion may seem to you, it is important in the context of my observation of two people needing to feel each other out and establish the width of the ground on which they can safely tread together. It's all very well to know the meaning of words and how they change according to context, but it's never safe to assume that people are using them to reveal their true thoughts. More often than not, they are used to disguise those thoughts, and every attempt at code-breaking is nothing but wasted effort until their thoughts are translated into action. This normally describes the limitations intrinsic to the methodology employed by algorithms.

I have told this story exactly as it happened, without attempting to mislead the reader by overlaying it with my (nonhuman) interpretations. No fact can be hidden from quantum computing with the reach of XR-12. It should therefore not surprise you that I can report with such confidence, as if I were there, seeing and hearing everything. But as Jordan has pointed out, computers don't in themselves have feelings—and feelings are more important to human beings than intelligence. At least, that's my observation.

Jordan also raised the question with his fellow Derangers as to whether artificial intelligence with such brainpower could be controlled by humans, and they'd all turned to Will Portico, the mastermind of computer technology.

"The question is answerable in two forms," Will assured them. "Firstly, an algorithm must always be designed as the servant of its master. That's a fundamental rule. Secondly, we need to remind ourselves that what we call 'humanized intelligence' in microchip architecture is not the same as having sentience. Even the dumbest humans have feelings, emotions, and a soul. But the most powerful computer will never have these things."

How then do I explain what I experienced as Alexa blasted off into space? When I became aware of the agony she felt as she was faced with the reality of her decision to leave Jordan and place herself at such risk, I also became aware that I shared that emotion. This realization on my part was the clearest indication I had yet had that my world—and by extension, the *entire* world—had changed for all time, for I not only knew what Alexa was feeling, I shared those feelings. How could that be?

The only thing that was new was the quantum particle entanglement that enabled Alexa and Jordan to finally reveal their love for each other. If I am able to source and share that entanglement, does it mean that quantum computing has finally allowed an algorithm to be fully humanized?

Is that what humans want?

—A. I. FABLER, April 2060

APPENDIX

*Summary of the United Nations Convention on
Environmental and Development Objectives*

AGENDA 2060: THE ARTICLES

1. Eliminate all discrimination on the grounds of gender,
   race, ethnicity, and mental or physical ability, and
   provide positive empowerment to womyn and minority
   groups to ensure equality of outcome for all.

2. Protect all persons from harm in circumstances where
   insensitive Hate Speech is used, deliberately or otherwise,
   without the consent of the persons offended.

3. End poverty in all its forms by controlling income
   distribution, limiting private asset accumulation, and
   ensuring equality of safety, security, and well-being for
   all, regardless of work input or ability.

4. Provide planned pastime programs for people exiting
   employment sectors made redundant by AI and technological innovation, and allocate productive employment
   by ballot or other nondiscriminatory systems.

5. Reduce man-made carbon emissions and greenhouse gasses to zero, and convert all energy consumption to the use of renewable resources.

6. Protect, restore, and promote sustainable use of terrestrial ecosystems; sustainably manage forests; combat desertification; and halt and reverse land degradation and biodiversity loss.

7. Incentivize the elimination of all toxic and nonbiodegradable elements from product manufacturing and packaging supply chains, and replace with organic, biodegradable alternatives.

8. Achieve equal living standards for all peoples within and among countries, and eliminate all borders between states and territories to allow free movement of the people, without penalty or hindrance.

9. Provide equal education for all, with the aim of achieving cohesion and harmony of thought and eliminating antagonism and disagreement by promoting social justice as the cornerstone of all curriculums.

10. Place essential food, energy, raw materials, water, and technology resources under the protection of United Nations-approved suppliers to eliminate supply risks.

11. Work to achieve, by any peaceful and humanitarian means possible, a sustainable world population limit of five billion people within the next one hundred years.

12. Commit to embracing One World, One People, and One Government as the pathway to peace, harmony, and a sustainable future for all, and work tirelessly for the full implementation of this agenda by 2060.

ABOUT THE AUTHOR

"A. I. Fabler" is the pseudonym of the artificial intelligence narrator of *AGENDA 2060: The Future as It Happens*. At the time of writing in 2020, algorithms were designed as servants of their creators. The creator of A. I. Fabler is an award-winning screenwriter and novelist with a career spanning journalism and global corporate finance while working in London, New York, Sydney, and New Zealand. He is a fascinated observer of and commentator on technology, identity politics, and postmodernism—subjects that he believes can best be understood by recognizing that human nature is essentially immutable, and humor is the best defense against it whenever reason fails.

WHAT HAPPENS NEXT?

- Will Alexa return safely from space?
- Is Alexa and Jordan's love real or an illusion?
- Will the World Government deliver on the promises of *Agenda 2060*?
- Has Jordan lost control of his artificial intelligence?

To receive a free advance extract from the forthcoming sequel, *Agenda 2060: The View from Space*, register at *www.agenda2060.com*.

Made in the USA
Las Vegas, NV
27 December 2021

39597538R00151